my way,
al fixing buddy Cw

(signature)

C. W. WINTER

THE SENTINELS

FORTUNES OF WAR

Published by Greenleaf Book Group
Austin, TX
www.greenleafbookgroup.com

Distributed by Greenleaf Book Group
For ordering information or special discounts for bulk purchases, please contact Greenleaf Book Group at PO Box 91869, Austin, TX 78709, (512) 891-6100.

Design and composition by Greenleaf Book Group LLC
Cover design by Greenleaf Book Group LLC

Publisher's Cataloging-In-Publication Data
(Prepared by The Donohue Group, Inc.)

Zuckerman, Gordon.
    The Sentinels : fortunes of war / Gordon Zuckerman.

    p. ; cm.

    ISBN: 978-1-929774-64-7

1. Industrialists--Germany--Fiction. 2. Conspiracy--Germany--Fiction. 3. Germany--Politics and government--1933-1945--Fiction. 4. Germany--Economic conditions--1918-1945--Fiction. 5. Transnational crime--Fiction. I. Title.

PS3626.U25 S46 2009
813/.6
                                                        2009920764

Printed in the United States of America on acid-free paper

09 10 11 12 13 14   10 9 8 7 6 5 4 3 2 1

First Edition

GORDON ZUCKERMAN

THE SENTINELS

FORTUNES OF WAR

GREENLEAF
BOOK GROUP PRESS

PROLOGUE

Karl von Schagel paced the drawing room. In the last five minutes, he had probably consulted his pocket watch a dozen times. He walked over to the sliding doors that opened onto the dining room, with its long, mahogany table polished to such a finish that a woman could probably use it to reapply her lipstick. Usually the table glistened all down its length with crystal, silver, fine bone china, and linens folded into place as crisply as a starched dress shirt. Tonight the table glistened, all right— but only for about a third of its length. This evening's dinner party guest list was limited. Von Schagel gave the dining room a final, critical glance and turned away from the door, tugging his watch from his vest pocket.

Like his father and his father's father, Karl von Schagel was a trusted financial adviser to Germany's wealthiest and most influential families. Karl had lost count of how many elegant dinner parties he and his wife had hosted here, parties that had been attended by the cream of German society. But tonight there were only seven guests, the seven most powerful men in Germany.

Erhart Schmidt was first to arrive, as usual. For well over a century, the Schmidt family name had practically been synonymous with steel in Europe. Schmidt steel had been forged into long-range, precise artillery weapons since the time of the Napoleonic Wars. Guns made from Schmidt steel had been used in China, in America's revolutionary and civil wars, by the Spanish, French, and Dutch armadas, during the Boer Wars in Africa, and by both sides during the Great War. Much of the rail and rolling stock that transported the fruits of the Industrial Age in Europe, Asia, and America was produced from Schmidt smelters.

Erhart, the current head of this powerful, proud, and arrogant family, was well over six feet tall; he was also heavily muscled and weighed more than 250 pounds. Like the big guns he produced, he commanded respect. He expected his word to be the last in any discussion, and his powerful presence alone was often enough to intimidate the worthiest adversaries. Tonight, he was the unquestioned leader among the illustrious group of men who would be seated around the von Schagel dining table.

A servant politely took Herr Schmidt's heavy woolen overcoat, hat, and gloves, and another, appearing from nowhere, caused a tumbler of single-malt Scotch to materialize in the steel mogul's hand. Karl and Schmidt spoke meaningless pleasantries for a few moments, until the other guests began to arrive.

Heinrich Bimmler, head of Germany's dominant automobile manufacturer, came in next, followed in a minute or two by Wilhelm Schenk, the chairman—some, out of his hearing, preferred the term "tyrant"—of Reichsbank, the nation's largest financial institution. Boritz, the railroad magnate; Klein, the shipbuilder; Fleischer, holder of the nation's most extensive mining interests; and von Steuben, who had grown rich by supplying the electrical infrastructure demanded by Germany's burgeoning industrial buildup, completed the party. Karl bowed his guests into the dining room and more servants appeared, bringing in steaming trays that drifted mouthwatering aromas in their wake.

When the last course had been served, the men retired to the privacy of Karl's library for the customary cigars and vintage Napoleon cognac. The congeniality from dinner carried over until the last Cuban had been lit and the last snifter served. Only then did the atmosphere turn serious.

Schmidt initiated the conversation. "Karl, we want you to listen carefully to what we have to say. Each of us has had the opportunity to discuss privately what we now want to discuss with you as a group. And we are all in agreement that your family's years of loyal service to each of our families uniquely qualify you for the sensitive assignment that we are hoping you will accept." Schmidt held Karl's eyes for a moment, then glanced at Bimmler and nodded.

The tall, thin, carefully dressed auto manufacturer, coal-black hair combed straight back, adjusted his glasses and began to speak in his quiet voice. "Karl, you probably understand better than most of us that any hope of reversing the failing prosperity of Germany will require some drastic changes. Following the war, the inflow of international financing and the corresponding improvement in our economy were, for a time, creating real hope. But now that the depression in America has spread to the rest of the world and the financing that we so desperately need is drying up, new solutions are becoming necessary. Many of our factories lie idle, unemployment is rampant, and public disillusionment is approaching historic highs. The Weimar Republic is unstable and the Social Democratic Party is losing its appeal. At the same time, membership in many reform political parties is fragmented but rising. In short, we think these circumstances indicate that time has come for us to start making some . . . discreet adjustments in the German government."

As Bimmler spoke, Karl felt the others watching him. He focused on Bimmler's words and maintained eye contact with him, however, and nodded at the expected moments.

"We have been following the progress of some of the most active new political parties and there is one that seems to be gathering more public support than the others." He paused to pull a piece of paper from his pocket, but Karl noticed that Bimmler never looked at it as he continued speaking. "According to my figures, Adolf Hitler and his National Socialist German Workers Party had an enrollment of 108,000 in 1928. In the recent elections, just four years later, they received 810,000 votes, an increase of almost 800 percent, and they now control twelve seats in the Reichstag. Experts agree that current economic difficulties will generate even greater public support for Hitler, whose fresh rhetoric and promise of change are having a mesmerizing effect on our discontented public. Disregarding the fact that many of his viewpoints may conflict with ours, the reality of the situation is that increasing numbers of our countrymen are convinced Hitler has some new answers to some old problems plaguing this country."

Klein coughed discreetly. Karl shifted his focus to the gray-bearded, stocky shipbuilder. "We believe that we can orchestrate the expansion of Hitler's support among the German people, allowing him to become our next chancellor. Once he is in office and has time to consolidate his power, we will already be in a position to use our influence over him and his party to introduce our own agenda."

After a pause, the railroad industrialist spoke. "Karl, some of us believe that by playing on the public's fear of invasion by the French from the west and the Bolsheviks from the east, Germans as a whole can be persuaded to support the establishment of an initiative we are calling 'Arsenals for Peace.' We think Germany can renounce the Treaty of Versailles and suspend the heavy burden of financial reparations from the last war. Rearmament of Germany means revitalizing our businesses. And . . . it goes without saying that putting Germans back to work is good for Germany," Boritz concluded.

As the following silence lengthened, Karl knew they expected him to respond. "Gentlemen, I agree with everything that has been said, but I fail to understand what all this has to do with me. I am a financial specialist, not a political strategist."

"Karl, your family and mine have been friends and business associates for a very long time," said Schenk, the banker. "Your loyalty and ethics are beyond reproach, and your assistance has, quite frankly, helped us survive this damned recession. Put quite simply, you are the only man we can trust to represent our collective interests *inside* Hitler's government."

"Just what is it you're all expecting from me?" Karl asked.

"It is absolutely imperative that our interest in Hitler's government remain anonymous," answered the electrical manufacturer. "Should the German public become aware of our involvement, their confidence in the National Socialist German Workers Party would be destroyed, and the backlash would frustrate the control we seek. We want you to be our representative within Hitler's government. With your expertise, no one will question your role there," said von Steuben. "Become acquainted with him and his top people. Find out how much money they need to fund their agenda, then create a conduit whereby we can provide the money. In short, do what you can to connect us with Hitler. He needs what we can provide—and he can, in turn, give us what we need."

"Once the National Socialists come to power, we can do our share to return our once-proud country to its rightful position as the true economic leader of Europe," said Fleischer. "When that occurs, we'll need to have you in the innermost circle. The generosity of our contributions will ensure that Hitler will want to keep you around, not only to preserve our economic backing, but to utilize your considerable financial skills."

Karl gave a modest little smile and made a dismissing motion with his hand.

"Funding their military arsenal will require selling a lot of debt to the outside world," the mine owner went on, "and they will want to take advantage of your relationship with the international investment community. To further all these ends, we should have you appointed deputy minister of finance."

Karl took a few moments to consider his words before he spoke; after all, he had not built his success based on rash answers. "Your explanations make it apparent that you believe the achievement of your goals will remain consistent with the interests of Germany and the aims of the National Socialist German Workers Party." He carefully considered his next words. "But . . . what happens should these things become incompatible? What would I do then?"

Rising to his full, imposing height, Herr Schmidt took a small step toward Karl. "That is a problem that could indeed occur later on," Schmidt said. "But the decision we are asking you to make *now* is whether the importance of what we are concretely attempting outweighs your need for answers to hypothetical situations."

At that point, Karl realized, there really was very little more to be said.

BERKELEY, CALIFORNIA, 1938

Jacques Roth strolled across the campus dressed in his semiofficial uniform: starched khakis, white Oxford cloth shirt with button-down collar, highly shined Bass Weejun loafers, white sweat socks, and a well-worn Harris Tweed sport coat with leather patches on the elbows. He looked every bit the aspiring academic. His black curly hair, blue eyes, tall athletic frame, and chiseled features typically drew attention, even on his cross-campus strolls. Some recognized him; there had been a few articles in the *Daily Cal* about the heir to the Roth banking empire who was also the former captain of France's national soccer team and a notorious Parisian playboy. A walk across campus that would take anybody else no more than ten minutes could take Jacques half an hour or more, depending on how many people would want to stop him and say hello. Today, knowing it would be his last walk through campus, he felt like taking his time.

As Jacques stopped to talk with friends, Dr. Tom waited with five other students across campus. The group had been studying, researching, and preparing for this afternoon's public presentation and defense of their work for three years, almost since the moment of their arrival at Berkeley to begin their doctoral studies. Tom Burdick had pulled them together very soon after they were accepted into his special, cross-disciplinary program in political economics. It was he who had molded them into a sort of mini–think tank and who had challenged them to reach beyond their privileged backgrounds and tap into the deep wells of intelligence, intellectual curiosity, and altruism that he said he knew existed in each of them.

It also didn't hurt that he had previously met each of their families or knew them by reputation. In his wide travels, Dr. Tom had collected friendships among most of the influential families of Europe and Asia. A charming storyteller in five languages, he knew somebody somewhere who knew something about almost anything you could imagine. Jacques and the others never ceased to be amazed during his lectures, when he would begin an anecdote with words like, "Once, when I was hiking through Nepal, I met a village elder who told me . . ." And the crux of the story would be the perfect illumination for the point he was making.

The learning didn't stop in class. The home of Dr. Tom and his beautiful wife, Deborah, was the regular weekend venue for dinner parties attended by Jacques, the other team members, and some of their more interesting friends. The conversation might wander across the economic reasons for the downfall of the Babylonian Empire, take a quick lap around Napoleon's five worst political mistakes, and end up headed in the general direction of the implications of long-range air travel for diplomacy in the Far East. The parties often lasted until the wee hours of the morning.

They all admired and respected Dr. Tom and were eager to please him and receive his praise. Tom Burdick was the hub of the wheel, and the six of them were the spokes. And today, with their major collaborative research presentation, the wheel would take a major turn toward its destination.

Lost in his thoughts, Jacques started up the front steps of Wheeler Auditorium, practically bumping into Dr. Tom and the rest of the team, who had been awaiting his arrival. They had all learned the hard way that despite his brilliance and strong leadership, Jacques was never predictable. Today, that trait was especially annoying. The crowd was already filing into the lecture hall, past the impatient presenters.

"Where the hell have you been?" Claudine demanded, stepping in front of Jacques and snapping him out of his reverie. "We've been waiting for you for almost a half hour. People are already being seated for the lecture."

Claudine Demaureux was Swiss, the daughter of Henri Demaureux, the chairman of Demaureux Bank, one of the most influential of Switzerland's financial establishments. She was brilliant, had a memory like a steel trap, and at this moment looked like she was thoroughly incensed by Jacques' playboy casualness.

"Sorry, guys," Jacques said, smiling and holding up his hands in a gesture of surrender. "I was just going over everything in my mind one more time. I'm ready. Are you all ready?"

"Ready as we'll ever be," said Mike Stone, the son of a very old New York banking family. In many ways, he was the most unassuming member of the group and was often required to play the role of peacemaker between the strong-minded and outspoken Jacques and Claudine.

"Remember, you're going to be talking to a room full of academic skeptics," Dr. Tom said. "This 'Power Cycle' of yours is going to sound like something out of a science fiction story unless you explain, verify, and back everything up with solid fact. Your thesis isn't some pie-in-the-sky academic theory; it talks about a real and present danger. You six have got to make them see and understand the importance of what you present."

"Gee, Dr. Tom, I never thought of that," said Tony Garibaldi with a wide grin. "I thought we could just pass out a little wine and have a nice, comfy chat, like we do at your house."

"Okay, I'm glad you're all nice and loose," Dr. Tom said, "but it's time. Now go in there and make yourselves proud."

The headline of the next morning's newspaper screamed at Dr. Tom as soon as he unwrapped it.

GERMAN INDUSTRIALISTS PUSHING EUROPE INTO WAR, SAY SIX CAL-BERKELEY RESEARCHERS

Berkeley, June 8, 1938. Six doctoral candidates at the University of California at Berkeley's influential Institute for World Economic Studies claim they have discovered a pattern that explains and can even predict repeating cycles of the rise and fall of world powers.

The scholars claim they have identified seven distinct steps that make up the repetitive cycles of political corruption, driven by economic and financial motives, that have occurred throughout history. They call this seven-step process "The Power Cycle." In a startling conclusion, the six assert that when viewed through their "power cycle" lens, the current political and economic situation in Germany, if left unchecked, will plunge Europe, and perhaps the world, into war. Jacques Roth, the group's moderator, concluded that the German industrial complex's continuing rearmament of Germany will inevitably result in the country's pursuit of a Western European Aryan Empire. Germany's invasion of the Ruhr and the Rhineland demonstrates that the process has already begun, Roth says.

The Power Cycle in History

Miss Cecelia Chang, a scholar from Hong Kong, started the group's presentation. Miss Chang, daughter of one of Hong Kong's most influential trading families, presented an analysis of 5,000 years of Far Eastern history that demonstrates repetitive sequences of the seven-step Power Cycle, she says.

Anthony Garibaldi, of Garibaldi wines, next traced three millennia of European history, showing how the continuous occurrence of power cycles could be used to explain the rise and fall of kingdoms and power coalitions in Europe and the Middle East.

Ian Meyer, scion of the founding family of one of London's most respected auction houses, Meyer & Co., used his analysis of the seventeenth-, eighteenth-, and nineteenth-century British, Dutch, and French empires to reinforce the findings of his colleagues and to more clearly define each of the seven phases of The Power Cycle.

The Power Cycle in Modern Europe

Next, Mike Stone, son of Morgan Stone, chairman of New York's Stone City Bank, listed details of recent events occurring in Germany that closely correspond to the early phases of previous power cycles. "Left unopposed," he said, "German national ambitions will almost certainly evolve into a quest for a pan-European empire. If allowed to occur, what alternative, other than another world war, will be available to restore political and economic sovereignty to Europe?"

Miss Claudine Demaureux, daughter of Henri Demaureux, the well-respected chairman of the Swiss bank of the same name, began her presentation by questioning whether this German military-economic-political power process was limited to just Germany. Referencing Swiss banking practices, she described some of the interlocking business agreements and investments that have been consummated between German industrialists and their counterparts on both sides of the Atlantic. Miss Demaureux concluded her remarks by asking, "Will these oligopolies, designed to restrict production, control markets, and concentrate capital, threaten the objectivity of the foreign policy of the United States and Great Britain? Have Germany's relationships with these nations' industrial and financial communities become so pervasive as to prevent these two great powers from opposing Hitler's aims on the rest of Europe?"

Is Now the Time to Act?

Jacques Roth, heir to the great French banking fortune, concluded the group's presentation. Using stories originally reported in European newspapers, Mr. Roth illustrated the fact that German military forces of limited strength have already invaded and successfully occupied the Ruhr and the Rhineland valleys, two regions that separate France from Germany. He asserted that by not understanding Germany's true agenda of imperialistic conquest—and the economic imperatives of its principal financiers—the governments of France and England failed to respond in sufficient force. Roth theorizes that by preferring policies of appeasement rather than utilizing their superior military advantage, a pacifist France and England and an isolationist America are allowing Hitler's pursuit of an Aryan Empire to proceed.

"Maybe it's important that we step back and examine what is really happening to our ever-shrinking planet," Roth said. "If and when we do respond, how much more violence and loss of life will be required than if efforts to eradicate these problems had taken place in the early stages of corruption? Big governments, burdened with their many dams of bureaucratic inertia, have historically never been able to identify, process, and react to new threats with the same degree of alacrity as the perpetrators. History is demonstrating that these power cycles are commencing much more quickly. The cost of war, measured in dollars and the killing capacity of new weaponry, is advancing at an alarming rate."

Roth concluded, "Our research suggests the need for some kind of watchdog organization funded independently of national and private politico-economic self-interests. Such an organization would be responsible for identifying these emerging pockets of corruption in their early stages, exposing them to the broader world, and finding solutions that can be used to eradicate these cancers when lower-level means can still be used effectively."

Government spokespersons in attendance left before the question-and-answer period that concluded the session. At press time, none of them could be reached for comment.

Dr. Tom was not surprised to learn the government spokesmen had left so soon. In the environment created by the Sentinels, it was highly likely that questions might be asked which the government wouldn't want to answer.

Chapter 1

TWO OLD FRIENDS

GENEVA, SWITZERLAND, MARCH 17, 1943

A conservative, precise man of reason and logic, and the seventh-generation president of the highly regarded Demaureux Bank of Geneva, Henri Demaureux inspired confidence in his investors and fellow bankers.

Henri valued his daily routines. Each morning, he would begin by sorting his own mail, separating the letters into three stacks. The first pile he would deal with personally, the second he would give to the appropriate vice president, and the third would be handled by his trusted secretary of many years.

As he sorted the day's mail, a hand-addressed envelope from his old friend Karl von Schagel caught Henri's eye and disrupted his morning ritual. The envelope was odd. Ever since Karl had been appointed Germany's deputy minister of finance, he had proudly used his official German government letterhead to communicate with both his friends and his business associates. Henri wondered why, on this occasion, he would choose to use his personal stationery. Curious, he quickly opened the letter.

Rising from behind his desk, Henri carried the letter to the large bay window overlooking a blustery Lake Geneva. The extra light made it easier for him to read Karl's cramped handwriting.

Dear Henri,

Please forgive my boldness in inviting myself to your chalet in St. Moritz. Recent developments in the war have made my job even more strenuous, and I would benefit greatly from a brief holiday. I am planning to visit Geneva the week after next on state business, which should not take more than a few hours. If it is convenient, I would look forward to combining some business with a weekend of relaxation with you and Julia.

Karl

Henri rubbed his hand over his thinning hair. This was certainly a strange communication—especially since Karl knew very well that Julia, Henri's wife, had been killed three years ago in a terrible skiing accident. Karl and Anna had attended her funeral! What would prompt him to mention her name and talk as if she were still living? And Karl could not have forgotten that the chalet was in Chamonix, not St. Moritz; he had been there several times. Henri read and reread the note, growing more puzzled. Finally, he lifted his eyes and gazed out the frosted window.

Karl's note and the weather outside turned Henri's thoughts to his beloved Julia, whom he still couldn't remember without tears welling from his eyes. Forcing himself to return his attention to the cryptic letter, he speculated about what could be bothering Karl. *Is it the war? This request has to involve more than a relaxing weekend. The pressure of serving two masters—Hitler and his industrial affiliates—must be making Karl's life very strenuous.*

Henri picked up a pen.

Karl, my friend,

I, too, would enjoy yet another occasion of challenging skiing on the slopes of St. Moritz. It would be less than hospitable if Julia and I refused your request. The backgammon board waits as well. Let me know when your train will be arriving in Geneva, and I will meet you.

Henri

━━

Declining to tell even his wife the true purpose of his visit to Geneva, Karl von Schagel left home with a farewell kiss from Anna and her request that he give Henri her warmest regards.

He arrived at the station half an hour before his train was to depart. Anhalter Bahnhof, once known for welcoming Berlin's most important arrivals, was now called *Tränengleis*, or "Track of Tears." This was the place where many of the Jews who had been taken from their loved ones were placed on trains, never to be seen again.

Escorted by the senior member of his staff, Karl boarded his private car, which was attached to one of Germany's crack expresses. It was wartime; nothing was spared in facilitating the movement of Hitler, his High Command, or his senior government officials.

Karl couldn't forget his amazement the first time he'd traveled in this car as the deputy minister of finance. It had been specially modified; it was half again as long as a regular passenger car. Its glossy, royal burgundy exterior, embossed with the gold government seal, elegantly covered hardened steel alloy panels, and bulletproof windows. It contained a full galley, a dining area that sat eight, and a library bar stocked with the finest wines and distilled spirits. Master suites were located on one end of the car, with staff facilities at the opposite end.

Karl breathed in the rich smell of leather and the hint of the flavorful dinner being prepared in the galley. He tugged off his gloves and took off his heavy leather topcoat before sitting in a well-cushioned chair and propping his carefully polished leather boots on the nearby ottoman. Unbuttoning his collar, he looked around at the richness of the mahogany paneling, the polished oak flooring covered with rare, Oriental area rugs, the gleaming brass lamps and fixtures, and the paintings by Renaissance and Impressionist masters. These were the special amenities afforded to men in his position.

But Karl was no longer impressed. Recently, he had begun to wonder from whose home or from which museum these priceless possessions had been stolen. Most likely, they had been the personal property of productive and responsible Jewish citizens of Germany, some of whom might have been friends of his family and clients of his firm. These spoils of war only served to remind him of how far astray the policies of Hitler and the Third Reich had gone.

A member of the car's staff brought Karl a well-chilled martini made with British gin, French vermouth, Italian olives, and a twist of Spanish lemon, served in a long-stemmed crystal glass made in Ireland. Karl registered the irony that Germany was engaged in war with three of these countries, had aligned itself with the fourth, and had supported a destructive civil war in the fifth. As he sipped his drink, he reflected again on the decisions that had brought him to this moment. *How many more times, I wonder, will I regret not having insisted that the seven gentlemen gathered in my library, all those years ago, answer my question?*

Karl stared out the window as the train left Berlin. The industrial areas on the outskirts of the city, the recently favored targets of British and American bombers, were beginning to show the ravages of war. Even the white frosting of a winter storm could not hide the devastation of Karl's once-proud country.

Sighing, he sat back and tried to put the troubles of Germany out of his mind. A second martini failed to dull the horrors he had been forced to witness. He envisioned German troops lying strewn across the frozen plains of Russia. *Our armies are trapped in Stalingrad, and another regiment faces defeat in North Africa. The tides of war are changing. It's only a question of time before the Allies invade Europe's mainland.*

He remembered Herr Schmidt's blue eyes boring into him during a recent "meeting." In reality, the occasion was more like a summons. "Karl, we've all discussed it," Schmidt had said, "and we want you to develop a plan that will allow us to remove our personal wealth from Germany while there is still time.

"You know how dangerous it will be to attempt this transfer. It is absolutely critical that we avoid detection by Hitler or any of his High Command. A man I knew, acting in concert with two of Admiral Canaris's *Abwehr* agents, was caught smuggling a modest amount of money across the frontier into Switzerland. Rumor has it that all three received fast trials and even faster executions. I wouldn't want to guess what would happen if Hitler became suspicious of what we are planning."

And so, I have now become their smuggler, Karl remembered thinking as he began writing his cryptic note to his old friend, Henri Demaureux. Now he was on the train that would take him to Henri and the next phase of this latest distasteful secret mission.

Lost in thought, he was startled by the sudden announcement of dinner. He rose and walked over to the carefully arranged dining table. But even the 1935 Chateau Margaux and pheasant, his favorite entrée, couldn't stop him from thinking about his forthcoming meeting. *Will Henri understand? Will he be willing to help? Can he be trusted?* That last question was the most important of all.

After a second glass of wine, Karl began to reflect on the events of the last eight years. In 1935, everything had seemed so promising. With the financial support of Karl's clients, Hitler and his National Socialist German Workers Party had risen to power. Once their power had been consolidated and Hitler's virtual dictatorship over Germany had been established, it wasn't long before the industrialists' influence was being exercised over the new government. Karl's cohorts had been busy supplying the armaments to satisfy Hitler's unquenchable thirst to rebuild the German military machine. Driven by the relentless demands of the buildup, enormous profits were generated for the industrialists. The German economy began recovering from its disrepair following the Great War, and mutually profitable arrangements had been made among right-wing industrialists on both sides of the Atlantic.

By 1938, Hitler and his new armies were reaching out and occupying neighboring countries. By 1940, Germany controlled most of Western Europe, exceeding the reasonable expectations of even some of the nation's leaders.

Now, three years later, why were things so different? How had Karl and his clients lost the influence they had once enjoyed over Hitler? How had Hitler-the-puppet become Hitler-the-puppetmaster? Why hadn't they predicted his rising popularity with the German people?

Hitler and his government were no longer dependent on the support of the elite industrialists. Over the years, the combination of a reviving economy, an appeal to German national pride, military victories, and the convenience of the Jews as scapegoats for all that was wrong had consolidated Hitler's popularity with the working people of Germany.

At that moment, Karl felt a cold shiver run down his back, even in the climate-controlled comfort of his private car. It was clear to him that he would have to make a choice: Would he commit treason against his beloved Germany by helping his clients transfer private wealth out of the very country that had made them rich and that needed capital now more than ever, or would he abandon them in their self-serving attempts? Either way, he would no longer be the loyal servant. He would be left standing on his own—if he was lucky.

Chapter 2

A CALL FROM GENEVA

As was her habit, Claudine arrived at her office in the Demaureux Bank building promptly at eight o'clock each morning. But her mental state today was anything but ordinary. Instead of sorting her correspondence—a habit she had acquired from her father—she sat in her leather desk chair, chewed her thumbnail, and stared pensively out the window at the gray, rainy early spring day.

She spent much of the rest of the day attempting to appear focused on her work. Fortunately for Claudine, her father, who was more attuned to her moods than anyone else she knew, was relatively preoccupied with some matter of his own, and no one else appeared to notice her unease.

Now, as the time approached, she was becoming agitated. *How could Father even consider the idea of helping preserve the capital of the very same people who financed Hitler's rise to power? Getting their money out of Germany to shorten the war is one thing, but freeing it up so that they can do the same thing somewhere else is quite another. Doesn't he realize it will only be a matter of time before these depositors find a new opportunity to start the next Reich?*

She felt her father should have trusted her sooner with the plan involving Karl von Schagel. Then, the two of them together could have developed a plan to tie up the Germans' capital for a very long time, preventing it from being used for more malevolent political purposes. Any plan that didn't accomplish this wasn't acceptable. Her research at Berkeley told her what would surely happen if the German industrialists were allowed to retain their wealth to use as they wished. The Power Cycle would simply begin again in a different guise, in a different place.

She sat back in her chair. She could still remember, as if it were yesterday, when she'd first met the five colleagues who would become, over the course of her study at Berkeley, both her best friends and her most challenging intellectual sparring partners.

Mike Stone, though unassuming and gentle in many ways, was tough, driven, and determined to succeed. He'd told her once that he used to sneak out of his house and down to the local YMCA for boxing lessons.

"Why did you have to sneak?" she'd asked.

"It was something my father never understood or approved of."

"So, why do it?"

"Well, let me put it this way. There were always plenty of street-wise guys in the gym who wanted to knock some sense into the rich Jewish kid. And they did. I literally had to fight my way out of there every day, but I learned something in the process. When we climbed into the ring, there were no such things as social class, color, or even family names, for that matter. I couldn't tell whose father earned how much. None of that counted there. You were judged only by what you brought to the bout.

"All I could see was an opponent who had to be beaten . . . an obstacle that had to be brought down. Fighting each different person was like solving a complicated problem, and that served me well outside the gym too. Even now, I equate challenges in my life to opponents in the ring. I can't rely on anyone else to do my fighting. It's just them and me."

Claudine smiled faintly. *Just them and me.* Mike would understand exactly what she was up against. She picked up the phone.

———

"Mr. Stone, there's a call for you and Mr. Roth from Geneva—a Miss Claudine Demaureux. Will you take it in the executive conference room?" the secretary asked.

"Yes, Carole, thanks. Would you please ask Mr. Roth to join me?"

Mike Stone quickly walked down one of Stone City Bank's long corridors to the room with the transatlantic telephones. It had been a while since he'd talked to Claudine, and he wondered why she was calling. She was not one to make social calls.

The first time Mike had ever laid eyes on Claudine, she'd been sitting in front of a large plate-glass window. The sunlight on her silver-blond hair made it appear almost luminous. Even from across the room, he could see her blue eyes set perfectly in that gorgeous face of hers.

Mike had quickly realized it would be a mistake to judge Claudine as some sort of pampered, rich European coquette. Underneath her cool Nordic appearance lay more intelligence and intensity than any three other people.

Mike's thoughts were interrupted by Jacques, who rushed into the conference room. "Mike, we have to do something about those elevators," he panted. "They are so . . . slow that I couldn't wait. I ran . . . up three flights of stairs . . . when I heard Claudine was calling."

Jacques slumped down in a chair next to Mike and each of them picked up a phone.

"Claudine, greetings from New York. Jacques and I are both here. To what do we owe the pleasure of this call?"

"Mikey!" Claudine's voice sang over the line. "I was wondering if you and Jacques are still planning to attend the International Bankers Gold Conference in Zurich during the second week of April. The economic climate in Germany appears to be changing quite rapidly, and I think we should meet before the conference to discuss the effects it's had on the banking business. Since you are going to be so close, Father and I were wondering if you could come early and spend a few days skiing at our chalet in St. Moritz. I know you are both busy, but I simply won't accept no for an answer."

Claudine had no sooner gotten the words out than the line went dead. Mike and Jacques stared at each other in confusion, still holding the receivers in their hands.

"St. Moritz?" Jacques said. "Their chalet's in Chamonix. What is she—"

"Something is wrong," Mike said. "Claudine's a smart girl. She probably knows German agents are monitoring international calls. What's she trying to tell us that she doesn't want them to know?"

Half to himself, Jacques said, "It's like that nonsense code we used to have at Berkeley, when we thought someone might be listening in on our research discussions. She asked if we were attending the IBG Conference in Zurich. I'm sure it's to be held in Geneva. But Zurich is where she and I had such a bad experience trying to introduce the concept of gold bearer bonds to the banking community. Things were going so badly that I said I would never come back to Zurich, even if the *streets* were paved with gold." He looked at Mike. "Maybe she's telling us that we need to go to Geneva to talk about something to do with gold."

"Well, I was struck by the fact that she called me 'Mikey.' She *knows* I hate being called that," Mike said. "When we were at Berkeley, she would only call me by that name when she had something serious to discuss and wanted me to really focus on what she was saying. I agree with you . . . Next month, she wants us in Chamonix, and she obviously couldn't discuss details over the phone."

Jacques nodded. "Actually, it wouldn't hurt us to get out of old New York, the city that never lets us sleep."

"That's true. I'm flying out someday within the next week to meet Cecelia, but beyond that, I haven't got anything scheduled. We haven't seen Ian in five years, either. Let's leave a little early and spend a few days with him in London before heading to Geneva. It'll be like a little group reunion."

———

Claudine stared at the phone. The call hadn't taken long. She wondered if it had gone well and if Mike and Jacques would remember that silly code they had used at school. *We used to joke that we were all becoming paranoid. I guess it wasn't so silly after all.*

Jacques was the son of one of her father's closest friends. Long before arriving in Berkeley, she had heard "Jacques stories," accounts of his exploits on and off the soccer field. The sports sections of French newspapers would frequently publish pictures of Jacques pursuing the ball toward the goal with such reckless abandon. Often, in the same edition, she would find photos of him in the society section, escorting his latest companion to a charity ball, the opera, or his favorite nightclub. Left unreported were his academic achievements at L'Ecole d'Administration in Paris and, later, at the London School of Economics.

Working so closely together for the three years at Berkeley, they had become good friends. Yet, always mindful of Jacques' reputation as a womanizer, Claudine preferred to maintain their relationship on a professional level. More than once, however, she wondered what might have happened if she had allowed things to be different.

Well, never mind all that. I'm about to get in over my head here, and Jacques and Mike are the only people who can help.

Chapter 3

SPIES AND LOVERS

As excited as Mike was to see Cecelia, he knew he wouldn't be able to enjoy their time together until he got some answers, even if it cost him their relationship.

I'm going to ask her about all the mysterious phone calls and unexplained visits to Chinatown. I know she's hiding something . . . I just don't know how bad it is.

As the skyline of the city appeared beyond the left wing, his mind drifted back to that day nearly eight years ago when he and Cecelia had first met. He'd seen her sitting across the table from the glamorous Claudine. The two women appeared to be having a serious discussion.

It wasn't Cecelia's physical appearance that had first attracted Mike, although even now, he could still envision what she'd been wearing: a plain white blouse with a Mandarin collar, a Chinese-red blazer, and a black, pleated skirt. What had attracted his attention were the sense of serenity she had and her aura of great personal strength and determination. He could tell immediately that she was a very special person.

As she'd spoken, Cecelia's facial expressions had seemed to mirror her every thought, giving her ideas a life of their own.

Almost immediately upon reaching the table, Mike had felt the surge of personal chemistry passing between them. He must have been staring rather impolitely, because Claudine had broken off her conversation.

"Oh, excuse me. Cecelia," Claudine had said, "I want to introduce you to Mike Stone from New York. His father and mine are great friends." She'd turned to Mike and continued, "And this is Cecelia Chang. She has come all the way from Hong Kong to join our study group."

In one fluid movement, Cecelia had risen, dipped into a slight bow, extended her hand, and in her quiet, clipped British accent, said, "Hello, Mike Stone."

"Nice to meet you," he'd said. "I'm sorry. I didn't mean to interrupt."

"Not at all," Claudine had said. "We were just—"

"—rallying against a male-dominated regime." Cecelia had shrugged. "You know, the usual girl talk." She grinned; Mike was hopelessly smitten.

The two women had motioned for him to sit down. "I was just telling Claudine about my life in Hong Kong," she'd continued. "I attended a private school where we were required to wear uniforms, the kind with pleated tartan skirts and white blouses—long sleeves in winter, short sleeves in spring and fall, just for a little variety. But it was those long, blue knee-length socks that bothered me the most. They always seemed to itch and make my legs look fat. Someday, I would like to meet the man who designed those . . . and I'm *sure* it was a man." They'd all laughed.

The two women compared notes on their sheltered—they considered them stifling—upbringings. Claudine expressed gratitude that by making the Swiss women's Olympic ski team, she'd at least gotten the opportunity to travel and escape the constant pressure to conform to her society's expectations of "proper" young ladies.

"Claudine, you really were lucky," Cecelia had said. "The only way I could learn more about life beyond Hong Kong was to *leave*. That's why the idea of visiting the United States and attending an American graduate school became such an obsession."

"And now you're here," Mike had interjected. "How did it come about that our study group would be graced by your presence?"

"Well, I earned it," Cecelia had said simply, "same as all of you." She said the words with a self-assurance and directness that Mike found totally disarming—and would come to admire more and more.

"Dr. Tom and his wife—"

"—are friends of your family," Mike and Claudine said almost simultaneously, and the three of them began laughing.

"It's true," Cecelia said. "How did you know?"

"You'll come to find out that Dr. Tom is the main thing we all have in common," Mike said. "Let's just say he gets around."

"At any rate, it was during a visit to our home in Hong Kong by Dr. Tom and Deborah that I first learned about the doctoral program he would be teaching the next year. Violating my society's strict 'seen but not heard' policy, I asked so many questions that my father reached over and put his hand on my arm. It was a clear signal to stop, *not* a suggestion."

"Your father sounds a bit like mine," Mike had said, remembering sneaking out of his window to go to the boxing gym while his father had thought he was upstairs, studying.

"Without telling anyone, I wrote for the course information, applied for admission, and took the tests," Cecelia said. "A few months later, I received my acceptance in the form of a personal invitation from Dr. Tom. Though I was elated, my concern over my father's reaction prevented me from truly enjoying my success. For weeks, I wondered how to best broach the issue."

"What did you do?" Claudine had asked, wide-eyed.

"As chance would have it, shortly thereafter, our long-time friends, Sir Edmond Meyer and his son, Ian, were visiting us during one of their art-buying trips to Asia. One night at dinner, Sir Edmond proudly announced that his son had been accepted to Dr. Tom's program the following fall. Without thinking, I blurted out that I had been accepted into the same program. The shock and disbelief on my father's face were almost audible amid the stunned silence from the dinner table. The time to get his approval had arrived, just not exactly as I had planned."

Cecelia had a serene smile on her face as she thought about her father, the all-powerful Ivan Chang. He loved his daughter deeply and had marveled at her intelligence and tenacity, telling her once, at a young age, that it was easier to give up and answer all of her questions than it was to keep sending her away.

"After an hour of highly energized debate," Cecelia had said, "I finally hit upon the right question to ask him. 'Father, do you want me to remain in Hong Kong and marry some older man whom I won't love, or will you set me free to study in America and realize whatever human potential I might possess?'"

"And he agreed?" Mike had asked, impressed.

"How could anyone in his right mind refuse?" Cecelia said, with a slight shrug and a smile.

———

The line in front of Mike moved slowly as passengers filed off the plane. Finally, he reached the exit, looked out at the gate area, and saw her. Any suspicions about mysterious phone calls and visits disappeared. *How could anyone in his right mind do anything that might destroy a relationship with her?*

Cecelia had pushed her way past the gate attendant and was waiting at the bottom of the stairs as he took that last step.

Throwing herself into his arms, this modest woman gave him a passionate and lingering kiss, unaware of the smiling passengers around them.

As she and Mike disentangled and started to walk arm in arm toward baggage claim, he asked, "Have you told anyone in your office where we're staying?"

She looked up at him and said, "Why would you ask that?"

"Because almost every time I've been out here, we get interrupted by one of your special meetings. I just want to spend six unbroken days with *you!*"

She stopped, looked him straight in the eye, and said, "I promise, there will be no meetings and no interruptions. In fact, Mr. Stone, you'd better get used to the idea of having to pay attention to me nonstop for the next six days."

The look in her eyes as she said it made Mike tingle in all the right places.

After they had claimed his luggage and were driving south on U.S. 101 toward Carmel, Mike remembered another mysterious phone call. "You'll never guess who called Jacques and me. Claudine telephoned from Geneva. You know, she can be so dramatic at times, but it seemed to us that she was trying to convey a very serious message."

"Trying to?"

"Remember our code from school? She used that. All we know is that she wants us to come to Switzerland next week."

Cecelia took on a worried look. "Here on the Pacific Coast, we're seeing a lot of money moving around. There are some very wealthy families throughout China and Southeast Asia who are concerned about protecting their savings from the Japanese. For years, they have been selling off their plantations, their companies, and anything else that couldn't be easily moved, and converting their wealth into gold. Perhaps Claudine wants to do something similar. After all, as the one who helped develop them, she certainly has a firsthand knowledge of the use of gold bearer bonds.

"If the Jews were still trying to move their wealth out of Germany, I would understand what's happening. But in this instance, I got the feeling she was talking about someone else. You don't suppose it could be German industrialists? Could it be that the fox and the chickens are seeking financial refuge in the same henhouse?" she asked.

As Cecelia leaned into him and he breathed the heady scent of her, Mike hardly noticed the long ride. Carmel-by-the-Sea was a quaint little village sustained by the Big Sur artist colony, golfers who came to play the great Monterey Peninsula courses, many wealthy retired residents, and tourists who frequented its collection shops, art galleries, and restaurants. It was the perfect place to get away from the bank, the war, and the world, if only for a few precious days.

Quickly, he and Cecelia fell into a lovers' routine. They spent days on the sand and nights in each other's arms, and he started to believe that nothing could intrude on their bliss.

On the fourth day there, they were returning from the beach when Cecelia suggested, "Why don't you go back to the room? I want to stop in a gift shop I saw the other day. I'll meet you in a few minutes."

"I don't mind going with you," he said.

"How's a girl supposed to buy a surprise gift if you go with her? By the time you shower and change, I'll be back. You'll hardly even know I was gone."

"You're wrong about that," he said, kissing her cheek and slowly backing away. "But you've convinced me."

"Good. Maybe later I can convince you to take me to that restaurant on the Monterey Wharf, the one we've been hearing so much about."

Back in the hotel room, Mike took off his clothes and climbed into the shower. He took an extra long time to wash off all the sand, then shaved and put on fresh clothes. Cecelia still wasn't back, so he sat down in a chair to wait for her. After a few minutes, however, he left the room and checked the bar and lobby. There was no sign of her. Growing increasingly concerned, he walked out the front door and turned toward Ocean Avenue.

He spotted her in a phone booth across the street from the gift shop she had wanted to visit. Her back was to him, but he could tell by the way she was gesturing that she was engaged in a heated conversation.

Suddenly, she slammed down the telephone, turned abruptly, and saw him looking at her. "Mike!" she exclaimed. "I thought you went to the hotel!"

"I did. But you didn't show up so I started to worry and came looking for you." Cecelia was clearly upset. Trying to defuse the situation, he glanced down at his freshly pressed sport shirt and trousers and said, "See? No more sand."

When she didn't reply, he said, "What was that all about, anyway? I thought you promised no business this weekend."

"I told the office I would check at least once for messages," she said, frowning a bit. Her face held a "no trespassing" sign, but then her mood changed. Giving him a charming smile, she took his arm, stepped off the curb, and started walking toward the hotel.

"Come back to the room while I get out of my bathing suit. If you aren't too mad at me about talking business, changing clothes could take a very long time."

———

Famished from no lunch and an afternoon of lovemaking, Mike and Cecelia drove to a small seafood restaurant that overlooked the lights of the bay. But even the romantic afternoon, the ambiance of the rustic restaurant, a bottle of good wine, and same-day fish all failed to dissolve Mike's lingering concern about the phone call. *I've been up against bigger opponents*, he thought. *But they could only break my nose—she could break my heart.*

He took a deep breath and started in. "Cecelia, I can't help it . . . I know talking about that call with you is trespassing on forbidden territory, but you have to understand my side. I have tried to accept the unexplained trips and urgent calls, but I find it increasingly difficult to ignore them. So difficult, in fact, that I am beginning to question how we can continue to build a relationship based on secrets. I think it's time that you let me know what's going on."

Her ensuing silence was deafening; he was sure she could hear the pounding of his heart. But after what seemed like an eternity, Cecelia began to talk. "If I didn't love you so much, I wouldn't tell you. I can't even imagine how many federal laws I'm breaking by doing this. When I'm through, I'm sure you'll understand why my need for confidentiality had nothing to do with our relationship."

She looked him squarely in the face. "During our last semester at Cal, I was approached by an agency of the United States government. They asked me if I would be willing to use my family contacts throughout Asia to assist them in establishing a network of people who could help the enemies of Japan remove their wealth from probable confiscation. That's how I guessed what Claudine's phone call was probably about."

Mike stared at her, his mind beginning to whirl.

She continued matter-of-factly. "Our networks were used to convert their proceeds of sale into gold and smuggle it into Hong Kong. In earlier days, I would like to think my work was essential, but for the last year, the need for my services has been steadily declining. Everything is already in place and running smoothly, and that's why I've been trying to resign. I am learning, however, that it's difficult to walk away from classified government work. That phone call this afternoon was another in a long line of fruitless efforts to free myself. Believe me, I'm more frustrated about all this than you are."

Mike was stunned speechless. *It's hard to believe that my not-so-quiet little friend from Hong Kong has been acting as an American secret agent.*

Chapter 4

OVER THE ATLANTIC

Just before the Pan American Airways Clipper flight took off, their attractive stewardess brought Jacques what he hoped would be the first of several Boodles gin martinis. He sipped it appreciatively as the craft's takeoff pressed him back in his seat.

When the airplane had begun to level off from its initial ascent, Jacques turned to Mike, seated beside him. "I can't tell you how envious I am of your relationship with Cecelia. You make me feel that for the first time ever, I would really like to have someone to share my life with. Picking the right girl for the right event no longer seems so important. Maybe, just maybe, I think I would enjoy taking an interest in someone else—for the long term."

"These things must be stouter than I thought," Mike said, eyeing his martini.

"I'm serious. Hearing from Claudine again after all this time has got me thinking. You know, it's been three years since I saw her in Europe. It was strictly business, of course. We traveled around Europe talking to bankers, answering their questions, preparing for meetings, responding to inquiries, trying to get the gold bearer bond program she was initiating off the ground."

"Sounds like loads of fun."

"Well, that's the odd thing," Jacques said. "It was the first time I can remember deriving that much enjoyment from working so hard—not for profit or for my own glory, but to help someone else."

"Not just 'someone else.' *Claudine*."

Jacques nodded and sipped his drink. "And as much as I was physically attracted to her, I was determined to keep our relationship strictly *professional*. Thinking back, I must have cared more about having her as a friend than as my latest conquest. What's wrong with me?"

"Jacques, my old friend, I do believe that you are finally on your way to becoming a decent human being."

A few more hours into the flight, Mike interrupted Jacques' reading. "I thought I would share this with you now, when we're high over the Atlantic with no chance of escape." He was holding some documents that he had removed from his briefcase.

Seeing Jacques' irritated expression, Mike went on. "It's not *all* business. It has to do with Tony. Cecelia and I stopped by his vineyard in Napa Valley. Seems he bought up all the land that his family's money could cover. Altogether, I'd say he has assembled more than five hundred acres of the best grape land that the valley has to offer, at very attractive prices. He's even got an enormous limestone cave for storing wine under controlled temperatures. You really need to see the place to appreciate it. It looks like an old European feudal estate."

"Doesn't surprise me," Jacques said. "Knowing Tony's ambition, it's not difficult to understand how he could accomplish so much in such a short period of time. The question is, will he be content transplanting his family operation from Italy to California, or will he want to conquer the whole West Coast?"

Mike laughed. "He has already picked out another five thousand acres he hopes to develop. It's not greed, though. He's convinced he needs that much land to produce a premium quality wine. These papers," Mike said, handing them to Jacques, "are part of an investment memorandum he has prepared. It calls for twenty-five million dollars to be spent over a seven-year period. That's the amount of time he thinks is required to complete the development, bring the early plantings into production, age the wine, and generate enough revenue to make the entire operation break even. I think Tony is relying on us to raise the twenty-five million dollars."

Jacques raised his eyebrows. "That's a tall order."

On Friday morning, one stop and fifteen hours after takeoff, Mike and Jacques awoke to freshly squeezed orange juice, softly scrambled eggs, and an unparalleled view of the Irish coast. The Clipper had begun its gradual descent toward the port of Southampton.

The landing on the waters of the Thames River was smooth and uneventful. As they taxied toward the docks, Mike nudged Jacques and asked, "When did we start calling Ian 'Father Time'?"

"I'm not really sure. Always, it seems. The name just seemed to fit. Who else do you know that drove around in old cars, wore a tie to school every single day, and used both a belt *and* suspenders?"

Mike smiled and nodded. "Ah, but the women all loved him. Unlike wise guys like us, he was never interested in conquests or bragging rights. He seemed to like getting to know them as real human beings."

"Yes," Jacques said. "Unfortunately, like me, he seemed to want to get to know them *all*. Ian was never content to date just one woman at a time. He wanted various women to share in each of his various interests. It was like—"

"—grocery shopping!" they both burst out at the same time.

"Remember when he came up with that idea?" Mike said.

"He was a genius!" Jacques said. "Where else, on any given day after work, would we find all the single girls, secretaries, bookkeepers, and typists? But Ian had it figured out. We'd walk the aisles of the local grocery store, pretending to be helpless bachelors trying to shop."

"Pretending, huh?" Mike said.

As the plane neared the dock, they caught a glimpse of Ian standing next to his family's vintage Rolls Royce limousine. His very posture was British. Even from a distance, Mike and Jacques could see Ian's aristocratic profile, his long, thin, crooked nose that was the oddly perfect complement to his habitual devil-may-care attitude. He was dressed in his traditional gray and maroon tartan hat and freshly pressed, unbuttoned mackintosh. From the ground up, he wore his standard uniform: well-shined brown wing tips from Church's, gray flannel slacks, a white dress shirt, school tie, and brown Harris Tweed jacket, all to suit the English weather. With not a strand of his sandy hair out of place, he looked like a male model from a Harrod's catalogue.

Ian was waiting for them at the top of the gangway. "Can it really be five years since we've seen each other?" he asked.

They all began talking at once, and continued until Ian noticed they were holding up the line. The other passengers were patiently waiting, trying to figure out who these three young men, accompanied by a Rolls Royce and a chauffeur, might be.

Without missing a word, the three of them moved over to the car, waited for the baggage to be loaded in "the boot," and settled into the backseat.

An hour and a half, two bottles of champagne, and many stories later, the limousine pulled to a stop at the front entrance of Claridge's.

The hotel manager was waiting curbside to greet them. "Good afternoon, Mr. Meyer—it's good to see you again. The suite is ready for you and your guests."

He gave a little bow as he snapped his fingers for help.

The manager accompanied them to the top floor, unlocked the door of the suite, and ushered them inside. Mike whistled his appreciation. "Wow, this is some kind of campground! How were you able to arrange all this on such short notice?"

"Finding the right furniture and paintings for this suite was one of my first assignments when I reentered the employ of Meyer & Company. In exchange for my continued services at the hotel, the owners let me make use of this suite whenever it's not otherwise occupied."

The Royal Suite occupied the southwest corner of the top floor. From the balcony, they had a wonderful view of London and Hyde Park. Three master bedrooms opened onto a large sitting room, complete with piano, bar, and refrigerator. The ceilings were fourteen feet high, and the furniture appeared to be mostly composed of original Victorian and French provincial antiques. French Impressionist and Dutch Masters paintings graced the walls. Noticing his friends' appreciative looks, Ian said, "They call it 'the Royal Suite' for a reason. Why don't I call for room service? We have enough time for a late lunch, showers, and a short nap before we are due at the theater."

"Due at the theater! Have you lost your mind?" Jacques exclaimed. "We've come all this way, and with only three days in London, you want to take us to the theater? Boy, have you lost your touch."

Smiling his winning grin, Ian said, "Oh, didn't I tell you that we are hosting the wrap party for the cast and crew of *Red, Hot and Blue*? What better way to introduce you to some of London's loveliest sights? And I'm not just talking about the sets . . ."

Chapter 5

NATALIE OF SUSSEX

The theater had been sold out for weeks. Even in wartime, tickets were selling on the street for multiples of their face value. For Londoners, a good show made the war disappear, if only for a few hours. Tonight, the loyal patrons of the musical theater were out in force, standing in line to attend the closing performance of *Red, Hot and Blue.*

From the moment the curtain rose to the last of the standing ovations, Jacques couldn't take his eyes off the female lead. She was tall and buxom, with a small waist and long legs. But, more than that, she was blessed with an astonishing stage presence.

"Miss Natalie Cummins," as she was listed in the program, made Jacques feel as if he were the only person in the audience, and he knew from long experience that this was the true test of a great actress. His hands were sore from clapping when Ian suggested they go backstage.

So engrossed was he with the vision of Natalie, Jacques had, without realizing it, pushed any thought of Claudine completely out of his mind.

It was crowded and noisy. London's most ardent theatergoers were congratulating the exhilarated and exhausted cast. Almost immediately, Ian spotted his girlfriend, Emily, and guided his two friends over to meet her.

"You've already heard so much about each other," Ian said. "Allow me to make the proper introductions. Jacques, Mike, I'd like to introduce you to Miss Emily Smythe."

Giving them both a warm hug, Emily seemed genuinely happy to meet them.

"It's taken so long, I didn't think I would ever meet you," she said. "Ian talks about you all the time. I feel as if we've known each other forever."

"Emily," Jacques said, "Ian has been telling us that we are supposed to behave ourselves around you. He thinks you may be the 'real deal.' I can't speak for my friend, Mike, but I would like to apologize in advance, just in case."

"I accept, but I'm not sure that *we* shouldn't be the ones doing the apologizing. As theater folk, tonight will be our last night to howl before we have to return to the reality of finding new work. We even invited Natalie, our lead, to reprise some of the show's best songs. That should keep things under control, at least for the first hour."

"Speaking of Natalie, Jacques hasn't been able to pry his gaze from her all night. Will you please introduce them?" Ian asked Emily.

Seeing Natalie standing with a group of admirers, Emily walked over to them, made a brief excuse, and gently guided Natalie back to meet her new friends.

Jacques was fascinated. Up close, she was even more exquisite. Curly, cropped, caramel-colored hair framed her face. Her brown, doe eyes were large and expressive. She had the kind of clear, pink complexion that the English seemed to have invented. *I can understand why she has no trouble captivating an audience.*

"Hello, Jacques Roth," she said, extending her hand. "It's lovely to meet you." Suddenly London's most successful musical star disappeared and in her place appeared one of the most charming and unself-conscious women Jacques had ever met.

Eventually, he and Natalie drifted into a corner and fell into the kind of conversation normally reserved for old friends. The noise, crowds, and backstage confusion dissolved. They became so engrossed in their talk they lost track of time and failed to notice when people started to leave.

It was Emily who broke the spell. "Jacques, if you don't take this poor girl to her party soon, you're going to be late and your guests will be most unhappy."

The reception in the Royal Suite at Claridge's was in full swing by the time they arrived. Any thought that Jacques might have had of monopolizing Natalie's attention quickly evaporated.

"Sing us a song, love," was the constant refrain from everyone who saw her.

Seated on top of the piano with a drink in one hand, Natalie sang the best songs from the show, then their favorites from other shows, and finally some that had special meaning for all of them.

Standing in the rear, Jacques could see how the girl draped over the piano was a different person from the well-publicized star of the musical stage. She was among her friends, she was relaxed, and she was having a good time doing what she did best: entertaining.

After about an hour, Natalie eased down from the piano, swallowed the last sip of her drink, took a deep bow—to her friends' enthusiastic applause—and acknowledged the several musicians who had accompanied her. Then she grabbed Jacques in one hand and her purse in the other.

Heading toward the door, she said in a stage whisper, "If you don't take me away from here now, we shall never be allowed to finish our conversation."

They went to the bar downstairs. The hour was late; the place was almost deserted. The bartender stood behind the long mahogany bar, quietly cleaning and polishing glasses. A piano tinkled softly in the far corner. Natalie guided Jacques to a small table next to a wood-burning fireplace, where the bartender took their order of Napoleon cognac in warmed snifters, and then left them alone.

Natalie looked into Jacques' eyes and said, "In case you were wondering, I recognized you from your football—excuse me, soccer—playing days. As a young girl, I accompanied my brothers to most of England's matches. Whenever they played the French, I waited for the sight of the tall, handsome captain. Of course, I always hoped the best for England," she laughed. "But you were my prince. Then, eight years ago, you suddenly disappeared—no more newspaper articles, no more soccer games. I lost track of you. So tell me, prince, where have you been?"

"Never in my wildest imagination would I have expected you to recognize me, Natalie. I'm so flattered. But I'm afraid that I have turned into a boring banker." He talked for a few minutes about his recent history, and then abruptly said, "But enough about me. I would like to know more about you, the star of the London stage."

She smiled and looked away from him for a moment. "I'm really just a country girl from Sussex. I grew up on a farm with two older brothers, and I was always a tomboy. I took care of my share of the daily chores: milking the cows, stacking bales of hay, mucking out the animal pens. No special treatment—my brothers made sure of that."

"Wow! What happened to that tomboy?" Jacques exclaimed, eyeing her appreciatively.

Pausing to take a sip of her cognac, she continued. "At the age of eighteen, I became interested in the theater. I loved going to movies, particularly musicals. I would always be dancing and singing the scores as I worked around the house. It all seemed so natural, and I never really thought much about where it could lead me. Then, at twenty, I had had enough of Sussex. I just somehow knew that there was a different kind of life waiting for me."

"So you headed to London?"

"Where else?" She shrugged. "I found some part-time work waiting on tables, serving drinks in the pubs. Afternoon and evening jobs were never hard to find, but getting morning work was always more difficult. To fill up my spare time, I got into the habit of attending early theatrical rehearsals and auditions. I would just sit there in the empty theater, picturing myself as one of those women on stage. I used to think, 'What is it that they're doing that I haven't done a thousand times around our house?' So, one day I decided, the hell with it, and went up and stood in line. And I got in! It was just a part in the chorus, but that's how it all started.

"After that, I began to use whatever money I was able to save to pay for dancing, acting, and singing classes. I auditioned for every part that was open and was fortunate to get enough roles to keep me going. A few years later, I was chosen for the lead in *Red, Hot and Blue*. And here I am now, with the charming ex-captain of the French football team."

"What about your personal life?" Jacques asked. "Certainly, there must be someone special, or at the very least a long line of broken hearts?"

"Not really. You'd be surprised. Between work, singing, dancing, and acting lessons, there has been precious little time for much of a personal life. In my world, there is no such thing as a dinner date. By eight o'clock, I'm always on the stage."

Jacques felt an unexpected tremor of elation at that news. *Easy, boy; you've only just met her.*

As their conversation continued, they once again lost track of time. The bar was closing, and they were the only remaining patrons. Not wanting the evening to end, and not sure of what to say next, Jacques extended his hand toward Natalie. Naturally and without hesitation, she reached out and grasped it, and allowed him to lead her to the elevators. When the elevator doors closed, and he pressed the button for his floor, Natalie broke the silence. "My prince, I don't know where all this is headed, but I think I should warn you—I'm a healthy girl with healthy appetites."

Late the next morning, Jacques and Natalie were joined by Emily, Ian, and Mike for one of Claridge's renowned room-service breakfasts. Just as they were settling down to eat, the service china was rattled by air raid sirens and the sound of one of Germany's buzz bombs.

Mike and Jacques exchanged nervous glances. The three Londoners seemed content to continue the conversation and enjoy their breakfast undisturbed.

When the bomb hit, it must have been within a block of the hotel. The noise of the explosion was deafening, and the building shook. Almost immediately, they could hear the sound of another approaching bomb and people outside their room running down the hallway.

Near panic, Mike asked, "Where are they all going?"

"Oh, they're just heading for the underground right across the street," Emily said.

"I don't care how accustomed you all are to this sort of thing," Mike said, "it's scaring the hell out of me! Can we join the others?"

The Londoners remained calm but indulged their guests by making their way into the crowded tube station. Families and groups of friends sat huddled next to each other, trying hard not to show their anxiety about what was happening above. They were safe, but their homes, offices, and neighborhoods were at risk. All they could do was wait until the all-clear signals sounded so they could go street-side and inspect the damage.

A young man sitting on the platform quietly began playing his guitar. Almost out of instinct, Natalie and Emily joined him and began to sing upbeat songs, the kind people liked to hear during wartime. Those who had been huddled together, talking quietly among themselves or lost in thought, began to listen. Gradually, they sat up, more erect and hopeful. They even started to request their favorite songs. It was not long before everyone was singing and smiling, and for a short time, the war overhead seemed to have been forgotten.

Jacques realized that Natalie's singing for the scared, war-weary Britons wasn't about work—she clearly loved doing it. This was her true theater.

It was mid-afternoon before the all-clear siren sounded.

"Hungry?" Ian asked, brushing himself off.

"Famished," Emily said, taking his arm and heading for the exit.

"A little change of scenery would be nice," Natalie added.

Mike and Jacques followed behind, shaking their heads in wonderment. "I guess that stiff-upper-lip image isn't an exaggeration," Mike said.

"Oh, you Yanks did *fine*. Experiencing a bombing for the first time can be terrifying." Natalie laughed.

"Well, I don't know about a stiff upper lip, but I could sure do with a stiff drink," Mike said.

The five friends made their way to the French Club, a meeting place for the free Poles, the free French, the French Resistance, and loyal neighborhood patrons. The French Club was known for its colorful clientele, its generous drinks, its onion soup, and Maggie, its legendary proprietress.

When Maggie saw Ian and Emily, two of her regulars, she let out a "whoop!" which was part of her legend. The six-foot-tall, fifty-year-old peroxide blonde gave Ian a big bear hug, almost smothering him with her enormous breasts. Then she planted a wet kiss right on his mouth.

"Where have you been? I thought one of the air raids had finally done you in!" she said, releasing him. Then she turned to Emily, extending her hand and politely saying, "Good afternoon, Miss Emily, it's nice to see you again."

Mike smiled to himself. Maggie and the other patrons spotted Natalie as soon as she turned from hanging up her coat. "Welcome to the French Club, Miss Cummins. It is *always* such a pleasure to have you here," Maggie said cordially.

All eyes were riveted on the popular star when Maggie let out her second "whoop!" louder and longer than the first. The proprietress was staring at Jacques, halted in her tracks.

She and Jacques stood still, looking at each other. They hadn't seen each other for eight years. In his soccer-playing days, Jacques had spent a lot of time at the French Club. After their matches, win or lose, he and his teammates would always go to Maggie's place. Still dressed in their soccer uniforms, they were always looking to celebrate—victory *or* defeat, it didn't seem to make much difference.

As the team's captain and most energetic member, Jacques had usually been the one in the center of trouble. Maggie would call him her "naughty little boy" and make him stand on a chair and apologize to her other patrons for his "discourteous" behavior. They loved each other as only longtime friends could.

"Jacques Roth, you have broken poor old Maggie's heart! Where the hell have you been for the last eight years?" she asked as she grabbed him in her best bear hug, kissed him on both cheeks, and gave him a big wet one right on the mouth. Pushing him away from her, she held him at arm's length and looked him right in the eye. "Jacques, have you been faithful to your dear old Maggie?"

"*Mais toujours*, Maggie!" he answered in his most seductive voice. Mike thought it was possible, for just an instant, that Maggie blushed.

Maggie turned away, eyeing the other member of their group. "Who else have we got here?"

"Maggie," Ian said, "I want you to meet an old friend of ours, Mike Stone. You had better be nice to him. His father owns a great big bank in New York."

"Come 'ere, then," she said, walking right over to Mike and giving him her customary kiss, just to make sure that he didn't feel left out.

Some of the regulars already knew Ian and Emily; others wanted to meet Natalie; and they all wanted to meet France's legendary center forward. Maggie had no choice—she closed the front door and ordered free beers all around. Next, she placed a large cauldron of her famous onion soup on a long table, along with bowls, spoons, and napkins so people could help themselves. It was going to be a hell of a party.

This time, the music would be French. One of the patrons started to play "La Marseillaise" on an old upright piano, long forgotten and stuck away in the rear of the restaurant. For the third time in twenty-four hours, Natalie found herself singing for her friends. To Jacques' amazement, she knew his country's songs and could sing them in French.

Who is this incredible woman? One minute she is the celebrated star of the London musical stage, the next she is the warm, witty girl who enjoys entertaining her friends and fellow patriots, and then the next instant she is the amazingly noncomplex tomboy from Sussex—with healthy appetites.

Finally, as the sun was beginning to set and everyone had talked themselves out, an exhausted Natalie excused herself, grabbed Jacques' hand, and said, "Prince, take me to your castle!"

———

Still a farm girl at heart, Natalie had risen early Sunday morning and had begun preparing the orange juice and coffee while the others were still sleeping.

Alone with her early morning chores, she began to think about the two days she had spent with Jacques. *Today may be the last that he and I will spend together for what could be a very long time. I feel that we've shared something special, intimate. Wouldn't it be nice if we could spend the rest of the day taking a drive down to Surrey? I would like to show him the real me.*

Suddenly, her thoughts were interrupted by a loud, persistent knocking. Half asleep, Jacques staggered out of his bedroom to the door of their suite and opened it. He was greeted by a large, uniformed man with bright orange hair.

"RAF Sergeant O'Halloran, at your service," he stated, clicking his heels together and giving his snappiest salute. "I've been instructed to fetch a Mr. Stone and a Mr. Roth to Brookings Field as quickly as possible, sir. It seems that your scheduled flight on the Demaureux Bank plane has been canceled due to mechanical difficulties. We've been instructed to fly you across occupied France to Geneva in two of our fastest fighter planes, flown by two of our most experienced pilots. Believe me when I say you are in for one hell of a ride."

Surprised, Jacques stood there for a few seconds with his mouth agape before he went to wake the others. He and Mike showered, dressed, and quickly packed. Just as Jacques was looking around the room for anything that he might have forgotten, Natalie entered, carrying a cup of coffee.

"Here, you might need this," she said. "This is not the way I would have preferred to say good-bye, but it's been a lovely two days."

"Natalie," he said, taking her by the hands, "I'd like to think that we are not saying good-bye. I hope we are saying, 'à bientôt, mon ami.'"

Chapter 6

LEAVING LONDON

Arriving at Brookings Field, Jacques and Mike noticed the two British Spitfires warming up on the tarmac. It was impossible to miss them.

One glance told Jacques that these were frontline planes: the repairs to their outside skin showed where bullets or flak must have penetrated. Several black swastikas were painted below the pilot canopy of both planes. Grease and oil stains were everywhere. Painted on the nose of each plane was an image of a scantily clad woman: one was holding a Union Jack, the other was wearing the hat of Uncle Sam.

Sergeant O'Halloran escorted Jacques and Mike into a small locker room inside the hangar. There, he helped them change into flight gear, fitted them with parachutes, and explained how to pull the rip cord on each chute.

Leading them out to the planes, he introduced them to their pilots, helped them get belted into the rear seats, and stuffed their luggage under their feet, the only available space. He then showed them how to eject, should it become necessary.

This all happened in what seemed like a split second, before the two civilians could fully absorb what was happening to them.

O'Halloran backed away, and the two planes taxied into position, receiving immediate permission for takeoff. Totally unprepared for the noise, the acceleration, and the sharp rate of ascent, Jacques hardly had time to catch his breath before realizing that they were well out over the English Channel, heading directly toward occupied France.

Just as he was becoming accustomed to the secure feeling of level flight, both planes began to dive toward the surface of the channel. At just the moment when it seemed they were going to hit water, the planes pulled up and leveled off.

They were now crossing France at maximum speed and minimum altitude, in a constantly darting motion. Jacques didn't know what to fear most—the sound of ground fire passing so close to the plane or the violent twisting of the plane itself. *I guess we're beginning to learn what war is all about*, he thought. *Buzz bombs in London, burning buildings, enemy flak, and attacking fighters are starting to make war very real and very personal.*

He needed to get his mind off his immediate circumstances—but how?

Luckily, he could still smell Natalie's perfume, drifting up from the scarf she'd given him as he was leaving, which he'd carefully tucked inside his flight suit. He could still imagine the touch of her warm, soft skin and hear her voice singing only to him. Perhaps it was the war; perhaps it was the fact that they'd both known they would soon be oceans apart. Whatever it was, it was obvious that they had grown incredibly close, both physically and emotionally, in a matter of only a few days.

How refreshing it was to be with someone else who was the center of attention for a change. The last time that had happened was three years ago—with Claudine.

Claudine . . . What's happening to me? For years, I've been content to play the field, never allowing myself to become emotionally involved. Now, there are two women I really seem to care about!

He smiled to himself. *I'm a fool. What am I worried about? I've only known Natalie for forty-eight hours, and I've never even had a real date with Claudine. Besides, I could be dead within the next two minutes.*

Just then, the plane twisted sharply.

———

Mike was more scared than he had ever been. Any unexpected, sudden movement of the plane—which happened every few minutes—any gunfire, or any sighting of an enemy fighter compelled him to use the intercom to ask the pilot what was happening.

Unable to answer all Mike's questions and still concentrate on the task at hand, the pilot began to ignore him. The silence on the other end of the intercom only added to Mike's anxiety. He wasn't sure whether his stomach was going to handle all the motion. *I sure don't want to be the sissy who vomits in the back of the plane. Jacques would never let me live it down. That is, if we live . . .*

Sergeant O'Halloran had explained to them that once their planes were discovered, the pilots would increase altitude for more room to maneuver. Higher up, they could change their direction and speed to avoid flak attacks from the artillery below. *Very reassuring*, Mike thought to himself at the sound of the engine's acceleration. The increase in their angle of ascent and their sudden rise in altitude told Mike they were coming under fire.

"Hang on, Mr. Stone," shouted the pilot over the intercom. Warned, but unprepared for the sudden movement, the noise of exploding flak, and the thud of it hitting the plane, Mike was becoming more terrified by the moment. Despite the fact that he was tightly strapped in, he was being thrown around his tiny seating area. *You've got to find your legs, Mike, just like in the ring.*

After surviving the first barrage, he was becoming a little more assured. But just as he thought he was learning to accept the danger of the artillery below, they encountered their first enemy aircraft—in the air beside them.

His pilot executed an abrupt rolling dive to the right, and Mike could hear the noise of the twenty-caliber bullets whizzing past. The sharp deceleration of the plane, as the pilot activated the air brakes, pushed him forward in his seat. From this position, he could hear the noise of the attacking plane before he actually saw the black monster pass above them. The ear-shattering sounds of wing guns were the last thing he experienced before seeing the German fighter explode directly in front of them.

When they finally leveled off, Mike heard the pilot's calm voice over the intercom: "Mr. Stone, the trouble should be over. We'll be flying around Paris to avoid the antiaircraft fire and should arrive in Geneva in about forty-five minutes."

———

As the two Spitfires taxied toward the military hangar, Jacques could see Claudine. She was waiting for them just inside the big door. As they climbed down from the planes, she walked forward to greet them. After giving them each a warm and enthusiastic hug and a kiss on both cheeks, she stood back and said, "Well, let's have a look at the two of you. You certainly don't look the worse for wear!"

Jacques wasn't listening. Her hug seemed a little tighter and her kisses a little longer than a customary greeting between two old friends. *Or maybe I'm just wishing . . .*

"Nothing but the best for you bankers," she said. "How did you enjoy the ride?"

Mike's experience had left him in no joking condition. "I certainly wasn't planning on anything like this. Whatever happened to the slow, smooth DC3s? Surely, we could have waited until your plane's mechanical difficulties were fixed!"

But Jacques' and Claudine's attentions were fastened on each other. Dressed in heels and a business suit, hair arranged in her customary French twist, Claudine seemed taller to Jacques, more beautiful, and more . . . professional than he remembered. *Maybe I've just been fooling myself to think she ever felt anything for me.*

"I'm so glad you made it here safely," she said. "Father and I are relieved that you saw through my gibberish and figured out the importance of our message. We have a lot to talk about. We're anxious to spend a few days with you—that is, if you can tear yourselves away from the banking conference," she concluded, wearing that mischievous smile Jacques remembered from so long ago.

"Claudine, if you and your father are in some kind of trouble, tell us what we can do to help," Mike said.

"No, it's nothing like that. A special . . . opportunity has arisen. Once we arrive at the chalet, we'll discuss it. But enough of that for now. Tell me what you two devils have been doing."

———

As Claudine turned south toward Chamonix, she was trying to concentrate on her driving, but her mind was focused on the handsome Frenchman sitting next to her.

Am I beginning to see Jacques in a whole new light? Has he matured, or is he still the old love-'em-and-leave-'em cad from college? This is the second time he has come all the way to Europe to assist me. How many girls can say that?

Chapter 7

ROOTS OF EVIL

The Alpine village of Chamonix was nestled comfortably along the northern base of Mont Blanc. It was part of the politically neutral network of ski resorts that crisscrossed the frontiers of Switzerland, France, Italy, and Austria. Skiers and vacationers could move across the borders with ease, even during wartime.

Henri stood outside the front door of the chalet, waiting to greet Jacques and Mike when they arrived. Both of them were sons of two of his oldest friends and banking colleagues. He had been following their impressive careers ever since they had graduated from Cal Berkeley in 1938, along with Claudine.

"Welcome to our mountain home. Mike, I'm pleased to finally meet you. For years, I've been listening to your father and my daughter talk about you."

"It's nice to meet you, sir," Mike said. "They both have certainly told me a great deal about you."

Shifting his attention to Jacques, Henri asked, "Son, what has it been . . . three years since your last visit? Thank you for coming all this way on such short notice."

"Of course, anything for you . . . and Claudine."

"Why don't you leave your bags inside the front door and join Father out on the deck while I prepare lunch?" Claudine suggested. "We're lucky—it's a beautiful, warm spring day."

Henri chose to keep the conversation light, although he could see that the two travelers were anxious to learn what was so important. Jacques and Mike took turns telling him about their work with gold transfers and currency exchanges. Before they could ask Henri any questions, Claudine announced that lunch was being served. "If we don't eat immediately, the trout that Father caught this morning will cool."

The trout was accompanied by fresh bread, fresh green vegetables, *pommes frites*, and an ample serving of wine. As they ate, the four discussed the recent events of the war. Rumors were starting to circulate about the increasing likelihood that Axis forces in North Africa were facing surrender or annihilation.

"A toast to the British and the Americans," Henri said, raising his glass. "A victory in North Africa could mark the first time the Allied forces will have achieved a victory after three years of battle with the Germans.

"Let's not ignore the Russians," Mike said. "The newspapers are picking up on the trouble they're giving the Nazis at Stalingrad. If the German army fails to reach Moscow before winter, Hitler's worst nightmare could be realized."

Claudine said, "Maybe that's it. The prospect of a turning tide could be the reason why the Germans are trying to get their money out of Germany."

Mike and Jacques gave each other a confused look.

"Before we get into all that," Henri said hurriedly, "I would appreciate it, Jacques and Mike, if you would allow me to ask you a couple of questions. For years, Claudine has been talking about The Power Cycle concept you worked on in California. When she returned from school, I don't believe I had ever seen her so enthusiastic about anything. In fact, this is the reason we asked you to come here."

"Excuse me, sir, but why, after all this time, are you so interested in our graduate research?" Mike asked.

"I've just concluded a series of communications with an old friend whose clients want to move some two billion dollars out of Germany while they still can. These Germans are high-ranking members of the industrial elite. His request raises other questions that I would like to discuss.

"When this war is over, public opinion will place the blame for it on Hitler and the Nazi party," Henri continued. "We will forget that it was conservative industrialists on *both* sides of the Atlantic—aided by the international financial community, and supported by right-wing sympathizers within various governments—that were the real force behind this war."

"Yes, sir," Jacques said, "that's exactly what we were trying to tell people five years ago."

"The problem goes a lot deeper, though," Henri said. "Perhaps I should explain. Even after the outbreak of war, many companies in Allied countries continued to do business with the Germans. Titus American Oil sold fuel to the German government. They routed the petroleum through Spain and moved the money through Switzerland. There are other examples, as well. These practices demonstrate how the influence of these international oligopolies is so powerful that even after the American Justice Department found out about these illegal oil sales, it was forced to withhold any lawsuits. Otherwise, Titus threatened to restrict its supply of oil to the Allied war effort."

Jacques couldn't contain his shock. "Are you telling us that the power and influence of these companies is so pervasive that they can override national priorities and *blackmail* the American government?"

"That's exactly what I mean," Henri replied. "And Germany's defeat will not eliminate the problem. These sources of corruption are like the roots of some evil weed. You can cut them down, but you can't kill them. In fact, these roots are capable of remaining in a dormant state, waiting for the right conditions to reappear."

"So, if you help them move their money, they're liable to use it to establish another self-serving system of tyranny," Jacques said.

"Yes," Henri said. "As I understand it, your presentation mentioned the need for a watchdog organization outside the influence of national and private interests. It's this subject that I would like to learn more about."

Jacques and Mike looked at each other for a moment, and Mike nodded for his friend to begin.

"The purpose of such an organization would be to identify sources of potential corruption in its early stages, when peaceful means can still be used to eradicate them. Had such an organization existed in 1938, the Second World War might have been averted."

"Well, what stopped you from putting this idea into effect?" Henri asked.

"Money," Jacques said. "Not only could we never figure out how much funding was needed, we couldn't identify any sources that would support us and still allow us to remain independent of national and business self-interest."

"Tell me, what would you do if a hundred million dollars were made available, under the proper circumstances, to fund such an organization?" Henri asked.

Jacques seemed confused. "Why talk to us about this, sir? Why not make this proposition to someone more experienced?"

"There is a second issue we need to address," Henri said. "Although my friend thinks that the loss of sixteen billion dollars' worth of purchasing power could seriously affect the outcome of the war, my daughter seems to think that the transaction still doesn't pass her 'higher purpose' test. She is convinced that by helping the German industrialists remove their money, we are simply making it possible for them to finance the next Power Cycle. This concern represents the second and far-more-complicated part of the problem. Somehow, you'd need to come up with a plan that prevents their capital from being used to re-create history."

There was a long silence.

"Well, I think I've given you young people something to think about for awhile," Henri said. "I need to return to Geneva. Claudine, why don't you and your friends get some rest and give some thought to what we have been discussing? We can pick things up when you come back to the office."

Chapter 8

A CHANGE OF PLANS

After Henri left, Jacques and Mike showered, changed into fresh clothing, and joined Claudine downstairs. "I bet you could use a cocktail," she said, handing them their glasses.

"It's as if you could read my mind," Jacques said.

"Amen," Mike said. "That is, unless you've got something stronger."

"Well, Jacques, it's obvious you *can't* read my mind or you'd see I wasn't suggesting that we unwind just yet," Claudine said.

"Then what's the purpose of these?" Jacques asked, sniffing the strong drink.

"To brace you," she said.

"For what?"

"*My* part of the plan."

Claudine walked over to the sofa and sat down, crossing her legs. Jacques immediately realized how difficult it was going to be to force himself to focus on German industrialists and gold bearer bonds.

"Ever since I called you two," Claudine said, "I've been developing an idea. Now, I know it's bizarre, but I would appreciate it if you would hear me out before responding."

"That's quite an opening," Mike said, after quickly downing half his drink.

"Don't worry, Mike. It's no more dangerous than, say, flying in a fighter plane over occupied France."

"Then where's the fun in it?"

"I'll tell you," she said. "The first step in this scheme involves the German families delivering their gold to Switzerland without being discovered. That would be their problem. The second step involves the transformation of the gold bullion into gold bearer bonds. That would be the responsibility of the participating Swiss banking group. The third step requires our obtaining the U.S. Federal Reserve's and the gold center banks' approval of the terms and conditions of this transaction. Finally, we must print the bonds and deliver them to the Germans. That would be our job."

"With you so far," Mike said.

"Then there's the fifth step, where the fun comes in. It's the part where we siphon off one hundred million dollars of the *ownership* of the gold."

Mike immediately choked on his drink.

"Ah, Claudine—" Jacques began.

She held up a hand. "Let me explain. Stealing the gold physically would be impossible. Stealing a portion of their *ownership* is possible." She was speaking slowly and clearly; Claudine had obviously given this a great deal of thought. "I know from the fraud prevention difficulties we've had within our own bank that properly forged bonds can be very difficult to detect. I am proposing that we find a way to duplicate one hundred million dollars of the gold bearer bonds."

Mike and Jacques took turns staring at each other, then at Claudine. Jacques was the first to speak. "Claudine, do I understand that you are proposing we steal one hundred million dollars of the Germans' money?"

"I told you it was a bizarre idea."

"Yes, but . . . Maybe your plan is not so strange after all," Jacques said after some thought. "I mean, would we really be committing a crime by stealing money someone else has illegally smuggled out of Germany?"

"Ah, excuse me, you two? The last thing we have to worry about with this deal is law enforcement," Mike said. "We're talking about stealing from some of the most powerful people in Europe. The real question is, can we cover our tracks well enough to keep from getting killed?"

"That's the beauty of my idea," Claudine said. "They wouldn't be able to expose us without exposing themselves. When our bonds show up at a gold center bank with the same serial numbers and denominations as the originals, all hell will break loose. The banks will refuse to honor any additional bonds of that particular series—ours or theirs—until the problem can be cleared up. So even if the industrialists had to absorb a five-percent loss, wouldn't that be preferable to the risk of having their capital tied up indefinitely, or, worse, being exposed to the reprisals of Hitler and his High Command?"

"I don't know," Mike said, shaking his head. "I think we have to assume that the German families will have both the will and the means to find out who is responsible. And if they are already willing to take such a risk to remove their money from Germany, I can't even imagine what they might resort to in order to remove any cloud that we might place on the liquidity of their bonds."

"That's why, for this scheme to work," Claudine said, "the forged bonds must be of such quality that not only will the most expert bank authenticator be unable to distinguish them from the originals, but no one would even think to trace them back to a bunch of young professionals, barely out of graduate school and with such good family backgrounds."

"Then maybe it would be prudent to discuss how we'd go about producing these duplicate bonds," Jacques suggested.

"Shouldn't we wait to include Ian Meyer in that conversation?" Claudine asked. "After all, I seem to recall that his company's restoration of first-edition books involves operations quite similar to what we'd need."

"I still can't believe we're having this conversation," Mike said. "Forging a million dollars' worth of bonds still seems to be a preposterous idea!"

———

Not much later, Mike excused himself and went to bed with a lot on his mind. Something was also weighing heavily on Jacques— something more precious to him than gold. He watched as his friend went toward the stairway leading to the bedrooms, then walked over to the sofa and sat down beside Claudine.

"I've got to say that you seem to have it all figured out," Jacques said, looking at her with admiration. "You always do."

"Not all of it. That's why I need you."

I need you. She hadn't actually meant to say it. Her words hung in the air between them. Embarrassed, she tried changing the subject. "Jacques, you must be exhausted. Why don't you go to bed? I'll clean up the rest of the dishes."

Their eyes met and held; a silent question was asked and answered. Jacques leaned in and their lips met. He could feel her body pressing into his until suddenly she pulled away.

Her cheeks were bright pink, and she was obviously flustered. "I—I'm tired," she said. "I'd better get some sleep before . . ." Without finishing her sentence, she quickly got up and left the room.

———

Watching her leave the room, Jacques thought, *It's been only twenty-four hours since I left London, yet I'm totally absorbed by a different woman. What's happening to me?*

———

The next morning, the three friends convened in the kitchen. While Mike was preoccupied pouring juice, Jacques stole a quick look at Claudine's freshly scrubbed face. She turned away. Today, she was all business.

After a good night's sleep, Mike was feeling better, more assured about their prospects. Chewing on a piece of toast, he said, "As I see it, this is a risk-opportunity problem. It's not all that different from what bankers do every day."

Claudine looked at Jacques, then away. She busied herself with pouring juice into her glass. "I'll tell you how it's different," she said. "In business, we are betting only money, generally someone else's. If we proceed with this, we will be betting our lives. We damned well better know what we are doing. That's why you two are the only ones I've told about my part of the plan."

"The way I look at this whole thing is, when will we ever have a better opportunity to realize our dreams?" Jacques said. "If all we wanted in life was to play it safe and follow in our parents' footsteps, we already have that option. We wouldn't have gone to Cal Berkeley in the first place. What we worked on all those years wasn't just theory, was it? Here's our chance to do something. We just have to develop the right plan."

They exchanged looks of understanding. "Well, our research determined that there needed to be some kind of watchdog group," Mike said. "I guess we're it." He looked at Claudine and Jacques. "So, the two of you, me, and Ian . . . the world's four guardians against the abuse of power."

"Don't forget about Tony and Cecelia," Claudine said. "I've got a feeling that before this is all over, we'll be needing their help as well."

Jacques raised a glass of orange juice. "Friends, a toast: to the Six Sentinels."

With a wry smile, Claudine raised her glass. Mike grabbed his coffee cup and hoisted it. "The Six Sentinels," he echoed. "I hope to God we can figure out what we're supposed to do next."

The drive back to Geneva certainly is different, thought Jacques. *On the short trip to the chalet, it was all I could do to contain my curiosity. Now, I couldn't be more amazed by what we are considering.*

It was nine o'clock sharp when they were shown into Henri's office. After a few minutes of small talk, Henri noticed that the three of them looked worried. Before he could comment, Jacques spoke. "We've given your suggestion some thought, sir, and I believe I speak for—"

Henri stopped him midway through the speech he had been rehearsing. "I can see by the look on your faces that you have weighed your choices carefully. That's all I could ask. If you've concluded that the risks are too great, please don't worry. I'll find another way—"

"No, sir," Jacques interrupted, "that's not what I meant. Your daughter, Mike, and I are very excited about the opportunity to make such an important contribution."

Henri smiled.

"We are prepared to proceed, as soon as we come up with a satisfactory plan to manage the risk," Mike added.

"What he means," Claudine said, smiling at Mike, "is a plan that we can all live with."

Or live through, Mike thought.

Chapter 9

THOUGHTS OF TONY

No one spoke during the drive from Henri's office to the airport; Claudine was deep in her own thoughts, and she assumed Mike and Jacques were as well. For her part, Claudine could not get her mind off last night's kiss. Did she really not want to get involved with Jacques, or was she simply not prepared and didn't know how to respond?

Damn it, do you have to control everything, Claudine? Do you really want to go through life as the "Nordic Ice Princess"? You may have the blond hair, blue eyes, and high cheek bones of a Scandinavian, but inside you're still an affectionate girl from Switzerland.

She drove slowly onto the tarmac and parked next to the bank's plane, which, to Jacques and Mike's great relief, was warmed up and ready to take off. "I wasn't relishing another literal game of dodge the bullet in a British Spitfire," Mike said. Jacques laughed and agreed. Claudine smiled, but she had to admit that her heart was sinking at the thought of their departure. Or was it the thought of *Jacques'* departure?

The funny thing is, he thinks I've got it all figured out, but I can't even figure out what I'm afraid of in our relationship.

She made sure to say good-bye to Mike first. Then, turning toward Jacques, she looked directly into his eyes before embracing him in the kind of hug that left no room for interpretation.

"Claudine . . ."

"I'll see you soon," she whispered, not wanting to let go.

On her drive back to the bank, Claudine thought about the first night she'd ever met Jacques. Dr. Tom had hosted a get-together for his grad students and Jacques, naturally, was the center of attention. She, along with the rest of them, had been asking him questions, which had triggered his telling a story, which had triggered even more questions and more stories.

For reasons she couldn't fathom, she had hoped Jacques would not have been so self-centered and would have been more interested in her.

Though he had been charming and charismatic, Claudine grew tired of the routine. As her attention had begun to fade, she'd shifted her gaze toward Tony Garibaldi, the quiet, olive-skinned gentleman sitting across from her.

They had been introduced earlier and, recalling the Garibaldi wines that were served in her family's home on special occasions, Claudine had asked, "Are you connected with the Garibaldi family of Tuscan wine fame?"

"Yes, as a matter of fact," Tony had said with a smile as he poured each of them another glass of beer from the seemingly bottomless pitcher.

Throughout the course of the evening, Tony had slowly unfolded the story of his life. She remembered telling him she was confused as to why someone with such a heritage in the wine business had joined an intensive political economics program.

His brow furrowed. "Believe me when I say that my family and I have personally seen the dark side of fascism for a very long time. At first, we didn't pay too much attention to Mussolini. We regarded him as a foul-mouthed, bombastic political aspirant. We were so preoccupied with resolving an epidemic of phylloxera in our vineyards that we didn't have time for much else.

"Once we became aware that certain Italian industrialists used their influence with Mussolini's government for their own self-interests, we began to take notice. It wasn't long before stories began to filter out of Rome describing the government's nationalization of companies whose owners failed to align themselves with the government. Even industries that had nothing to do with national defense, like the wine industry, were being targeted."

"Your family was threatened?"

"In 1932, everyone in Italy was living under constant threat. As the oldest son, I was already set to study enology and viticulture at the University of California at Davis. But by the time I completed school, things had gotten so bad that my family asked me to stay in the United States and help them prepare for the possible transfer of our wine operations to the Napa Valley."

"But still . . . what made you join Dr. Tom's program? I mean, why would you want to divert so much time and energy away from your primary mission?"

"It's just as we have been talking about. My family was a responsible maker of fine wines, an employer of hundreds of people, and an influential force in our community. Unfortunately, we didn't spend the effort to remain well informed or to initiate action when there was still time. We have learned the hard way that it's not enough to concentrate on producing great wines. It's important also to pay attention to what's going on around you. We don't want to make the same mistake twice. That's why this program is so important to me."

For Claudine, that conversation marked the start of what was to become a strong personal relationship. It wasn't long before Tony invited her to accompany him on his weekend trips into the Napa Valley. She could still remember carrying the heavy surveyors' instruments up and down the hillsides. The weather was hot, the distances were long, and the footing was unsteady. It wasn't exactly romantic, but it reminded her of her summers in Switzerland, when her family would go on long hikes.

Together, she and Tony had mapped the elevations, taken soil samples, and set up small weather stations to record wind currents, rainfall, and air temperatures. Everything had been faithfully recorded in one of Tony's coded books.

One day in particular she would never forget. Tony was trying to determine the presence of underground water on a parcel of land he thought to be particularly well suited for growing cabernet sauvignon grapes.

"Come on, let's get serious. You think that little piece of wood is going to help you find water?" she had asked him.

She remembered sitting on a rock under a tree, watching Tony hold the Y-shaped willow wand by its two forks, extending the main stem out in front of him as he walked over the areas where he believed underground water might exist. If she hadn't seen the wand actually dip—indicating the probable presence of underground water—she wouldn't have believed it. Still not convinced, she recalled asking, "Tony, can I hold one side of that wand?" Putting one arm around his waist, she made sure that she had a strong enough grip on one of the forks to prevent him from manipulating it with his other hand. They had moved only a few yards before she could feel the pull on the fork as it dipped toward the ground. "Well, I'll be damned, it really does work!" Two weeks later, with the help of a local water-drilling company, they found water under four of the five locations they had established with the witching wand.

The nights were her favorite part of the day. After a long day's work, they would search for a small restaurant known for its local wines and good Italian cooking. She would watch as Tony first consulted with the waiter in an effort to learn which wines best reflected the unique growing conditions of that particular region. He would then engage the waiter in a long and sometimes active debate over which food selection would best amplify the qualities of the particular wine he had ordered.

The waiters had learned to recommend wines that would best complement the food, just the opposite of what Tony asked them. In dim candlelight Claudine and Tony would sample the local wines, test a different wine with each course of the dinner, talk about their day, and faithfully complete making their notes in the little notebooks.

They would always wait until after dinner to look for a place to spend the night. Claudine recalled how Tony would drive around until he would hear her say the magic words, "Now there is a place where a girl could relax and enjoy herself."

She could still feel his warm, strong arms wrapped around her, his special smell, but most of all his gentleness. It was as if he knew that there was a sensitive little girl trapped in a young woman's body that needed to be recognized and understood. That was the girl to whom he made love.

━━

By 1937, the economic backlash of Prohibition, continuing Depression problems, and the absence of a market for anything other than brandy were creating financial difficulties for many of California's oldest and proudest wine-making families. California banks that had faithfully supported the businesses up till then could no longer extend credit. Reluctantly, the banks began to force customers to begin the liquidation of their property or face foreclosure. Repossessed properties were resold to anyone with a minimum down payment and a history of vineyard and winery operations. Tony had both.

Tony's time had come. He was one of a very small group of able and willing buyers. The deposits from Italy were growing. The banks liked him. He was a high-energy, well-educated, experienced vintner who was supported by his family's capital. Braced with the information carefully recorded in his books, he knew which parcels best fit his program. Unsure of how long this opportunity to acquire prime lands at such low prices would last, he moved quickly. It wasn't long before analyzing each new opportunity, communicating with his family, and using their capital to acquire only the highest potential lands had become a full-time job.

His fellow graduate students had watched Tony's academic work suffer. Knowing that someday he would regret not completing his doctoral studies, they had felt they had no choice but to help carry him. They had divided the workload by five instead of six.

Claudine now realized that the demands of the extra work had prevented her from seeing the changes that had begun to occur in their relationship. Trips with Tony to Napa had become less frequent. When they had gotten together, Tony had always seemed preoccupied with his business. He had no longer had the time or interest to think about Claudine or her feelings.

She had never been sure if he had noticed when she began to withdraw. After they had completed their doctoral work and the demands of study were behind them, she had hoped that Tony might realize what was happening and come to his senses. To make certain that she hadn't misread the situation, she made arrangements to stay with Cecelia in her San Francisco apartment. He never called or visited.

Claudine frowned as she thought of the pain he had caused her. *I really loved that man. If he had asked me to remain in California, marry him, and share in his life, I probably would have said yes.*

Maybe it's time that I take a fresh look at my life. My victories seem so hollow. It was never my intent to forge an independent career, I always thought of myself as someone's partner.

She forced herself to change the direction of her thoughts, and began imagining the feeling of Jacques' lips pressed against hers, the way her body had responded, with no conscious decision on her part. She shook her head. *Come on, girl, Monsieur Jacques Roth has broken way too many hearts. You'd best keep your mind on your business.*

Chapter 10

AN ABDUCTION

Sighing in frustration, Cecelia stood in the hallway outside her apartment, rifling through the contents of her handbag. The "business" dinner with her government contacts had been grueling, and all she wanted to do now was to get inside her apartment, kick off her shoes, and relax. *How can I not even be organized enough to keep track of my keys?*

Whenever she had to help with the network or set up a transaction from Hong Kong, she'd be met at the bank by some "friends" who escorted her to Johnny Kan's restaurant in San Francisco's Chinatown. She often thought bitterly that the restaurant was becoming her second office.

Johnny Kan's was well suited for their meetings. The stairs leading to the second-floor private dining rooms were just inside the entrance, directly opposite the maître d' station. Anyone following Cecelia or any of the others could be readily noticed.

There was a panel near the rear of the private dining room that separated it from a staircase leading to the back alley. People who wanted to arrive and leave without being observed could use the rear entrance.

At tonight's meeting, shortly after their dinner had been served, Ted Lee, the San Francisco manager of the Bank of Hong Kong, had quietly entered from behind the panel. Nodding to Cecelia's companions, he'd chosen an open seat next to her. After waiting for the waiter to finish organizing his place setting, Lee had reached into the inside pocket of his linen suit, extracted a plain white envelope, and handed her the two sheets of paper that were inside. Excusing herself, Cecelia had gone to the restroom, where she could study and commit to memory the content of the pages before tearing the papers up and flushing them down the toilet. One sheet had contained a list of coded names and the other a column of figures.

What a glamorous life, she'd thought, studying her face in the lavatory mirror. *Working all day at the bank, spying at night for the government, and carrying on a coast-to-coast relationship with Mike. What else could a girl want?*

Still, Cecelia thought, she was getting her wish, as she had expressed it to her father: she was pursuing her own destiny, mostly on her own terms. She couldn't deny how different her life was from that of the traditional Chinese woman forced to remain in Hong Kong. When the U.S. government had first approached her to help, she'd known it was only a question of time before the Japanese would invade China, Hong Kong, the Philippines, Malaysia, and Indonesia. It would take years for the American public to recognize the true imperial motives of Japan and vote for the larger military budgets required to take action.

Cecelia had apparently attracted the attention of a group within the U.S. government that knew something had to be done. Political and business leaders, teachers, and professional people in and around China, people whose participation would be of critical importance in postwar reconstruction, had to be smuggled out of harm's way. Their wealth had to be secured also, and it was a wonderful feeling for Cecelia to know that she—a single Chinese girl—could make such a difference in so many lives.

But these days, Cecelia was feeling she had done more than her share, and the need for her services was declining. Her old desire to retire from the government work was constantly on her mind. She wanted what she had always wanted—freedom to make her own choices. And one of those choices involved spending a lot more time with Mike Stone.

"Finally!" Cecelia said, wrestling her keys from the depths of her purse. She opened the front door, placed her purse and keys on the hall table, and walked into the living room.

After slipping off her shoes, she sat down on the sofa and flexed her tired feet, then stretched like a cat. *Maybe a glass of wine would help me relax. Anyway, it couldn't hurt.*

Sighing, she got up from the couch and moved to the antique bar, where she poured herself a glass of port. As she turned to set the glass down on her lacquered coffee table, she stopped.

The table legs are a few inches off the indentations in the carpet.

Cecelia cocked her head to one side, slid the table back into its regular place, and walked over to the window nearby. It didn't make sense; there was never anyone else in her apartment. Despite the fact that she checked that the window was locked, she felt the beginnings of fear growing inside, and immediately chided herself for it. *It was probably just the super who came in to fix something.* Cecelia refused to be one of those women scared of living alone—not after she had worked so hard to get here.

She returned to the couch, leaned back into the sofa cushions, took a long sip of wine, and stretched her feet out on the coffee table. But instead of relaxing, she noticed a small snag in one of her stockings.

After taking another sip of wine, she set the glass down, got up, and walked into the bathroom.

She reached beneath her skirt and unsnapped her garters, letting the nylons fall around her ankles before reaching down and carefully removing them.

Since she didn't have to share bathroom space with anyone, Cecelia had gotten into the habit of hand-washing her nylons in the bathroom sink and hanging them to dry on the rod of the shower curtain. She turned on the water and studied her reflection in the mirror above the sink as she waited for the water to warm. Suddenly she had the feeling that someone was watching her.

This is crazy. I'm imagining things. I just need to calm down. She forced herself to take deep breaths. She would fling the shower curtain open to reveal nothing more threatening than the cream-colored tile of the shower. She started to reach for the shower curtain, then hesitated. *Just do it, Cecelia. You know there's nothing there except your imagination.*

She could hear the blood pounding in her ears and . . . breathing. She could swear she heard someone breathing.

Her fingers lightly touched the curtain. Then, she gave it a sudden tug. A man with a pockmarked face sprang forward and clamped his hand over her mouth before she could scream. From somewhere else, another man grabbed both of her hands and twisted them behind her.

"Look, lady, we have instructions not to hurt you—unless you give us trouble," the pockmarked one said in a low voice. Cecelia felt the other man's huge hand pressing between her shoulder blades as he pushed her against the bathroom sink.

"Are you going to be a good girl?" continued the man in a menacing tone.

Cecelia quickly nodded her head. As soon as he took his hand away from her mouth, she spoke as calmly as she could. "Take anything you want. I won't tell a soul."

"What we want is you," he said.

They're going to rape me.

Cecelia took a breath to scream, but the man clamped his hand back over her mouth.

"Shhh! If you behave yourself, we won't hurt you," the man said, his face close enough to read the terror in her eyes. "Not that I wouldn't like a piece of you, darlin', but we have instructions to deliver you to the boss man unhurt. I'm going to take my hand away from that pretty little mouth of yours, and you're going to keep your head about you, okay?"

Cecelia nodded her agreement again and tried to show a look of resignation in her eyes. The man in back released her hands but twisted one of her arms way up behind her. She winced in pain but said nothing.

"Good," the pockmarked man said, showing her his gun. "Now, we're all going to walk out of your apartment like a happy little threesome, and nobody will be the wiser."

The two men flanked her on both sides and walked her into the living room. She looked over at the mantle, at a picture of Mike, and wondered how long it would take him to realize she was missing.

Chapter 11

IAN THE MAGNIFICENT

Following an easy, uneventful flight, the Demaureux Bank DC3 landed at London's Hanworth Park airfield. After clearing customs, Jacques phoned Ian while Mike retrieved their luggage.

"Jacques, you can't be serious!" Ian's voice crackled over the line. "What do you mean you want to meet me alone? Since you left four days ago, Natalie has done nothing but ask Emily when you would return."

"Ian, it's just that there's a certain . . . business proposition I'd like to—"

"What kind of proposition could take precedence over the most beautiful woman in all of London? My good man, I don't know what's come over you. What am I going to say when she learns that you were here and didn't see her?"

"Fine," Jacques said. "Let's have our meeting first, sort things out, and if there's time, Emily and Natalie can join us later."

———

Ian arrived at the French Club within minutes of Jacques and Mike. It was packed, as usual. Maggie greeted them at the door, but she could tell from the looks on their faces that their visit was business. No whoops, no hugs, no big wet kisses; these would have to wait until next time. Without another word, she escorted them upstairs to a small, private room, set tankards of beer on the table, and respectfully retreated, leaving them alone.

"So tell me, how is our sweet Claudine?" asked Ian.

"She's even more beautiful than ever," Mike said. "And she enjoys the admiration and respect of the entire European banking community. Her work developing the gold bearer bond has been well received as a landmark piece of work."

"That all sounds quite lovely," Ian said. "But how is she? The woman—our friend? What's going on in her life?"

Mike shrugged. "I . . . I don't know. I guess it never really came up." He looked at Jacques.

Thinking about the kiss, Jacques decided to keep his own counsel. He gave Ian a shrug. "Nothing doing on the romantic front, as far as I could tell."

"Well, that's a waste," Ian said. "It's difficult to imagine that someone as beautiful as Claudine doesn't have a personal life! Tony must have hurt her more than we realized."

"Oh, I don't know," Jacques said. "Claudine has a very rich life and is still able to come up with innovative ideas on the spur of the moment. In fact . . ." He gave Mike a meaningful look.

"Yes, of course," Ian said. "So what is it that you gents need so urgently to discuss?"

When Jacques finished explaining the situation with the German industrialists and their money, including Claudine's plan, Ian sat in silence. "One can't possibly live in London and not be deeply worried about what will happen when this blasted thing is over," Ian said slowly. "Ever since I finished my military service after returning from Berkeley, I've been buying art, antiques, and first editions from frightened people—good people who feel they have no choice but to sell their precious possessions to survive in Hitler's new world. What I find especially heart wrenching is that most of these people are old friends of my family's. Many had been among our best customers."

He lifted his glass and set it back down without taking a drink. "Every day, I witness the high cost of war. You've seen the bombings firsthand. Regardless of how hard we Londoners try to appear calm, we know that more are on the way." He looked at them both for a moment, and then took a long pull at his beer. The loud noise he created when he slammed the heavy beer mug down on the table sounded like a judge pounding a gavel. "I would welcome the chance to help put a quicker end to the war and to prevent this horror from happening again. Nothing would please me more!"

"Ian, are you sure you understand the implications of what we're planning?" Jacques asked. "Once we start, there'll be no turning back. No matter how painstakingly we duplicate the bonds, it will only be a question of time before they're discovered. Although it's a risk that we'll all be taking, your position here in London will leave you the most exposed."

"In London, we are risking our lives every day," Ian said. "At least I'll be doing something that matters, instead of standing on the sidelines."

"That's settled, then. Let's get down to details," Mike said. "Exactly how are you going to create these bonds so that they will pass the test of the most skilled authenticator?"

"Reproducing the bonds won't be our biggest problem," Ian said thoughtfully. "Doing it in such a way that they can't be traced back to us will be our greatest challenge. I believe our best course is to break down the total process into four parts, making each appear as normal, everyday work."

"I don't know about you, but stealing one hundred million dollars isn't exactly something I do every day," Mike said.

"No, and that's why we need to not make it look like some amateur undertaking. The mechanics are straightforward enough," Ian said. "Not too long ago, we had to solve a similar problem. Why don't I describe what we did in that situation? First, to prepare the plates, we will need originals of the exact types of bonds we plan on duplicating. I should think Claudine could take care of that end."

"After having heard her detailed description, I'd certainly say that's possible," Jacques said.

"The second step involves the actual printing," Ian went on. "To complete it, I must have precisely the same serial numbers and denominations used by the issuing bank—all of the duplicate bonds need to match up with the master list."

"That step could be difficult," Mike said. "Those lists are provided to each major bank to aid in any verification process they may need to perform. Demaureux Bank will certainly receive a copy. The problem is that this information only becomes established after the bonds have been printed. We'll have to wait for the printing before that data can be produced."

"I can live with that as long as everybody understands the necessary delay," Ian said. "The third step requires copies of each bank president's signature. If you can get me those, along with the exact sort of pen they'll be using to sign, I can approach the special—what should we call them—artists our company sometimes employs. These chaps are so good, the bank presidents themselves won't be able to tell which bonds they signed and which they didn't."

"How do you know these, um, artists will do what we're asking *and* keep it confidential?" Mike asked.

"This may come as a surprise to you," Ian said, "but not all the first-edition restoration we are asked to do is on the level. Parts of some rare book to complete a long-sought collection can be missing or damaged beyond repair. We are occasionally asked to re-create them in such a manner that their insertion can't be detected by even the most discriminating authenticators. The fees for the professionals whom we use to do this work are very high for the relatively few who can afford to hire them. Any future use of their services depends upon them being totally discreet, and they know it."

"Ian, never in my wildest imagination was I expecting such a forthcoming answer," Jacques said.

"Well, we still have one more problem," Mike said. "How will we transport the duplicates out of England to the countries where the gold center banks are located?"

"And now, we come to the fourth step—the first editions," Ian responded. "Meyer & Co. regularly receives damaged books from customers all over the world. We have them shipped directly to London, restore them, and ship them back. Customs officials are so familiar with our work that they rarely inspect our incoming or outgoing shipments."

"But surely you won't just tuck the bonds into the books?" Mike said.

"Not quite. We've been asked to forge a few minor papers in the past—historical notes, mostly. For that, we have developed a technique in which the old pages in a book can be split and documents can be placed between the two sides. Then, we glue the sides back together and rebind the pages into the book. No customs agent has ever discovered this technique."

"Can you still move around during wartime with the same freedom you described last week?" Mike asked. "You may have to take delivery on the other end."

"As long as my travels involve the appearance of legitimate business activity, no one seems to question my movements. Now, tell me, who else is involved in all this?"

"A few more familiar faces," Jacques answered. "As long as none of the money we get is deposited into the banking system, a trail won't be established. That's essential to our safety and success, and that's where Tony comes in. His wine business would give us a great place to bury at least twenty-five million dollars. Only thing is—we haven't asked him yet."

Pausing to reach into his briefcase, Mike extracted another copy of Tony's investment memorandum, which he had given to Jacques on the plane. "This is what gave us the idea. It describes Tony's whole setup. You might want to read it in your spare time."

Ian eyed the small print dubiously. "I doubt I'll ever have that much spare time. But I do have a question. What are your plans for the rest of the money? Seventy-five million dollars in bonds would be rather a lot to keep in safe-deposit boxes."

"We might cash another fifteen million dollars for short-term operating expenses, leaving sixty million dollars in bonds to remain bound in the first editions. The question isn't the money, it's where to keep that many books," Jacques said.

Ian said, "I have friends and clients in many countries who have been more than happy to store first editions in their private collections for safekeeping. It would be like hiding trees in a forest. In addition, we would have the ability to retrieve those editions anytime we needed to do so."

"My goodness, man. I do believe you've thought of everything," Mike said.

As if on cue, Emily and Natalie entered the room. Ian smiled. "I do believe this celebration calls for something stronger than beer."

"What are we celebrating?" Natalie asked as she flowed into Jacques' arms. "Is the war over? Someone's getting married? Or is it simply the return of my prince?"

When it became obvious that Jacques and Mike were not going to divulge anything, Emily looked straight at Ian, expecting some kind of an explanation.

Just then, Maggie walked in with a tray of glasses and the best Scotch in the house. "All right, that's enough business for one night," she announced. "It's time for all of you young folks to start having fun."

That they did. The five, with Maggie in tow, closed down the French Club; the after-hours jazz spots in Soho were next. It seemed as though Emily, Ian, and Natalie knew most of the jazz clubs in London. Maggie knew the rest. It was obvious to Jacques they were intent on visiting them all in one night.

———

The next morning, Jacques woke up in a Claridge's suite with a real hangover. His first thought was, *I will never allow Ian to lead me astray again.*

His second thought was, *Who is this beside me?*

Slowly, the fog began to clear. He looked over at Natalie's smiling face, waiting for him to awaken.

Natalie brought him a Ramos Gin Fizz in a tall glass with an even taller straw. "Here, drink this while I rub your back."

He watched Natalie in the mirror. *She looks as fresh as a daisy. How does she do it? She matched me drink for drink.*

"What time is it?" he mumbled.

"It's time for you to take a shower and buy a hungry girl brunch."

"Brunch? Is it that late?" Jacques groaned and sat up.

Later, as he stood in the shower, he tried to piece together the events of the prior evening. By two in the morning, things had started getting hazy, and by four, his memory was a total blank.

I can't even remember if Natalie and I had sex. Worse, I can't think of a tactful way to ask.

As he stepped from the shower, he hoped that she'd fill in the empty spots over brunch.

It has only been a week since we left New York, but it feels like a lifetime. I just wish I hadn't blanked out during the best parts.

Chapter 12

WHAT SHE SAW

Doris Claybourne had been watching, as usual, when Cecelia disembarked from the elevator, hunted for her keys, and entered her apartment. *That silly girl. Doesn't she know she ought to have her keys in her hand when she gets out of the cab?*

Doris was lonely. She lived by herself in an apartment on the same floor as Cecelia. She liked to know what was going on, so anytime she heard the elevator doors or apartment doors on her hall opening and closing, she would climb on the stool she kept by her front door and peer out the transom. She watched as Cecelia fumbled in her purse, finally found her keys, and went inside. Doris climbed down from her stool, shaking her head. *Silly girl.*

But then, only minutes later, Doris heard Cecelia's door open again.

Normally, when she comes home this late, it means she is in for the night. Stepping onto the stool, Doris got a good view of two men escorting Cecelia toward the elevator.

Now, that is strange. Why didn't I see those men when they arrived?

The men didn't much resemble any of the usual visitors at Cecelia's apartment, that was for sure. *And why wasn't she carrying her purse just now?*

The more Doris thought about what she had seen, the more worried she became. She stepped down from the stool and started to pace around her apartment. *It really isn't any of my business. But how could I live with myself if something happened to her?* She reached for her phone.

———

The sergeant on duty received the call and wrote down what Doris Claybourne had seen, assuring her that it was probably nothing. He handed the report to the new lieutenant, Carlson, who was heading home after a long shift.

"Lieutenant, this call we just got . . . looks like it's on your way home," the sergeant said, smirking. "Should only take a few minutes."

———

Arriving at the address on the complaint, the lieutenant took the elevator up to Doris Claybourne's floor.

Doris, hearing the elevator come to a stop, had already mounted her stool. She saw the young policeman looking at the apartment numbers. Climbing down, she opened the door and invited him in.

Politely declining her offer of tea and cookies, Carlson asked, "Would you mind telling me exactly what you saw this evening?"

She did, in detail.

Almost an hour later, after finishing his notes, the lieutenant left, a little miffed at the sergeant. *Only a few minutes, huh, Sarge? Now I gotta check out this old lady's story.*

Fighting sleep, he headed straight for the superintendent's room, hoping to gain clearance to enter Cecelia's apartment.

Carlson knew right away that something was wrong. Suddenly alert, he scanned the young woman's apartment, noticing keys sprawled on a small table next to a purse.

———

The night sergeant on duty was clearing his desk for the next shift when Carlson's call came in.

"Sarge, that call you got from Doris Claybourne turned out to be for real. It looks like we have an abduction on our hands."

"Write up anything you've got and leave it on the captain's desk. She still has a while to go before we declare her a missing person."

Carlson's report was sitting neatly on the desk when Captain Philips walked into his office the next morning. He glanced at it casually until he saw Cecelia's name. Then he picked up the phone and called the FBI.

———

Hours later, Roger Malone, chairman of the U.S. Federal Reserve, was sitting in his office in Washington, D.C., carefully reading the report the FBI had compiled. Due to its serious nature, he had read it twice before deciding to contact Cecelia's employer, Pete Ferrari, chairman of California's American West National Bank, who also happened to be his old friend.

"Pete, I'm calling with some bad news. It seems one of your employees may have been kidnapped—a Miss Cecelia Chang."

"What? That's horrible. How can that be?"

Roger briefly explained the police report and asked, "Do you know anything that can help me on this?"

"Well, I don't know much about her personally, other than that she is in charge of our Pacific Rim operations and is the daughter of one of our biggest clients in Hong Kong. Could that have something to do with it—ransom?"

"I'm afraid it's something more serious than that. Pete, what I'm about to say is in the strictest confidence."

"I understand."

"Here in Washington, we think there may be a much larger and more dangerous game going on. For some time, we've been receiving vague reports and hearing rumors about a paramilitary organization operating in the United States, code-named Samson—sort of a modern-day Pinkerton Detective Agency, only these guys are selling their services to our enemies."

"What does that have to do with Cecelia?"

"For the last five years, Miss Chang has been involved with a highly classified U.S. government operation that moved the private wealth of many enemies of Japan for safekeeping. Her work has been invaluable, but our shadow reports tell us that Japanese officials may have caught on to this program and retained Samson's services."

"Roger, this is all a little hard to believe."

"I can imagine what you're feeling," Roger said. "But there have been other recent attempts in Hong Kong, Singapore, Sydney, and Manila—all by the Japanese government and all designed to stop the flow of unauthorized shipments of gold bullion and gold bearer bonds out of these financial centers."

"Who are these Samson members? I mean, exactly what are we dealing with?"

"Unfortunately, we know exactly how this organization came about," Roger said. "Even worse, the British and American governments were initially involved in providing financial support."

"What do you mean?"

"If you remember, in the '30s, a military coup took place in Venezuela. The new government was threatening to nationalize the country's oil industry, similar to what had occurred in Mexico.

Had that happened, it would have threatened the entire Western hemisphere's supply of petroleum. At the time, the American government was already concerned about possible involvement in a European war. To ensure access to oil, the British and American governments, together with local oil companies, funded a paramilitary organization, Samson, to protect their interests."

"That's unbelievable. It sounds like a very professional organization, capable of carrying out some real harm."

"It is. As it turned out, Juan Pablo Perez, a young Venezuelan engineer educated in America, succeeded in negotiating new contracts between Venezuela and the oil companies, and the oil was never nationalized. Since there was no further need for Samson, the governments suspended funding and it was believed, until recently, that the organization had been disbanded. But if, in fact, they are involved with Miss Chang's abduction, it means we have a well-trained paramilitary group, employed by the Japanese government, operating right here inside the United States."

"And what does it mean for Cecelia?" Pete asked.

"They may have been hired to abduct her, find out what she knows, and possibly kill her."

"My God! If they're capable of that kind of action, what are you doing to get her back? Why haven't I heard a word about this kidnapping in the news?"

"We don't want to alert Samson or their clients that we are aware of their existence. The less they know about what *we* know, the better our chances are of recovering her unharmed."

"What can I do to help?" Pete asked.

"Believe me when I say that this case has Washington's full attention. All the stops are being pulled out. But it's a very sensitive matter. Since you know Miss Chang personally, is there someone you could contact close to her, to tell them *only* of her suspected kidnapping? You might learn something, no matter how insignificant it may seem, that could help us immensely."

"If I find anything out, I'll call you immediately," Pete said.

"Thanks. And try not to worry. We have our best men in the Federal Bureau of Investigation working on it."

———

Pete Ferrari hung up the phone, then instantly lifted the receiver again. He had to get through to his friend, Morgan Stone, in New York—immediately.

Chapter 13

GETTING IN DEEP

The first person Mike saw as he walked through the gates at New York's La Guardia Airport was his father, standing in the waiting area. As Morgan Stone moved toward him, Mike could hardly believe his eyes. *What would prompt Dad to come all the way out to the airport in the middle of the night?* Mike's chest suddenly felt cold with apprehension. *Something must have happened to Mom.*

He hurried toward his father. "Dad, what—"

"Son, I received a call from Mr. Ferrari. He's as confused as I am . . . but he said Cecelia's been kidnapped."

Mike halted in his tracks, staring at his father. "What? Cecelia's been . . . is she okay?" Jacques, who had just caught up with Mike, quickly put a supporting arm around him.

"Try to take it easy, Mike," Mr. Stone said. "No one's heard anything yet. The San Francisco Police Department got a report from a neighbor who saw two men escorting her out of her apartment and into an elevator. That's all that Pete knows. But he thinks it might be connected to something big. He couldn't say."

Images from Carmel suddenly sprang into Mike's mind: Cecelia at the phone booth, all that talk about smuggling money through Asia, how hard she said it was to get free from government work . . . It was something big, all right.

Reaching into the inside pocket of his overcoat, Mr. Stone pulled out an envelope and a folded sheet of paper. "I made arrangements for your flight and registered you at the Clift Hotel. Here's a list of contacts and phone numbers you'll need when you get there. I'm sure you'll want to do everything you can."

Mike felt numb. He took the ticket, stepped toward the gate, then turned around. He hugged his father for the first time in a long while.

———

The next morning, in New York, as Jacques sat behind the stack of mail piled atop his desk, his secretary barged into his office unannounced, with a rather perturbed expression on her face.

"Mr. Stone requests your presence immediately. I can't think what you've done to warrant his concern this time. You've only been back in the office for half an hour. That would be quick work, even for the likes of you."

Grabbing his notes on his trip to Geneva, he headed down the hall to the elevators. He rode up to the top floor and quickly walked down the long hallway to the desk of the chairman's personal receptionist. He had rarely met with Mr. Stone without Mike being there, and Jacques was actually feeling a bit nervous.

"Mr. Stone is expecting you. Please come with me," the receptionist said, leading Jacques into the chairman's palatial office.

"Jacques!" Morgan said, smiling. "Come in. I am sorry about all that business Mike is involved with, but I wanted to find out how things went in Switzerland."

"Well, as I'm sure Mike told you . . ." Jacques began hesitantly. *What had Mike told him, exactly?* "We met with Henri

Demaureux to discuss the issuance of a sizable sum of bonds for gold from the Swiss banks."

"Yes, Mike mentioned that, and it sounds very promising," said Morgan. "But in order for this transaction to take place, we need to discuss what you're going to present to the United States Federal Reserve tomorrow."

"*I'm* going to present? Sorry, I don't understand."

"Well, I'm telling you now. They have just made a new ruling requiring special approval of any Allied bank issuing gold bearer bonds in excess of a hundred million dollars. A transaction like the two of you are proposing is going to require a lot of explaining."

Before Jacques could speak, Morgan continued. "Let me fill you in. The Fed has become convinced that certain limitations need to be placed on the withdrawal privileges of large new gold deposits. The governors are particularly sensitive about what effect premature withdrawal of large deposits could have on the country's money supply. They need to know how long they can count on having that money there for credit purposes. Although the Fed hasn't quite come out and said so, I think its willingness to allow gold bearer bonds to be used for liquidity and portability purposes is dependent upon the long-term contribution they make to the money supply of our economy. They may be looking for precedent-setting terms tomorrow, ones that they can apply to all future transactions."

"Mr. Stone, as you know, I have absolutely no experience in dealing with the Federal Reserve," Jacques said. "Especially when it comes to a transaction of this magnitude."

"Then tomorrow could be a day of many firsts."

Jacques knew there was nothing more he could say; it was time to prepare. After receiving his itinerary, he took his leave of the chairman and headed to a place with which he had become intimately familiar during his dissertation days—the library.

After hours of poring over financial documents in one of the lone-liest sections of the New York Public Library, Jacques went back to Stone City Bank to sift through its archives. He was searching for a similar case with standards stringent enough to make the industrialists' money less accessible to them, yet attractive enough for everyone involved to go through with the deal. In short, it was like looking for a needle in a haystack—or a postage stamp among a stack of dusty old financial documents.

By two o'clock, his tired eyes signaled he needed to take a break. Looking at his watch, he thought, *It's only eleven in the morning in California; maybe I should give Mike a call.* Jacques dialed the number for the Clift Hotel. Mike answered on the second ring.

"Cecelia?" Mike's voice was thick with fatigue.

"No, Mike, it's Jacques. Sorry I woke you."

"It's okay," Mike said. "You got me out of a bad dream."

"No news, huh?" Jacques asked.

"No leads. No demands. Nothing. The agents and I all sus-pect this has something to do with Cecelia's 'other job' I told you about, but I haven't been able to be much help. Everyone here just thinks of me as the pain in the ass from the East who asks a lot of questions."

"Listen, buddy, I'll be there soon," Jacques said, feeling sorry for his friend. "Right after I finish my meeting in Washington, I'll head to the West Coast."

"What do you mean *Washington*?"

"Your father wants me to meet with the Federal Reserve. Turns out we've got to get their approval for a transfer of this size."

"Wow! Looks like you've got enough to think about. Don't worry about me. There's nothing I can do but wait. But Jacques,"

Mike's voice was almost a whisper now, "whatever happens tomorrow, keep in mind that these money transfers—especially the ones we're talking about—could be a very messy business. You've got to be careful, buddy."

———

Jacques took the overnight train to Washington. Arriving early in the morning, he checked into the Hay-Adams Hotel and made arrangements for them to store his suitcase. There was still time before the meeting, so he decided to take advantage of the beautiful spring weather and take a leisurely walk to the Federal Reserve building to help clear his mind, the way he used to do at Berkeley.

Forty minutes later, he found himself being escorted into the offices of the chairman.

"Jacques, welcome to Washington," said the chairman, shaking the young man's hand. "I'm Roger Malone."

"Nice to meet you, Mr. Malone. I must say it's an honor."

"I've wanted to meet you for a long time. Your father and I are old friends, and I've heard a lot of nice things about you from him and, more recently, from Morgan. This should be a very interesting meeting. The governors have already arrived and are waiting to hear what you've got to say."

Roger guided Jacques into the very private boardroom of the Federal Reserve and introduced him to the five governors, who represented each of the different banking districts of the United States.

Here I am in the same room as some of the most influential bankers in the United States. Okay, Captain, if you take things one step at a time, it's easier to control the ball.

After the introductions, Chairman Malone brought the meeting to order. "Gentlemen, we have a very important issue before us today. Mr. Roth, if you please, share with us your proposal."

Jacques spoke as directly as he knew how. "Gentlemen, we have been approached by a consortium of Swiss banks that want to convert two billion dollars into gold bearer bonds. We've been led to believe that the size of this transaction requires your approval. Since there is an elevated sense of urgency, I have taken the liberty of doing some research. Based on the results, I am here to present our recommendation for your approval. In essence, we would respectfully suggest that you consider terms and conditions that, among other things, call for a minimum term deposit of no fewer than ten years, with the proviso that not more than ten percent of the gross deposit can be withdrawn in any year. This proposed ten-percent, ten-year limit would effectively shift the long-term investment capacity of the transferred funds to the Allied banking system. We believe that such a deposit can be classified as a preferred debt transaction for credit purposes and, although the funds must be repaid like any other debt deposits, the limitations placed on withdrawals and the non–interest bearing terms effectively convert the debt into equity for lending consideration."

The men exchanged looks, then focused their attention back on Jacques. One of them raised a hand, and Jacques nodded at him.

"Your suggested terms would be considered quite demanding by some. Do you mind telling us how you came up with that particular recommendation?"

"Not at all, sir. Extensive research uncovered a transaction with similar terms that the Federal Reserve considered awhile ago, but never with such large sums. Should this transaction be allowed to occur, by our calculations the two-billion-dollar deposit would translate into a decrease in German credit capacity of fourteen billion dollars and a corresponding increase in Allied banking capacity."

There was some murmuring around the room. The next gentleman to speak was a governor from the west. "We've been debating minimum standards for several months. If we were to approve the terms you suggest, how do we know that we would not be adopting standards that are too difficult for the Swiss to enforce?"

"We don't, definitively. Before approaching the gold center banks, I would need to obtain the consent of the individual depositors and the Swiss banks. This may be a good opportunity to take advantage of an unusual situation. Without the cooperation of the American banking community, I doubt if there is sufficient financial capacity in the gold center bank system to complete this transfer. We are, in effect, the only game in town."

This got a good response from the governors all around.

Jacques continued. "As for the Swiss bankers enforcing the terms, I have done considerable research on that question and am not aware of any instance wherein they have failed to honor the stipulations of a major transaction."

A governor from one of the southern states spoke up. "I'm sure you understand that we can't provide you with any approvals at this point, conditional or otherwise, but let me just say that if this situation is as workable as you make it seem, I am prepared to give it my prompt and careful consideration."

Realizing that he had achieved what he'd come for, Jacques knew it was time to stop. "On behalf of Stone City Bank, I thank you very much for the opportunity to present our plan."

As the governors rose to shake hands with Jacques and exit the meeting room, Roger Malone put his hand on Jacques' shoulder and asked, "Would you mind remaining behind for just a minute? There's something I want to show you."

He led Jacques into his office, to a photograph hanging on the wall. "Have you seen this picture before?"

"Now that you mention it, I recall seeing that same picture on my father's desk in his Paris office, and, if memory serves, hanging on the wall in Mr. Stone's office." Moving in for a closer look,

Jacques said, "That's my father on the left. Next to him is Morgan Stone, you, Henri Demaureux, and a man I don't recognize."

"That's Pete Ferrari, chairman and president of American West National Bank."

Cecelia's boss. Jacques turned to face Roger. "Is there some significance to all this?"

"There is indeed. It's the story behind the picture that I want to explain to you. It was taken in 1932, thirteen years after the end of the First World War. The Bolsheviks had secured their control over Russia, and the economies of Great Britain and the rest of Europe were in complete disarray. The United States was just entering the Great Depression. Banks were being closed, and unemployment had reached record highs. Both domestic and international bankers knew they faced some very serious problems."

He paused, looking at the faces of his friends. "The five of us in the photograph began to meet informally, in an effort to improve international banking communications and coordinate our respective efforts. At first, we met on informal fishing trips, well away from the press and other prying eyes."

Roger motioned to Jacques to have a seat on the sofa under the photo. "We believed ourselves to be the 'young tigers' of the banking industry, just like, I suspect, you and your friends do. Even then, we could see the possibility that private and commercial self-interests might conflict with public interests in resolving postwar problems."

Just like our research. Mr. Malone is definitely trying to tell me something. Does he know more than he is at liberty to say?

"Anyway, it wasn't long before our unofficial organization became the nucleus of the Allied Bankers Association, the ABA. Even though we're not an officially sanctioned body, our collective influence makes it possible for us to speak authoritatively in resolving many international banking problems."

Roger paced about his office, then turned to meet Jacques' gaze. "As time passed, we tried to maintain a low profile and keep our activities as private as possible. But increasing public scrutiny and wartime conditions have made it impossible for us to get involved with certain . . . *issues*."

The chairman sat next to Jacques on the sofa. "Jacques, as with all holders of gold bearer bonds, these depositors are technically unknown, but it's not too difficult to guess what is really happening. Not only are we talking about a lot of money and the possible shortening of the war, but we may also alter future world history. An awful lot depends on what happens to that money.

"If you are able to coordinate the gold center banks and produce the deal you have proposed, it will set an important precedent in wartime wealth transfer and international banking cooperation. I can help open doors to make it easier, but I can't be 'officially' associated with what you're trying to do."

———

Following the meeting, Jacques decided to walk back to the Hay-Adams Hotel, hoping the cool spring weather would help him sort out what had just happened.

In less than a week, the Swiss banking community, the Federal Reserve, and the Allied Bankers Association have asked my friends and me to undertake missions of enormous importance. What is this world coming to when a few people like us are asked to undertake such an important mission?

It was seven o'clock in the evening in Washington and New York, already one the next morning in Geneva, and four o'clock in the afternoon in San Francisco by the time Jacques got back to his room.

The first call he placed was to Morgan Stone, who, Jacques knew, frequently worked late in his office.

Stone answered his own phone. "Jacques, I was hoping you'd call. Roger rang me just after you left. Apparently, you made quite an impression on the board of governors. So, what happens next?"

"Mr. Stone, it seems to me that I need to return to Geneva and work out the details of our proposal with the Swiss and their depositors. If it's all right with you, I'll make arrangements to pass through New York tomorrow, pack a suitcase, and catch the next flight out."

Jacques' next call was to Claudine.

"Jacques, have you any idea what time it is here?"

"Claudine, are you awake?"

"I am now. What's so important that you would call me at one in the morning?"

"I've negotiated a tentative acceptance with the Fed to act on our transfer. Step one is almost complete. But before we can proceed, we need the approval of the Swiss banking community and that of Karl's 'cousins.' Would it be convenient to have your plane meet me where you left me last time?"

"Of course." He could hear her sleepy chuckle. "*That* news was definitely worth waking up for."

Chapter 14

CLAUDINE AND JACQUES

The spring morning slowly warmed as Jacques, Claudine, and Henri enjoyed breakfast on the balcony of the Demaureux Bank's private suite in the Hotel du Lac. "Jacques, before we get started, tell us the latest news regarding Cecelia," Henri said.

"What's really weird is that it has been more than a week and there has been no ransom note and no communication," Jacques said. "All we can hope for is that she is still alive and that her kidnapping is some kind of government-to-government thing."

After a long silence, Claudine said, "Knowing Cecelia, she has found a way of proving to her captors that she can really be a handful."

Over coffee, Henri broached the real subject of Jacques' return. "I have just heard that the U.S. Fed is holding up its approval of all new gold bearer bond issues above a hundred million dollars. A substantial delay like this could kill our deal. I'm afraid my clients will panic and change their minds."

"Henri, as usual, your information is correct," Jacques said as he set down his coffee cup. "But as I'm sure Claudine explained, I met with Roger Malone, who, I gather, is an old friend of yours, and without committing himself, he was generally supportive of my ten-year/ten-percent terms."

"How did you arrive at those particular conditions? They're most restrictive," Henri said.

"In the past, the Fed approved a much smaller transaction to Stone City along those same terms. Because of its size and the impeccable track record of all the parties involved, it was not considered noteworthy at the time. But, as you know, our case is entirely different. I had to go with something they had already shown they were comfortable with accepting."

"Do you think there is any flexibility in the Fed's position?"

"You would know better than I, but I suspect that if we introduce softer terms, we would be taking a hell of a risk. We need to play by the 'laws of the game,' to borrow an old footballers' expression, particularly if we need them to act in an expedient fashion."

"Well, I guess we are going to find out how motivated Karl's clients are to complete this deal. Before I talk to him, I need to work things out with my Swiss colleagues, which may take a couple of days." Standing up, Henri said, "Look, instead of hanging around here, why don't you and Claudine go to Chamonix, and I'll let you know as soon as I have an answer. I understand that the snow on the back side of the glacier is still good."

———

Jacques and Claudine arrived at the chalet and took time only to change clothes and grab their ski equipment before heading up the gondola to the summit of Mont Blanc. Two lifts later, they were standing on the top of the world.

Staring out over the mountain, the two were standing close enough to be touching. Jacques put his arm around her.

After a few seconds, Claudine broke the spell. She pulled away and gave him a mischievous smile. "I'll be waiting for you at the bottom!"

Jacques watched her for most of the afternoon, amazed by her complete mastery of the mountain. *She makes it seem so easy, just like everything else she does.* In fact, he was so lost in his thoughts that he missed a turn and disappeared from view.

Claudine looked over her shoulder just as Jacques vanished. She couldn't see what happened next. All she could hear was a muffled thud, followed by, "Oh, shit."

Thirsty and soaked with perspiration, they were more than ready for a cold beer when they completed their final run. As Jacques ordered a second round, Claudine asked, "Are you ready for a hot shower, a good dinner, and a warm fire?"

The silent question of what might follow lay heavily between them. Neither of them voiced it.

"Yes to all three. Where would you like to eat?"

"I have a taste for a certain . . . intimate nightspot that I often frequent. Actually, I know the chef personally."

"Where's the restaurant?"

"Chez Demaureux—but I'm warning you, the food may not be the absolute best. In case you haven't noticed, I'm not the traditional domestic Swiss *Hausfrau*."

"I've noticed," he replied. "But perhaps you don't realize that you are talking to a famous French chef!"

"As a matter of fact, that information had escaped me. Do you think that between the two of us, we can manage one good meal?"

———

As she stood under the scalding shower, Claudine wondered, *Who is the real Jacques Roth? Is he still the inveterate chaser of women? Self-absorbed showboat? Famous French chef?* She smiled to herself. *Has he matured into a man I can depend on and trust? Will he let me share his life, or will he push me aside, the same way Tony did?*

So many questions, she thought, getting out of the shower and toweling off.

Still lost in her own thoughts, Claudine dressed in her old cable-knit sweater, gabardine slacks, and worn-out pair of sneakers, and she arranged her hair into a single braid that extended down to the middle of her back. Wearing no makeup, she looked like a healthy young woman, relaxed in her very familiar environment and at home in her own skin.

As she approached the kitchen, she saw a well-scrubbed Jacques, absorbed in chopping vegetables, pause to take a sip of wine.

Standing there like that, he hardly seems to be the internationally acclaimed banker, playboy, and heir to the Roth banking empire. He looks more like the very real man with whom I think I may be falling in love.

Hearing her approach, Jacques lay down the big chopping knife and poured chilled wine into a second glass. Claudine walked over to take it, standing close enough to feel the now-familiar current passing between them.

Uncertain what to say, she busied herself in the kitchen. "Let me see what we have for dinner!" Rummaging around the refrigerator, she found fresh trout, some small white potatoes, and a bunch of long, green onions.

"What can you do with these, Chef Jacques?"

"Trout happens to be one of my specialties. Wait until you have tasted Sauce Roth."

We have studied, worked, and played together, Jacques thought, *but nothing from earlier times is like the intimacy I feel standing in this small kitchen with Claudine at my side.*

When dinner was ready, he opened a second bottle of wine and they sat down at the tiny round table, illuminated by two candles. Everything in the world seemed complete.

Claudine took her first bite. "It's absolutely delicious. I'm surprised you can find your way around a kitchen, much less prepare such a wonderful meal!"

"My dear, you should never underestimate the talents of a totally spoiled French bachelor. Mike can't even find the stove's 'on' button in our apartment, so I'm forced to do all the cooking."

When they had finished their meal, Claudine wondered aloud, "Why do meals seem so much better when you don't have to eat them alone?"

"Sharing a meal is life's second best pleasure," Jacques answered. Seeing Claudine blush, he quickly changed the subject. "Let me pour you another glass of wine, and we'll sit in front of the fire."

They got as far as standing in front of the fireplace before he wrapped his arms around her. He could feel her leaning into him. Slowly, Jacques began to kiss her, his lips trailing a path from her hairline down her neck to her shoulder.

"So, what are we going to do about this?" she whispered, pulling herself free from his embrace.

As an answer, he pulled her back into his arms, nuzzled her hair with his nose and lips, and ran his hands down to the small of her back, drawing her closer. She floated into his arms. Jacques scooped her up and lay her gently on the couch.

Slowly, they began to undress each other, reveling in the contours of each other's bodies in the light of the fireplace. Claudine's eyes filled with desire; as he stared into them, Jacques was enraptured by their deep turquoise color.

Totally lost in the moment, Jacques felt as if he were making love for the first time. Claudine's hair, now free of the braid, was splayed across the pillow; he could see the growing passion in her face and feel the rise and fall of her breasts and the arching of her back as her body moved in concert with his. His dream had come true—Claudine was finally giving herself to him.

Their lovemaking lasted well into the night, leaving them spent and sleepy. For the first time in his life, he couldn't get close enough to a woman, couldn't get enough of her smell, her feel, and the way she made him feel.

This was no conquest—unless, maybe, a mutual one.

The sun shining through the window awakened him. At first, he didn't know where he was; then he realized that his arms were wrapped around Claudine, who was still asleep. Watching her peaceful breathing, not wanting to disturb her, he didn't move.

Could this be the Ice Princess who uses her career to insulate her from close personal relationships, so afraid of getting hurt? Is this the same girl who is seriously planning to steal one hundred million dollars from the Germans? Jacques, you'd better brace yourself. Getting involved with Claudine makes skiing down that glacier seem like child's play.

For the next two days, they were determined to make every minute count. They skied, talked, made love, and—most important— spent a lot of time just holding each other, lost in the moment. Jacques knew that things had irreversibly changed between them, and also that there wasn't much time left before the realities of war and their roles in the world would once again take over their lives.

The call came early on the third day.

"Claudine," her father said, "I've heard from our new clients—the terms are acceptable. As you can imagine, their biggest concern is moving forward as quickly as possible. My Swiss colleagues are also on board."

"That's great news," she said with an enthusiasm she didn't feel. *Back to the real world . . .*

"Yes," Henri stated. "It also means we've got to get busy. You and I will take care of the Swiss banking end of things, but I'm afraid Jacques is on his own with the Fed. We have to be careful not to do anything that will implicate Roger."

"I'm sure Jacques can handle things just fine on his own," Claudine said.

During their last night in Chamonix, the possible repercussions of what they were planning started to weigh on their minds in earnest.

"Claudine," Jacques asked, absently stroking her hair, "should we tell your father and Mike's father about our second agenda? After all, if something goes wrong, they'll be strongly affected."

"Nothing will go wrong."

"Still, we are planning to foul up the 'flight capital' of right-wing German industrialists, possibly infringe on the credit of the Swiss financial community, and upset the operations of some of the world's most powerful banks. Is this the kind of decision we have a right to make on our own?"

"Jacques, we *must* make this decision on our own. Any conversation would make them just as culpable as we are. And even if they believe as we do, they have more to lose." She turned to look at him. "In thinking through this problem, it was the possible losses that could be inflicted on the Swiss banks that naturally worried me the most. I would never want to put my father in that situation. So, I did some homework. The banks become exposed only if they unwittingly honor both the genuine and the duplicate bonds. That's a problem that I can control in my role as special accounts manager. I'll make sure that each bank receives a master list of the bonds, a complete set of instructions, and notifications every month that audits are scheduled, to ensure their compliance. In other words, it's already taken care of."

"Good. Then there's only one thing left."

"What?"

Laughing, Jacques took her in his arms. He didn't let go until the next morning.

======

Saying good-bye to Claudine at the airport was one of the hardest things Jacques had ever had to do. Still, he didn't allow himself the luxury of thinking about his relationship with her (or with Natalie) until he was safely ensconced in the comfort of his seat on the Pan Am Clipper headed back to New York. He leaned over to loosen his shoelaces.

How is it that a confirmed bachelor, never willing to subject his interests to the whims of one woman, has fallen in love with two entirely different women at the same time? Ordinarily, I would have been content not making a choice. Plus, it's wartime, and I probably won't see much of either one. Why not lie back and enjoy it?

His thoughts were interrupted by the same pretty stewardess he'd met on his trip to London with Mike.

"Mr. Roth, may I bring you a drink? Boodles gin martini?"

"Yes," he said, impressed by her memory.

Fifteen minutes later, he was sipping his second martini. *Is it my imagination, or is this one tasting even better than the first?*

More relaxed, he let his thoughts drift back to his female dilemma. Anyone would be privileged to have the kind of relationship he was enjoying with either Natalie or Claudine.

As difficult as it will be, I'm the person who will really be cheated if I don't make a choice. How I wish my life could be more like Mike's. He wins by loving one woman entirely.

Lost in thought, he barely noticed when the stewardess began to serve his dinner. Looking up into the eyes of this smiling woman, he asked impulsively, "Do you mind if I ask you a question about my personal life?"

"I'm flattered, actually. Let me finish serving the rest of the passengers, and you can ask me any question you want."

A short time later, she settled down in the empty seat next to him. "Okay, Mr. Roth, tell me what's troubling you."

He briefly described his dilemma to his captive audience.

"Do you know how unusual your question is?" she said, after a moment's consideration. "The men I know are so self-centered, they would never consider how much damage they are doing to each of those women. But put yourself in their places. If they are as independent as you say, how difficult do you think it is for them to let themselves be vulnerable to you? If you truly care about them both, you have to let one go."

"But how do I decide which one?" he asked.

"Now, that's a different question. You will never be confident about your choice until you reach a point of clarity. Though the situation is entirely different, the principles are the same ones you deal with every day in your professional career."

"So, the problem is how to achieve a sense of personal clarity without feeling forced to make a decision?" asked Jacques.

"Now you have it," she said, standing up. "And just so you know, I think they are both very lucky women. I'm sure I'll see you on another flight. Let me know how it turns out."

Chapter 15

A TEST OF WILLS

The rusty steel door squawked on its hinges and Cecelia's eyes snapped open. She watched the guard carry two fresh buckets into the small, poorly lit room—an empty bucket and one filled with water. He removed the old buckets, then returned with a bowl of soup, two pieces of stale bread, and a three-day-old newspaper.

With the benefit of some sleep, Cecelia's mind was beginning to function more logically. She had been held here for about a week. She was convinced that the kidnapping had something to do with her government work. *But what do they want? Information, the names of my contacts, money, or perhaps all three? And what can I do to make sure that I don't compromise the operation . . . but stay alive?*

Her survival would depend on staying alert and functional. That meant eating, but as hungry as she was, the foul-smelling soup made her recoil. Congealing fat floated on the surface of the soup. There were a few scraps of some unidentifiable meat.

Focusing on the soup, Cecelia realized that she was faced with the first dilemma to occupy her mind. *If I eat the soup, it will probably make me ill, but not eating anything will weaken me. I'll call that problem number one.*

She looked around for other things to divert her attention. *How much water should I apportion each day for both drinking and cleaning? Problem number two.*

She turned her gaze toward the newspaper, her mind reaching for problems to solve. *Every time I read the newspaper, I have to be careful not to allow the bad news of the war to depress me. I have to use the news to occupy my mind but not compromise my will. Problem number three.*

Now, I need to concentrate on solving the nightly issue of personal warmth. I could use the newspaper for insulation, but if my captors learn what I am doing, they might stop delivering it to me. Problem number four.

Personal interaction was her next problem. One morning, as she watched the guard complete the ritual of changing the buckets, she gave him a weak smile and said, "Thank you." He nodded his head at her in response. It was the first acknowledgment of her humanity that she had gotten.

How can I expand my conversation with the guard? Problem number five.

Each day, Cecelia would attempt small talk, usually centered around that day's weather. It wasn't long before extra pieces of beef had been added to her soup bowl, a third slice of bread accompanied each meal, and the newspapers were more current.

By concentrating on her five problems during the day and her most cherished memories by night, Cecelia learned to control the emotional turmoil of her incarceration somewhat. Each day blended into the next; days became weeks.

One night, in the middle of the night, the door to her room clanged open. A man handcuffed and blindfolded her before forcing her into another room and making her sit on a cold metal chair, clad only in her underwear.

From the sound of breathing, she could tell that other people were there with her. The warmth she was feeling on the front side of her body suggested that she was sitting in front of a very bright light.

Nothing happened and nobody spoke for at least five minutes. She was becoming aware of her semi-nakedness, the cold of the metal chair, the pain of having to sit in one position for a very long time, and the tightness of her handcuffs.

Suddenly, the blindfold was jerked from her head. The bright light was excruciating. She had to look down to reduce the pain. Finally, a voice from behind the light said, "Good evening, Miss Chang. As soon as you tell us what we want to know, we can all go home."

Cecelia wasn't sure how to respond.

"Miss Chang, it has come to our attention that you have been very busy helping enemies of Japan transport a lot of money out of China and other Pacific Rim countries. Would you like to tell us about it?"

They expect me to be disoriented and probably to lie. I must project a calm, controlled demeanor and tell as much truth as I can.

"As I'm sure you already know, I have been in the employ of the United States government since 1938," Cecelia said. "My job was to assist people in the path of Japanese imperialistic conquest to transport their wealth to safe harbors."

Judging by the long silence that followed, Cecelia guessed that her composure and candor must have put them off balance. *Good.*

A different man asked, "Do you mind telling us how you were able to accomplish this feat?"

"Not at all. Prior to the Japanese invasion of Hong Kong in 1941, we introduced a new financial instrument known as the gold bearer bond to the British- and American-controlled banks in Hong Kong, Sydney, Singapore, and San Francisco. Clients of these banks, fearful of confiscation by the Japanese, would convert their wealth into gold bullion, deposit it into gold money center banks, and convert that wealth into gold bearer bonds, which were smuggled out of the country."

"Miss Chang, don't you think that at this point, we know all that already?" a third voice thundered. "What we want to know are the names of the bond owners and how they transported the gold!"

"I am sorry, sir. I have told you all I know."

"Maybe another thirty days here will convince you to cooperate!"

As her guard dragged her back to her cell, Cecelia allowed herself a tiny smile. Being able to frustrate them wasn't much, but it was something.

Chapter 16
COMPLICATIONS

By the end of May 1943, the war was escalating. The easy German advances of the early part of the war were all but forgotten; the once-unstoppable armies of the Third Reich were pinned down on the Russian front and at the same time anxiously watching the western coast of Europe for the Allied invasion that everyone knew must be coming. The time was right for the Sentinels to initiate phase two of their plan.

Ian presented ten million dollars of the duplicate bonds to the London Bank of Commerce, Great Britain's largest and most active gold center bank. It would take a week for the bank to present the bonds to the corresponding issuing bank in Switzerland, wait for their experts to complete the authenticating process, and convert them into currency.

Two weeks passed after the first bond had been cashed before Ian received a phone call from the bank's chairman, Sir Desmond Muirhead, requesting his presence at their offices the following morning.

Something is wrong. Could the Germans have already tried cashing their bonds, causing the duplicates to be discovered?

He tried to convince himself that the call had something to do with his family's day-to-day business dealings with the bank. After all, Meyer & Co. had a long-term relationship with them. But down deep, he knew this meeting had something to do with the bonds he had cashed.

Ian was waiting apprehensively outside Sir Desmond's office when the chairman arrived at eight the next morning.

"Good to see you, Ian. Come in and have some tea," Muirhead said.

Inside, he gestured for the young man to sit next to a large bay window, joining him there in an adjacent chair. A tea service had been placed on the small table between them. Sir Desmond poured both cups.

"Ian, I'll get right to the point. Last week, we were presented with more gold bearer bonds of the same issue as the ones we cashed for your art-collector client two weeks ago. Two of these bonds had exactly the same serial numbers as yours."

Ian took a sip of his tea, hoping that Sir Desmond would not observe the cup shaking. "Surely there must be some mistake."

"No mistake on our end," Sir Desmond said. "My people examined the bonds and could find nothing wrong with them, apart from the two identical serial numbers. When we notified the issuing bank in Geneva concerning the second set, they checked their master list and verified the duplication."

Sir Desmond paused and took another sip of tea. "Although your bonds had been approved, they refused to honor the ones with the duplicate serial numbers. The terms and conditions, in case of any duplication, require banks to honor only the first bond presented. But I'm sure you'll agree that this arrangement is most unsatisfactory, since we cannot presently determine which bonds are authentic and which are forgeries. Until we clear up this problem, we may be denying the rightful owner his money by refusing to cash one of the bonds."

Why was the sunlight coming through the bay window suddenly so warm? Ian wondered. He began to perspire.

Calmly, Sir Desmond continued, "Accordingly, I felt I must advise you not to risk accepting any more of these bonds as art payments until we can clear this situation up with Geneva."

"Sir Desmond, I can't express strongly enough my father's and my own appreciation for your concern in this matter. You can be assured we will not be accepting any more payments of this sort," Ian said. He was very impressed by his ability to keep his voice even. *I almost convinced myself I was telling the truth!*

Jacques sat behind the desk in his corner office, high up in the Stone City Bank Building, looking out through the slightly cloudy sky. In a rare moment of relaxation, he watched all the empty ships, riding high on the water, making their way to New York's East River docks. The ships moving in the opposite direction rode low in the water, heavily laden with their outgoing wartime cargoes of fuel, military supplies, and equipment.

How vulnerable these slow-moving ships appeared, sailing by themselves. Although he knew things would change once they formed into convoys, escorted by naval war ships, he still couldn't help but think about all the tremendous losses that had been absorbed. Keeping open America's supply lines to Europe proved to be a costly operation.

By the end of the previous year, American wartime production had exceeded the total of all the Axis nations combined. In such a short span, the United States was able to supply a war being fought on three continents. An article in the *New York Times* reported that one cargo ship could be built in seventeen days, compared to a prewar schedule of one year. A maverick West Coast builder was promising to be able to produce a ship in only one day. Longer-range bombers were being produced fifteen times faster than when production had begun. Typewriter factories now made machine guns. Auto plants were producing bombers, tanks, and armored personnel carriers.

The world is changing fast. The industrialists on both sides of the Atlantic are getting rich. The winner will be the industrial economy that escapes most unscathed.

Recent reports were beginning to sound more optimistic. Allied troops won a decisive victory in North Africa and invaded Italy. The German invasion of Russia was stalled, and three of Hitler's armies had been defeated at Stalingrad. *More of these supplies are reaching their destinations, and Hitler is having trouble funding his war machine.* A faint smile appeared on his face.

Just then, his secretary was behind him, looking at a strange invoice statement from London. "Mr. Roth, we have received a letter from Meyer & Co.," she said. "I'm afraid I don't understand what it means."

Jacques took it and read:

> Please accept our apologies for your last invoice. Upon further review, we have determined that it was issued in error. The invoice in question seems to be a duplicate of another party's order, sent to you by mistake. We have notified our bank of this error, and the problem is being researched.
>
> —Meyer & Co.

Jacques had no trouble deciphering the true meaning of the invoice. Their duplicates had been discovered, and the Germans would start searching for their identity.

The leaders of the German industrial families had gathered once again in Karl's library. This time, there was no formal party, no fancy dinner, no cigars, only the well-filled snifters of cognac.

The atmosphere was strained. Germany was fighting on two fronts—something they had hoped would never happen. If their reports were accurate, the Allies would invade France in the spring of 1944. Already stretched thin, German resources would have to support a third front.

To make matters worse, Erhart Schmidt had just received a report describing London Bank of Commerce's discovery of the duplicate bonds. The war problems were serious, but the safety of their private wealth was far more personal.

Addressing his nervous friends, Herr Schmidt said, "Should more of these duplicate bonds begin to surface at other banks, it's safe to say that they'll adopt the same policy as the London Commerce. We have to ask ourselves which is worse—losing access to some of our own money or risking possible exposure to the government."

"But Erhart, our entire investment could become frozen, at least until the banks determine which bonds are duplicates," Heinrich Bimmler said. "That could put a real cloud over the liquidity of our capital for a very long time."

Karl Schagel considered for a moment. "Privately and quietly, we must find out who is behind this. Money doesn't just disappear. Once the bonds are cashed, we should be able to follow the money trail back to the source."

"Karl," Erhart said, "you don't seem to understand our priorities. It is much more important to bring this situation to a quick conclusion, regardless of what we have to do. Should Hitler or the High Command discover that two billion dollars in gold has been smuggled out of Germany, it won't take them long to figure out whose money is missing and come after us."

"If the war continues to go badly, and we wait too long, what will happen to us?" Heinrich chimed in. "The Allies could confiscate all our wealth, our factories. It's possible that we'll have to be ready to leave Germany at a moment's notice. That means that all our financial arrangements must be in order well in advance of our departure. Now, do you understand our sense of urgency?"

Before Karl could respond, Schmidt spoke again. "Karl, maybe your connection in Geneva could help us. In the meantime, we must do something to find out who is behind this forgery, and we must act immediately!"

Chapter 17

INVASION OF PRIVACY

Having received the urgent call from Erhart Schmidt's solicitor in London, the Insurance Fraud Investigation Company of London appointed their two top agents to the case. Kevin O'Sullivan had been with the investigation company, IFIC, for almost as many years as it had been in existence. It was rumored that he had underworld connections and wasn't afraid to use them, which didn't bother the executives at IFIC—provided they weren't directly implicated.

Considered trustworthy by snitches and street people alike, Kevin could rely on their cooperation. More recently, it was said that he had gained the cooperation of certain people inside the government intelligence agencies on both sides of the Atlantic.

Kevin was a bulldog of a man, both physically and emotionally. He was only five feet, six inches tall, but he weighed two hundred pounds and had well-developed muscles. His hair was cut short, and he had several mean-looking scars on his jaw, around his right eye, and near his right ear. These were the well-earned marks from a lifetime of brawling, much of it in neighborhood bars. All of it added to his legend—which suited his purposes quite well.

O'Sullivan was an intelligent man, meticulous and extremely detail oriented. Once assigned to a case, he would go at it with tenacity and tirelessness. He had never failed to solve a case, and IFIC believed that he was exactly the investigator to solve this one.

A large part of Kevin's success could be attributed to his partner, the thirty-five-year-old unmarried daughter of a Scotland Yard inspector, Katherine "Cricket" Williams. She was a tall, figureless woman with plain features whose main pleasure in life was derived from her work. She thrived on the intrigue, the excitement, and the large fees. If she had a personal life, no one seemed to know very much about it. Some wondered if she was a well-concealed lesbian; others saw her as a totally dedicated professional whose only personal pleasure was making money.

Cricket had previously worked as a bank data security officer, an accountant, and an auditor for the British government. She was also a tax fraud expert. Her technical and analytical skills were a perfect match for Kevin's street smarts.

During the five years Cricket had worked at IFIC, she had partnered with Kevin on more than several occasions. Together, they had recovered tidy sums for both the company and themselves.

It was common practice for IFIC to bill clients ten to twenty percent of what was recovered, depending on the size, complexity, and risk of the case. After recovery of out-of-pocket expenses, fees were then split fifty-fifty between the company and the members of the designated investigative team. Both Kevin and Cricket sensed that this case would involve the kind of fees that could change their lives.

For this investigation, as with all the others, Kevin and Cricket would pursue different trails. He'd follow the people; she'd follow the money.

"I think the place for me to start is with some people in the art community," he told her as they first began discussing the case.

"According to the bank report, Meyer cashed a number of bonds for one of his company's clients, who chose to remain anonymous. Despite the mysterious identity of the buyer, someone must know something. It's been my experience that once someone starts to pay big sums for art, word of his presence spreads quickly."

Cricket nodded. "And I'll begin by searching the records of the London Bank of Commerce and some of the other large banks capable of handling deposits of a multimillion-dollar magnitude. If the funds were deposited in one of those banks, a trail will have been created. Who knows how many more of these bonds there are? All told, we could be talking about a lot more than ten million dollars."

They grinned at each other. This was going to be fun.

———

Morgan Stone barked to his secretary, "Get me the bank commissioner. I'm going to get to the bottom of this right now!" He had already berated the security guard who was on duty.

"Sir, they were claiming to be bank examiners. They had badges and paperwork that appeared to be official. As a matter of fact, I recognized the blonde woman as the same one who visited Stone City a few years back."

"What else do you remember?"

"I remember having a friendly conversation with her when she signed in on her previous assignment. It was just a few days after my first daughter was born. If you'd allow me a few hours to search our records, perhaps I can find her name."

"Mr. Stone, the bank commissioner is on the line," the secretary said, trying to tiptoe around the boss's anger.

As Morgan grabbed the phone, the security guard took the chance to slip out of his office.

"Stone here. What do you mean by sending two examiners over without notifying me?"

"Unless I'm mistaken, Mr. Stone, we sent no personnel to your bank. If you'll give me their names, I'll check my records," the commissioner said.

"The visitors' logs are on their way up to my office," Morgan said. Just as he uttered the words, one of his young vice presidents came through the door.

"Here they are now," Morgan said, holding the receiver between ear and shoulder as he opened a book and found the signatures. He glanced in disgust at the VP, who backed slowly out the door. "Well, I can't tell you their names from these current signatures—they're illegible. But our guard recognized one of them from an earlier audit. Ah, here it is, backlogged. Her name is Eloise Cooper."

"I beg your pardon, Mr. Stone, but I have a list of our current examiners and that name is not on it. Whoever she was, she is not one of our people."

Outside the door, Jacques was listening to Morgan's side of the conversation. He suspected that the unauthorized search was related to the bank's cashing of another ten million dollars' worth of the duplicate bonds. The transaction had gone smoothly; the Swiss had verified the authenticity of the bonds, accepting responsibility, and Stone City had converted them into dollars.

The problem must be with the Germans. Perhaps they are searching bank records in an effort to identify the deposit of a corresponding amount of money. That magnitude would be easy to trace. Thank God Ian didn't deposit anything.

———

Erhart Schmidt's face turned almost purple as he read the initial IFIC report. Their undercover investigation of the records at four gold center banks revealed that not ten but forty million dollars' worth of gold bonds had been redeemed!

Worse still, there was no indication that any of the money had been redeposited into the banking system. There was absolutely no trail for IFIC to follow.

Whoever it is knows exactly what they're doing, the bastards!

Schmidt swore to himself that not a single person involved in the forgery would escape justice—swift and very final justice.

Chapter 18

PASSIVE RESISTANCE

Jacques dialed the number for Tony's California ranch. Tony answered on the second ring. "Hello?"

"Tony, it's Jacques. Have there been any new developments?"

"Not a word! Mike is driving himself crazy with concern. Not knowing what has happened is bad enough, but not being able to do anything about it is making things much more difficult for him."

"Maybe you should remind him it's Cecelia we're talking about. In many ways, I think she may be the strongest of us all. We've got to keep the faith that something will turn up soon."

"Thanks, Jacques. I'll try my best."

"As long as I have you on the phone, perhaps we could take a few minutes and talk a little business?"

"Mike and I have been talking a lot about old times—our thesis work, and how it relates to your recent plan. He mentioned that the two of you may have . . . found twenty-five million to invest in my development of, uh, Sentinel Wines."

"That's true," Jacques replied. "Of course, there's not much more we can do without a complete write-up of your business plan, but if this deal is going to happen, it will happen quickly."

"Well, that's the only good news I've gotten out here."

"Mike explained the details to you, right? You know what you'll be getting into? And you realize that any profit will go to the organization, not be used for personal purposes?"

"Stopping the pervasive misuse of wealth and influence is a lot more important to me than sharing in profits. I want to do it for a whole lot of reasons, not the least of which is for what my family went through." Tony paused, then added, "It's a good idea to invest the money in land here, Jacques. I can make it disappear like a drop of wine in a vat."

"I'm glad to hear you're on board," Jacques said. "We'll discuss it in detail when I see you. I would appreciate it if you would tell Mike I'll be arriving on TWA Flight 812 tomorrow, and while you're at it, tell him to keep his chin up."

———

FBI Special Agent Nate Green looked around the table at the senior members of the multiagency task force.

"All right, gentlemen, so glad you could all make it for our little get-together. I doubt you'll be surprised to hear that the only item on today's agenda is what the hell we're doing about the disappearance of Miss Cecelia Chang. This is our fourth weekly meeting since her abduction, so if she's still alive, her condition may be deteriorating. This little lady's recovery is of supreme importance to some pretty big guns in Washington and elsewhere, so you damn well better have some good news for me today.

"Commander Dunne, since you're the lucky bastard who's sitting to my immediate left, you're up first."

The crew-cut officer cleared his throat and glanced around the table. "The Navy has continued to apply pressure throughout the intelligence community in the Pacific. All that we know is that Samson has been using agents previously trained and employed by different government agencies. The men who have her know how to keep her hidden. But they also know that they won't get the information they want from a dead girl."

Green shifted his gaze to Jon Gersham, a U.S. Army major, and gave him a curt nod.

"The Army has been trying to identify the ex-agents who make up this organization. We've been investigating former government investigators, Army and naval special operatives, and Internal Revenue agents who have the kind of experience and qualifications that might satisfy Samson's requirements. For this case, we have narrowed our focus to those living on the West Coast and enjoying standards of living well beyond the means of a civil servant's income. At the present, we have managed to cull a long list down to a relatively short one."

The major glanced down at a sheet of paper in front of him. "According to our information, Samson tends to operate in cells, one of which may be in Northern California. We have recently assigned surveillance teams to track suspected members of that cell, and we are in daily receipt of their reports. Nothing we have learned so far indicates anything involving the kidnapping of a young Asian woman."

"Damn it, Jon, that's not good enough!" Green shouted. "I want your people to talk directly to the surveillance teams. Dig deeper. Somebody has seen something—they just don't know it."

"Beyond the filing of the initial report, my people have not heard or reported a thing. There's no talk on the street. We've given our snitches a thorough going over, and we've failed to discover even a sniff," reported Francis J. O'Connor, chief of the San Francisco Police Department.

"Well, Chief, the fact that you've heard nothing must mean something. Suppose you give us your best guess."

The chief glanced nervously at Green. "Well . . . maybe it's what we don't know that creates the more interesting questions.

If this were a San Francisco criminal operation, I think we would have heard something by now. So if I had to guess, I'd say it's happening outside the city."

Green nodded his head. "Okay, that's something, I guess." He looked at the map behind him and said, "That leaves the East Bay or the Peninsula as the most likely places." He turned around, slapping the table. "That's where we've got to concentrate our energies. Let's get to it."

The group needed no further encouragement to quickly leave the table.

———

The morning after her interrogation, a new guard had been assigned to Cecelia's cell. There was less soup in the bowl, only one slice of bread, and no newspaper. Obviously, her response, in addition to disappointing her captors, had demonstrated to them that their current tactics weren't producing the desired result.

Cecelia tried to guess the meaning behind these changes. *Is time working against my captors? They seem to be tightening the screws. I've just got to outlast them.*

But maintaining her alertness was going to be harder if they fed her even less. Cecelia thought about animals that hibernate during the winter; they slept, using as little energy as possible, until the warmer weather made it possible for them to forage more easily.

I have to conserve as much strength as possible. I have to find a safe place, like a bear in a cave, and go there in my mind.

Weeks later, the door opened and a man dragged her into the next room, again shoving her on to a cold metal chair. It was a different woman who faced her adversaries. Cecelia was thinner; she was pallid and frail. Her fingernails and toenails had grown to more than an inch long. There were large circles below her eyes.

Her head hung down. Her eyes were focused on the floor, away from the glare of the bright lights.

"Good morning, Miss Chang," a voice said. "We hope that you have brought us some better answers today. If you choose not to cooperate, I assure you we are prepared to continue this process for as long as it takes."

"Miss Chang, what are the names of the people you contacted in San Francisco?" a second voice asked.

Cecelia made no effort to respond. After what seemed an eternity but was, in reality, no more than a minute, she heard someone say, "Very well. Perhaps we will talk again, after you have had some time to think."

The next morning, her door didn't open at all. A small part of her mind considered that someone might be watching. *Stay in the cave—save your strength.* The only thing keeping her alive was the information her captors needed to get from her. She had to retreat from them, to a place they could not follow.

What do they call this? Passive resistance? I just hope I can keep it up long enough. I suppose that would make this current situation problem number six.

Chapter 19

CRICKET AND KEVIN

Cricket and Kevin sat in a pub in Kensington and stared past their fish and chips to see a mist falling in the glow of the streetlight on the damp August night.

"I've been mulling over this assignment," Cricket said. "We've been mucking about with this thing since June, and I think there's an angle we haven't thought of yet. There could be a real risk for our clients that's worth looking into."

Any time she hinted at something, Kevin knew enough to listen. "What kind of risk are you talking about?"

"I do believe we've gotten involved with the lives and personal fortunes of very high-level people in Germany. Though their solicitor led us to believe that the bonds belonged to the German government itself, I think the actual owners are some of the very same men who supported Hitler's rise to power and are now interested in removing their savings from Germany while there's still time."

"You keep saying 'think' and 'believe.' But you're pretty bloody well sure, aren't you?"

Cricket smiled and took a swallow from her pint.

"Gold bearer bonds would work well for that," Kevin mused, nodding, "providing these Germans had the cooperation of the

Swiss banks. In fact, I wouldn't be surprised if the people we're looking for aren't some of the same ones who helped arrange the transfer."

He took a draught from his glass, then placed it thoughtfully on the table. "There are only a handful of blokes who could organize a transaction of that size. That gives us a starting point for a second investigation."

"Kevin, there's a second question to consider." Cricket leaned in across the table. "What do you think *der Führer* would do to these German depositors if he learned of their plan? That is the risk our clients are taking, and it's certainly one worth exploiting."

Kevin stared straight into her eyes, beginning to understand.

"The High Command could be willing to pay a very substantial fee in exchange for our providing them with *certain* information," she said. "Think of it as an insurance policy. We would get paid to recover the bonds, but we could also earn a second fee from the German government."

Kevin sat back, studying Cricket's face. "You're not much to look at, but your mind is a thing of beauty."

"Sod off, you," Cricket said, smiling as she took a bite of her fish.

When Erhart Schmidt called the meeting two days after American bombers first hit Berlin, Karl Schagel immediately felt the beginnings of a headache.

"The lack of progress from London is alarming," Schmidt said, red faced, standing in front of Karl's desk. "All this time and the IFIC investigators haven't found a damned thing." He shoved the most recent report into Karl's hands.

Karl glanced at the paper. "Their search of recent deposits failed to produce useful information about Mr. Meyer or any unusual art sales."

"But when I threatened to terminate our agreement," Schmidt said, "their agents came up with a new theory. They are now suggesting that the art purchase was a cover story by this Mr. Meyer to mask a totally different agenda. Read what they sent me about him. It doesn't make sense."

"Their preliminary search of his background doesn't indicate any criminal activity," Karl said, staring down at the paper. He looked up suddenly. "Quite the opposite, in fact—his father is a duke whose title was bestowed."

Erhart nodded and paced as Karl kept reading. "Mr. Meyer is well-educated, with a doctoral degree in political science from the University of California in the mid-thirties . . ." His voice faltered but recovered once Schmidt turned to look at him. "Um, it says that ever since graduation, except for a stint in the service, he's been engaged in his family's business. I'm sorry, Erhart," Karl said, putting the sheet aside, "but he doesn't need the money. I don't think he's our man."

Schmidt took two big strides toward where Karl was sitting. Glowering over him, he said, "And this contact of yours at the Swiss Bank. Do you trust him?"

"With my life," Karl answered.

"Then right now, Meyer's the only lead we've got. And I won't let him slip away," Erhart said. He snatched the report from Karl's desk and stormed out of the room.

Once alone, Karl poured himself a cognac and sat down in his overstuffed armchair, staring into the dying flames in the fireplace. He had recalled that Henri's daughter had received a similar degree from the University of California at the same time.

I don't believe in coincidences. Could it be that Claudine, my own goddaughter, has something to do with all this? And how could the duplicate bonds be so perfectly forged without the help of a knowledgeable insider? Has Henri betrayed me?

Karl covered his face with his hands. *Does it even matter anymore? The war has made it impossible to trust anyone. But once Schmidt or his people make the connection—or imagine one—it won't take him long to make a move.*

He shivered, thinking of the hate he had seen in Erhart's eyes. *Should I try to recover the bonds myself and risk exposing Claudine and Henri? Or should I try to warn them?* He sat back in his chair and downed the rest of his cognac in one gulp.

How have I managed to get caught in the middle of yet another impossible dilemma?

Claudine looked out the window as her father drove them to their Chamonix chalet for the weekend. As she watched the passing scenery, she found herself regretting that they'd found so little time to enjoy the beauty and serenity of their surroundings.

Henri broke the silence. "Karl told me that his group has decided not to cash any more of their bonds until they can straighten out this mess with the duplicates."

"That seems extreme. In their place, I would take my money and run."

"That is what you would *want* to do, but don't forget, they have a ten-percent annual limitation clause in their agreement, courtesy of your friend Jacques. What they *did* do was get some help from the IFIC."

"Father," Claudine said, "Jacques said that some unauthorized persons, passing themselves off as federal bank auditors, inspected Stone City Bank's records recently. Do you think that had something to do with the IFIC investigation? And isn't it only a matter of time before the same thing happens to us?"

"Don't worry, my dear, the German families are going to have to be quite certain of what they know—or suspect—before they are willing to risk their relationships with the entire Swiss banking community. In any event, we have nothing to hide."

Claudine stared at the scenery to keep from meeting her father's eyes. "Still . . . I wonder if that's the reason for Uncle Karl's upcoming visit."

Chapter 20

A WARNING

Rail transportation across Germany to Switzerland was becoming more difficult and complicated. Overnight trips now took days to complete. Troop and supply trains absorbed almost all of the country's track capacity and received top priority in scheduling. Air attacks had further reduced Germany's operable rails. Henri had received several calls from Karl en route, letting him know of yet another delay in his arrival in Switzerland.

Still, as was his usual custom, Henri waited on the platform to meet Karl as he stepped from the train. *It looks as if my old friend has aged even more in the months since we last saw each other.*

As Henri gave him a welcoming hug, Karl leaned in and said, "Henri, I know that you've made arrangements for us to return to your chalet, but if you don't mind, I would prefer to walk along the lake. I have to leave by five o'clock, and that gives us less than three hours to talk."

Now Henri was really curious. What could be so important that Karl would spend three days coming to Geneva for just a few hours of conversation?

It was a short walk to the lake, but because neither man talked, to Henri it seemed much longer. It was also unusually cold for so early in autumn, and the two men pulled their hats low to protect their faces from the brisk wind and thrust their hands deep into their overcoat pockets.

Karl stopped, took a deep breath, and turned. "Henri, I have received two pieces of very disturbing information. I am sure that what I have to say will be very distressing to you. It certainly has been for me. This is a time when we really need to trust each other."

Henri remained quiet, waiting.

"Germany's national comptroller informed me that two billion dollars have gone missing from the government's national accounts. I will have to tell my clients as soon as I return that it will no longer be safe for them to remain in Germany. Our time to solve this problem of the duplicate bonds has just been shortened."

"Forgive me, Karl, but my Swiss colleagues and I kept up our end of the deal. What involvement do I have with the duplicate bonds?"

"Henri, this is the reason I'm here. The IFIC learned that Ian Meyer, of Meyer & Co. in London, employed book restoration specialists to forge the signatures of five Swiss bank presidents. We have all five of the forgers in our custody and they have identified a Mr. Duncan Melvin as their employer." Karl paused for a moment. "We had Mr. Melvin picked up and he told us that Mr. Meyer was his employer."

The two men resumed walking. Henri's mind was spinning. *Ian? One of Claudine's classmates from California? Dear God, surely Karl can't think that Claudine is involved.*

"Once they learned about Meyer, they started digging into his background. They found out that he participated in a doctoral studies program at the University of California. Henri, it's the same program Claudine was in," Karl said, stopping.

Henri realized in an instant that the whole situation had changed, but he did his best not to reveal his sense of alarm. "Karl, that's a tenuous connection at best."

Karl studied his friend's face. *I've got to hand it to him—I just delivered some of the worst news possible, and to look at him, you'd think he was having a normal day at the office.*

Karl continued. "The IFIC has connections with a security agency in the United States. This organization, known as Samson, was employed by the Japanese to kidnap Cecelia Chang, who was working for the American government, smuggling private wealth out of Asia. She was also a classmate of Claudine's."

"Karl, whatever you're alluding to—"

"Henri, I have to ask . . . Are you involved in this business with the forged bonds?"

"On my honor, I've nothing to do with it."

Karl exhaled again. "I knew that, Henri. Deep down, I knew." They started walking slowly around the lake. "An article I found refers to Claudine and her classmates making a presentation on the abuse of wealth and its connection with political and military history. I don't know what that fact has to do with any of this, but I know that once my very angry and frightened clients see that article, and they surely will, they'll put all the pieces together in a way to suit themselves. I don't believe that you yourself are in any particular danger. You are the only conduit that can be used for negotiating purposes. But Claudine and her friends could be in a lot of trouble. Their lives may be at risk."

Henri's mind was spinning. *Surely Claudine wouldn't do something so dangerous. But she is guided by her sense of "higher purpose." Is there really any length to which she wouldn't go to follow her convictions?*

"Karl, what can we do?" Henri didn't bother arguing his daughter's innocence.

"One purpose of my coming here," Karl said, "is to ask for your assistance in working an agreement to recover the remaining duplicate bonds, quickly and peacefully. My clients prefer not to take the risk of failing to track down the bonds before they leave the country. I haven't asked them outright, but I believe they'd make a deal. They can hardly afford the risk of discovery."

Henri felt slightly relieved. *If it's a business deal they want, that puts things back on familiar ground.*

Karl continued. "I propose a transaction whereby the people involved would be allowed to keep the forty million dollars they have already cashed. In exchange for tendering the remaining duplicate bonds, my clients will pay them one hundred percent of the face amount, which would be placed in an escrow account for a period of ten years. Should they disclose any information that would compromise my clients' positions, they would forfeit all rights to the escrowed funds. On the other hand, should your people live up to their side of the bargain, then at the end of the ten-year period, the entire amount would be distributed to them."

Henri considered the proposal. "Your offer is more than fair, as far as it goes. What concerns me is the possibility of your clients trying to seek revenge, either before or after the deal has been finalized. These industrialists are not exactly the most scrupulous people in the world. They should know that if anything happens to my daughter or her friends, I will turn all the evidence I have against your clients over to the international courts and use my influence to render their bonds worthless."

"Understood. I'll do my best to convince my clients to negotiate. But, Henri, you have the hard part. You must convince Claudine."

———

Henri returned to his office and immediately summoned his daughter. She sat down across the desk from him without saying a word.

"Claudine, I want you to listen very carefully to what I'm going to say. I've just left Karl at the train station. They know about Ian Meyer's involvement . . ."

She did her best to keep her face impassive, but she felt sure her father could see her guilt written on her face, in her posture. *Father always knows.*

"He also had a copy of an old article from the *San Francisco Chronicle* describing your presentations of your doctoral theses. It will only be a short time before the bond purchasers figure out what has happened—or what they believe has happened—who was involved, and why."

He fell silent and stared at her with those eyes that could always see straight through her. She held his gaze while her mind raced to prepare an explanation.

"Please, you've got to understand why we did it." Claudine described the details of their plan and what they hoped to accomplish with the money. She finished by saying, "I hope you will appreciate why we didn't take you into our confidence. After our meeting in Chamonix, we became convinced that the removal of wealth alone wasn't adequate to prevent the industrialists from reusing their capital to finance irresponsible future programs. We wanted to protect you and the others in the event that what has just happened ever happened."

"I understand perfectly why you felt as though it was the right thing to do—in fact, I understand better than you can possibly realize. One of the overriding reasons for doing this transaction in the first place was a desire to end this war. You and your friends have just taken things to a higher level. Believe me when I say that your problems aren't with me or with any of my colleagues. Your problems are with some very pissed off Germans."

The thought flitted through Claudine's mind that this was the first time she had ever heard her father use such vulgar language.

"Fortunately," Henri continued, "Karl and I were able to arrive at mutually acceptable terms and conditions for his clients' purchasing the remaining duplicate bonds." He explained these calmly to his daughter before adding, "Karl will try to get his clients to agree. As for you, Claudine, I don't see that the six of you have much choice. I doubt they will leave any of you alive if they catch you."

Her first thoughts turned to Jacques. After a moment, she asked, "What about you? Aren't you concerned that you may be on their list as well?"

"Oh, I'm sure that as long as they are convinced that my services are necessary to help them recover their bonds, I will be relatively safe. It's you and your friends I'm worried about. I know you have principles . . . I just don't think you need to die for them."

———

Three days later, after numerous delays, inspection points, and transfers, Karl's train pulled into Berlin. Half an hour after returning to his office, the door opened and Erhart Schmidt walked in.

"Karl, I'm glad you're back. Hopefully you bring us good news."

As if having to face an agitated Erhart Schmidt wasn't bad enough, having to tell him about the comptroller's report was even worse. Karl took a deep breath.

"Erhart, I am afraid I have good news and bad news. I have just gotten word from the comptroller's office that they've discovered that two billion dollars are missing from the national accounts. They haven't yet identified from whose account it was transferred. But an investigation is under way."

Erhart's face turned crimson, and Karl watched, unsure whether to call a doctor or a policeman. Instead, Schmidt took a deep breath and slowly sat down.

When he felt safe enough to go on, Karl continued. "Someone on Hitler's staff received a call from what was described as an impeccable source. They said that over the course of the summer and fall, several small, unauthorized shipments of gold bullion were transferred to banks in Switzerland under the assumption that they were consistent with the government's normal practices. The comptroller's office admitted that without the tip, they probably would have taken months to discover what had happened, if at all."

Schmidt clenched his fists but remained seated.

"Hitler is livid," Karl said. "He perceives the transfers as a threat to the country's money supply and a clear demonstration of a lack of confidence in his government and its war effort. It's been said that he used the word 'treason' several times in his assessment."

"Who would have something to gain by tipping off the comptroller?" Erhart asked, his expression distorted, despite his efforts to remain calm.

"Certainly not the Swiss banks," Karl answered, "not without implicating themselves. Nor the forgers, who would risk the liquidity of their own bonds by making the smuggled gold public knowledge." *That should clear Claudine and Henri.* "That leaves only the investigators you hired in London."

Schmidt stood and paced around the room like a caged beast. He finally replied, "After threatening them with losing a big fee, I remember thinking about how they might react. You don't think they're trying to ensure that they get paid either way?"

"Well, if IFIC is in fact playing both ends against the middle, any further investigation on their part may end up doing us more harm than good," Karl concluded, hoping this put Schmidt completely off the trail of Claudine and her friends.

Erhart took a deep breath and let it back out, then cupped his face in his hands. He let his hands fall and stared straight at

Karl. "My concern now is only with our capital. This development gives us only a very short period of time to free it up."

"That's the good news," Karl said. "Our Swiss contact believes that a deal can be made. He may know of a way to reach and communicate with the duplicate bond holders."

"Oh, he does, does he?" Schmidt's fingers twitched like claws. "Just how does he propose to do that?"

"He didn't say, and under the circumstances, I didn't ask. I don't want to alienate our only contact. He may be the only one who can help."

"Well," Erhart said, walking over toward Karl, "before we agree to any deals, I, too, have some good news." He reached into his jacket pocket and produced what looked like an old, yellowed newspaper article.

Without another word, he pointed to a photograph of Ian Meyer, standing among his five classmates.

"Look at that," he said, after Karl had time to adjust his glasses. "They are the sons and daughters of some pretty big names in the banking world, including one in Geneva you may have heard of."

Karl started to explain that the evidence was circumstantial, but Erhart simply took the article back, folded it up, and put it in the pocket of his suit jacket.

"I guess those agents at the IFIC did something to earn their fees after all," Erhart said with a twisted smirk. "Now it is up to me to protect the personal safety of our families, our fortunes, and the future of the Reich."

Schmidt left Karl's office and returned to his own. Unsure of whom to trust in his homeland, he decided to call on an American industrialist, Jack Hardy, chairman and president of Titus Oil, an old and trusted friend. They had had many dealings in the past. Prior to the outbreak of war, Schmidt and Hardy had orchestrated a transaction whereby Schmidt's company had become the second-largest shareholder in Titus Oil.

The war had not totally interrupted their working relationship, as the world believed.

Perhaps Hardy can give me some information I can actually use to settle this entire problem before I am forced to make a deal.

Chapter 21

RESCUE

Dr. Tom answered the knock at his door to find a courier holding an envelope. "Message for Tom Burdick," the young man said.

Tom took it and closed the door, curious to read the contents. Before sitting, he instinctively walked back toward the door and locked it.

> Tom, my old friend, please excuse this sudden and unusual message. It's imperative that each of the six members of your 1938 study group be warned that their efforts at gold bearer bond duplication have been discovered. Samson, a private organization operating within the US, has been employed to hunt them down and recover their bonds.
>
> —Karl von Schagel

Was this some kind of joke? Why would six talented, financially secure future leaders get involved in a scheme to duplicate bonds?

Tom stared out his office window at the green Berkeley hills rising majestically behind Memorial Stadium. *What are they up to? First I read about Cecelia's kidnapping, and now some group has been hired to track the rest of them.*

He flipped through the telephone directory in his desk and found the number for Tony's vineyards. He wasn't expecting Mike to pick up on the first ring.

"Hello, Nate, have you heard anything yet?" Mike asked as soon as he answered.

"Mike? It's Dr. Tom. Listen, I've just received a very odd message from an old friend of mine, who happens to be Germany's deputy minister of finance."

There was a long pause. "A message from the German deputy minister, during wartime? How can that be?"

"For years, we've been using bank courier services to communicate. It takes a little while for messages to get through, but the system works . . . and its privacy has so far proven reliable. Karl and I have used it to maintain a sort of pen-pal relationship. But, I have never received a note like this. Where can we meet tomorrow?"

———

Special Agent Nate Green stared out the window of his temporary San Francisco office in the Ferry Building. It was the end of the day and he was finding it difficult to concentrate on his work.

Out in the bay, one of Admiral Chester Nimitz's frontline carriers was returning to her home port at the Alameda Naval Air Station, on the eastern shore of San Francisco Bay. For weeks, the newspapers had been filled with stories of the hard-fought battles on and around Guadalcanal. According to all reports, the Japanese resistance had been much greater than anticipated. For a stretch, the outcome of the invasion had hung in the balance. Finally, the combined efforts of the American ground troops, the U.S. Navy's continued shelling of enemy positions, and the support of the American aircraft carriers were sufficient to overtake a brave, committed, and well-entrenched enemy.

Americans were excited. The successful invasion not only represented the Allies' first victory in the Central Pacific but also started what they hoped would become a long, island-hopping string of victories that would eventually link up with General Douglas MacArthur's forces in the south and take the war to the Japanese mainland. The end of next month brought Thanksgiving. Nate hoped there would be some war news to be thankful for.

From his office window, Nate had a bird's-eye view of the oil-stained aircraft carrier, which showed evidence of numerous attacks. She was returning for needed repairs, shore leave, and resupply. In preparation for their arrival, the crew was standing at attention along the sides of the flight deck, wearing their dress whites. Proud but bloodied, the ship and her men were returning home in victory.

Nate tried to imagine what the battles must have been like. But the sudden ringing of his private telephone interrupted his reverie. *God help whoever it is. This better be good.*

"Nate, this is Major Jon Gersham. You were right. When we restudied the reports from the East Bay team, we learned that they had been watching what they believed to be a subversive cell guarding an old machine shop in Albany, north of Berkeley. According to their reports, two shifts of machinists came and went five days a week. Until recently, none of us regarded this information as being sufficiently important to include in our reports."

You mean until I chewed your ass. "And what did you find?" Nate asked.

"We checked the town's industrial records. That factory shut its operations at the beginning of the war, and these buildings should be abandoned."

"Major, tell your men to stay put and out of sight. My men and I will come right over to check it out."

An hour later, FBI agents joined Major Gersham and his intelligence officers on their stakeout. While they were waiting, barely breathing, a prewar model black Buick pulled to a stop in front of the warehouse and three people got out—two big men and a smaller one. It was the smaller man who caught Nate's attention.

"That's Tony Clarke," he whispered, keeping the binoculars up to his eyes. "I knew him when he was in the bureau . . . A bad seed if there ever was one."

As they watched, Clarke and the two bodyguard types walked up the long stairs, went inside, and reappeared in less than thirty minutes.

"Whatever happened," Nate surmised, "something must have gone wrong. It looked to me like Clarke was upset and barking orders."

Green thought he saw a slight movement in one of the loft windows, and he quickly focused his binoculars on the window. *Someone is in the loft.*

———

It was nightfall, but it made little difference to Cecelia. In her dim room, what little light there was wasn't missed. One night ran into another. She was still in her "cave," but her sleep had become sporadic. She was having trouble with nightmares, which were becoming so real and horrific that she would wake up in a cold sweat and realize she was living them. Hunger had ceased to be a problem; her system had begun to shut down. The veins on her arms and legs could now be clearly seen. The bones in her shoulders, her rib cage, her hips, her arms, and her legs appeared to be covered only by a thin parchment of clear, white skin. Thirst was her biggest problem. Even with her careful rationing of water, she couldn't seem to make it last. None of it could be spared for cleaning. Her fingernails had grown at least another inch; her hair had become an oily, dirty mess. The hair under her arms had grown full, and she could smell her own odor.

Outwardly, she looked like a small, wild animal. Her eyes showed no expression of life or recognition of anything occurring around her. Cecelia was protecting her mind, though, guarding it the only way she knew—by keeping it in a safe place, far away from reality. She concentrated on her most cherished memories. They represented all that was left of her life. Nothing else mattered now.

Earlier, her captors had taken her into the room next door, and once more the bright light was turned on. She could see only dim silhouettes of the three men as they entered the room and sat opposite her, behind the big table. The interrogation lasted longer than usual. Three times, they had asked her the same question, and three times, she hadn't answered. Something seemed different—was it a tone of desperation in their voices? She allowed a very small part of her mind to engage with her surroundings. *Have they run out of time? Have they given up?*

After the questioning was completed, they returned her to the small room. She could hear the three men outside her door. One of them was especially angry. He either didn't realize that Cecelia could hear or he didn't give a damn.

"This is going nowhere. Our client is frustrated and time is running out. We need to try something new. If we can't wait it out, I say we beat it out of her!"

Overhearing the conversation, Cecelia couldn't be sure if this was simply a scare tactic or if, tomorrow, they would try torture. Either way, she knew it wouldn't make any difference. Whatever they did to her body, she would be far away in her mind.

She heard the steps of three men as they descended the outside stairs. The fourth—her regular guard, she assumed—remained posted outside her door. Cecelia nodded off into a light sleep. She was awakened not by her discomfort or by her bad dreams, but by a soft sound she couldn't identify.

She sat up, stock still, in the total darkness.

The skylight, painted an opaque black, shattered above her head. Instinctively, Cecelia held up her arms to protect her eyes as a blinding light flashed through the room, followed by the sound of a small explosion.

The guard unlocked the door and, gun in hand, came charging into the room. The first man who dropped through the skylight shot him. The second rescuer grabbed Cecelia, saying, "Don't worry, Miss Chang. You're safe now."

———

"Mike, you've got a phone call," Tony Garibaldi said, his eyelids just a tad heavier than his dragging feet. He stood in Mike's bedroom doorway, rubbing his face in a futile attempt to wake himself up. He looked at the clock; it was five AM.

When Mike didn't respond, he walked over to the bed and shook his friend awake. "Mike, wake up! You've got an important phone call."

"Yeah, okay, hang on." Mike dragged himself upright. He reached over for the phone and picked up the receiver. "Hello?"

"Mr. Stone, I'm Dr. Ross at the Peralta Hospital in Oakland. A Miss Cecelia Chang has just been admitted here. An FBI agent requested that we call you."

Mike's eyes shot open; he sat straight up in bed. "Is she . . . Is she okay?"

"There doesn't seem to be any evidence of physical harm. But she is badly dehydrated and in need of nourishment. We are treating her intravenously. It's her . . . mental condition that concerns us most. She's had a difficult time, and there's no telling how disturbed she may be. You may want to get here—"

Mike dropped the phone and bolted for his closet.

"Tony! They got Cecelia! She's at the hospital! She's going to be okay."

Catching the tail of his shirt in the zipper of his pants, Mike went on, "They didn't tell me much . . . We need to get there as fast as possible. Peralta Hospital in Oakland." Mike couldn't get dressed quickly enough. He ripped his shirt out of the zipper, leaving it undone, and jumped into his shoes—no time for socks.

"Do you want me to drive?" Tony offered.

"That would be great. In my state, I don't think I could drive across the street."

To Mike, the car seemed to be standing still. After what felt like an hour, they crossed over the Bay Bridge, drove through Oakland, and pulled up to the front of Peralta Hospital. Mike opened the door before the car came to a complete stop and nearly fell out onto the pavement.

"Take it easy," Tony called after him. "They'll be admitting you next."

Rushing through the entrance, Mike approached the reception desk. "Please, can you tell me where I can find Cecelia Chang?"

The receptionist looked down at the patient admission sheet. "I'll page Dr. Ross for you."

In a matter of minutes, a handsome, middle-aged doctor appeared. "Mr. Stone?"

At that point, a policeman stepped between them. "I'm sorry to ask you this, sir, but can you please show me some identification?"

"Yes, of course," Mike said as he began to sort through his wallet for his driver's license, which he dropped twice before managing to hand it to the officer.

The policeman examined it, handed it back to Mike, and stepped out of the way.

Dr. Ross said, "She's on the fifth floor, 517. It's a private room." He placed a hand on Mike's shoulder to stop him. "Before you go see her, let me explain a few things. We've cleaned her up and confirmed that she was not beaten, raped, or sexually assaulted.

Despite her appearance, she's in surprisingly good condition. But she's been totally unresponsive. She hasn't said a word, and there's no indication that she's even heard our questions."

Mike looked startled. "That's not like her."

"The human mind sometimes has a way of shutting down to protect itself from what it can't handle. That doesn't mean her brain is permanently damaged. It just means it's not ready to respond to external stimuli. We're hoping your presence might help, but you've got to be patient. It's been my experience that emotional traumas like these run deep and can last a very long time."

"But you *do* think she'll be okay, right?" Mike pleaded more than asked.

"I believe she will be, but she needs you." The doctor took his hand off Mike's shoulder.

It seemed that the elevator would never get to the fifth floor. When the elevator doors finally opened, Mike burst out and ran down the hall, searching for Room 517. Turning a corner at full speed, he nearly knocked over a nurse.

At the end of a long corridor, he finally located her room. Two uniformed policemen sitting outside asked Mike for identification. He handed it to them, said, "Keep it," and stepped inside.

Mike saw Cecelia sitting in the middle of the bed, dressed in a hospital smock. Her legs were crossed; her head was down; she was hugging herself. She didn't make a sound. She looked like a small, frightened, and very fragile child.

Mike crossed the room, sat down on the bed, and wrapped both his arms around her. He held her silently for a long time before lying down on the bed. He gently pulled her down beside him. Holding her in his arms, he began to describe some of their experiences together, hoping she would show some sign of recognition.

While he recounted their trip to Carmel, he looked at her face and thought he saw a faint smile form on her lips. It was enough to give him hope.

He held her closer, whispering in her ear. They fell asleep.

When Mike woke up the next morning, he had forgotten all about his appointment with Dr. Tom. The first call he made was to his father. The second was to Jacques.

Chapter 22

LUNCH AT JACK'S

Jacques' flight to the West Coast was delayed by mechanical difficulties, so he arrived at Peralta Hospital late in the afternoon—far later than he had intended. He poked his head inside Cecelia's room and whispered to Mike, "How is she?"

"She'll be okay." Mike sat beside her in the bed, stroking her hair.

Jacques could hardly believe that the figure huddled into a fetal position beside Mike was really Cecelia. But he did his best not to let his shock show; that wouldn't help Mike.

Realizing there was nothing he could do but be as supportive of Mike as possible, Jacques pulled up a chair and sat next to him at the side of Cecelia's bed. They spoke little throughout the early evening before visiting hours were over, or as Mike drove them to a restaurant for dinner after they left the hospital. It wasn't until he was finishing his second drink that Mike began to relax. "Jacques, I can't tell you how many times I prayed for Cecelia's return. I promised myself I would be so grateful to get her back that I would take care of her, no matter what her condition might be."

As Jacques drove to the Clift Hotel, he tried to pull his mind away from Cecelia and focus on the problem of the false inspections. *If the fake inspectors have made it to the West Coast, that's good. It means that they still haven't figured it all out. But it also means that they're running out of places to look. Either they'll be getting ready to deal . . . or they'll be getting desperate.*

———

Jacques arrived fifteen minutes early at the American West National Bank headquarters, overlooking Montgomery Street and the heart of San Francisco's financial district.

As he exited the elevator on the third floor, a lovely silver-haired woman greeted him. "Good morning, Mr. Roth. The chairman is expecting you," she said as she ushered him into Mr. Ferrari's office.

Turning toward Jacques, Pete Ferrari said, "This roguish-looking gentleman must be none other than Jacques Roth. I'm sure you probably don't remember, but we met briefly at your father's home, before the war. You certainly have come a long way from the young man not allowed to talk at the dinner table. What a pleasure it is to see you again."

Flattered that the chairman would remember him, Jacques stepped forward to shake his hand. "Mr. Ferrari, I only wish that I were meeting you again under more pleasant circumstances. As you no doubt have realized, Morgan Stone is really upset about what has occurred."

"Of course. If Morgan hadn't called, we might never have suspected that our bank had a similar breach. I took the liberty of contacting Ted Lee, the president of the Bank of Hong Kong here in San Francisco. It turns out that he's had the same trouble."

"We checked with our friends in the Swiss banking community," Jacques said, "and it seems as though someone is inspecting all Allied banks large enough to handle a transaction involving millions of dollars of bonds. They're trying to trace the identity of the owner."

"Why?" Pete asked, motioning to Jacques to sit down.

"There were some duplicate bonds circulating in London."

"Well, I can certainly understand the owner's concern if a significant block of those bonds have been stolen or forged."

"No, it's nothing like that, sir," Jacques said. "According to the Demaureux Bank in Switzerland, two bonds were presented for cashing at the London Bank of Commerce that had serial numbers identical to two that had been previously cashed. Authenticators examined both sets of bonds and determined that they were both authentic."

"A glitch, then? Or human error?" Pete speculated.

"Quite possibly. Still, sending in phony inspectors cannot be attributed to 'human error' or even a lapse in judgment. It amounts to an invasion of privacy, and Stone City is determined to get to the bottom of it. Do you think it would be possible for us to talk to Mr. Lee? You know Morgan—he's expecting a complete report."

Pete smiled, picked up the phone on his desk, and dialed a number. It seemed as though Mr. Lee answered on the first ring.

Jacques sat patiently as he listened to Pete making plans. *How is it that high-level business executives are always able to reach each other?*

Pete put the phone down and looked at Jacques. "All set," he said. "An early lunch at Jack's it is."

A few minutes later, Jacques and the chairman of American West were walking up Montgomery Street. They turned left onto Sacramento and walked the two blocks to Jack's, the meeting place of many of San Francisco's business and social elite. Although Jacques had never been there, he knew it by reputation. Even at eleven-thirty there was a line extending from the entrance out to the street.

Walter Taylor, the maître d'—himself a San Francisco tradition—immediately spotted Mr. Ferrari and escorted them past the line and into the restaurant. "Your regular table, sir?"

"Yes, Walter, thanks. And Mr. Lee will be joining us shortly. Would you be kind enough to escort him to our table when he arrives?" Pete said.

"Certainly, sir. Would you gentlemen please follow me?" Walter led them past a small bar on the right, and then headed toward the rear of the restaurant to Pete Ferrari's regular table.

As they passed through the famous eatery, Jacques took in the decor. Black-and-white tiles gave the floor a chessboard appearance. The ceiling was high, and the walls were paneled in alternating sections of floor-to-ceiling mirrors and gleaming white paneling. The tables were covered with crisp, white linen tablecloths. The waiters were dressed in tuxedos and sported dishtowels tied neatly around their waists. In the back of the restaurant, a flight of stairs led to the private dining rooms.

Several people rose to greet Pete as he walked by. The chairman knew them all by name and was very careful to introduce his guest to each one. Jacques was amazed at how many of their names, if not their faces, he recognized.

After they were seated, Walter motioned for the waiter. "Have a delightful lunch, gentlemen."

The waiter approached as soon as Walter left the table. "Good afternoon, Mr. Ferrari."

"Oh, hello, Harry. Would you please bring us a bottle of your house white burgundy? We'll have that while we're waiting for our other guest."

The waiter removed one place setting and put a basket of sliced French bread and small dishes of unsalted butter on the table. He then opened a bottle of sparkling mineral water, poured it, and disappeared downstairs to the wine cellar.

"Jacques, Ted Lee and I go back several years. He's been managing the Hong Kong Bank since before the war, about two years before Japan began its invasion of Indochina. His family moved here from Hong Kong when he was very young. Over the years,

Ted and I have worked together on many projects. I consider him a good friend as well as a very capable banker."

The wine and Ted Lee arrived at the same time. They all shook hands, and introductions were made. "Jacques, I understand that you are friends with Cecelia Chang," Lee said. "I've known her family for years and we've all been so worried about her. Mike called this morning to tell me she was found alive and has been rescued. Is there any more news?"

"It's too early to really know how well she'll recover," Jacques said. "Months of forced confinement can do some real damage."

Lee shut his eyes tightly for a moment, visibly pained by his report. "But if you know Cecelia," Jacques continued, "then you also know that she's one of the toughest-minded people on earth, pound for pound."

Pete said, "Jacques, the three of you—you, Ted, and Cecelia—have something in common. You all attended the University of California."

"We did, indeed," Ted said, seeing Jacques' surprise. "I was class of '31 and I know you were there from '35 through '38."

Pausing for a moment to allow the waiter to pour a second glass of wine, Ted continued. "I was in attendance when you presented your research. I came to hear Cecelia, and I must admit that it was a nice piece of work. Your predictions were, unfortunately, more accurate than anyone could have realized at the time. Tell me, whatever happened to your suggestion about some kind of watchdog organization to identify abuses of power?"

"Unfortunately, nothing," Jacques responded, taking a quick gulp of water.

I could be paranoid, but I get the feeling Mr. Lee knows more than he is letting on.

"With the pressure of starting new careers, the distractions of another world war, and our scattered locations, I am sad to report that we allowed the idea to die."

"That's too bad," Ted said. "Just like the rise of fascism that occurred so quickly after the First World War, I wouldn't be surprised to see the spread of Communism start shortly after the conclusion of this one. The Communist Revolution that was well under way before the Japanese invaded China has not been stopped by the outbreak of war, only delayed." Lee toyed with his fork for a moment, then looked at Jacques. "Just for the record, how would you have distinguished your watchdog organization from a contemporary form of vigilantism?"

Jacques was intrigued. "Mr. Lee, you have asked a very interesting question. It's one that we debated for two years after first thinking up the idea. Vigilantism implies taking the law into your own hands. At no time did we ever consider doing anything that would be illegal or outside the strictest letter of the law. More important, we concluded that internal checks and balances would never constitute a total solution, nor would the fact that the organization stood to gain nothing. Once we chased the problem all the way through, I think we concluded that nothing we hoped to accomplish could have been achieved without the cooperation of other people. Our only hope in obtaining their assistance depended upon their viewing our actions as being consistent with the public's best interests."

Pete Ferrari nodded.

Lee appeared satisfied with Jacques' explanation, as though it had answered another unasked question. "So, Jacques, I hear Morgan Stone has sent you here to discuss the problem we've been having with these unauthorized inspections."

"Yes, sir. Stone City Bank is determined to get to the bottom of this breach of security. In fact, I think it might be a good idea if I were to go to London and speak with Sir Desmond concerning this issue."

"Thank you, Jacques. That would certainly save us all a trip, not to mention a lot of time and trouble," Pete said.

"Well, then," Ted said, "I guess it's agreed."

As they finished lunch and rose to leave the restaurant, Jacques couldn't help but notice that a bill never came to the table.

Chapter 23

WINE COUNTRY

Hoping that he might jog her memory by bringing some of her personal items into the hospital room, Mike had gone to Cecelia's apartment and brought back some clothes, a few pictures, and a stuffed dog wearing a U Cal T-shirt.

Mike helped Cecelia change from her hospital gown into what he happily called her "out of Peralta" uniform: her favorite red sweater, an old polka-dotted skirt, penny loafers, and no socks. During the whole time he was helping her, she clung desperately to the stuffed dog.

Will leaving the hospital make her worse, or is it the first real step toward a full recovery? Careful not to let his anxiety show, he talked to her in a normal, conversational manner as he helped her change clothes.

"Cecelia, today we're going to have lunch at Larry Blake's. You remember the place—it's that beer bar and restaurant near campus. Would you like that?" He was watching her closely for any signs of recognition. *Still no reaction.*

Careful to keep up the one-sided conversation, he escorted her out of the hospital, walked her to his car, and drove to Berkeley. Along the way, he pointed out familiar places.

Mike was trying to keep his own spirits up and enjoy the fact that Cecelia was actually there, sitting beside him. He glanced over at her, sitting bolt upright with no look of comprehension. *How different this girl is from the one who snuggled close to me on the way to Carmel. I want Cecelia back . . . the real Cecelia. My Cecelia.*

The next day, he took her for a walk on the Cal campus. It was twelve o'clock, and the bells in the campanile began to chime. Turning to Mike, Cecelia said, "It must be noon. Let's go to the 'I' house and meet the others for lunch before class."

Mike looked at her. *Where is she? In her mind, it's still 1938. But at least she remembered and reacted. And that's something.*

For the next several days, Mike took her to all the old places, hoping to trigger more memories: Cal Stadium, Wheeler Hall, a college baseball game, dinner at the cheap student places near campus, and shopping at her favorite stores in Berkeley. At least once each day, she would respond to what she was seeing, occasionally asking questions. Each time she spoke, she had more to say. Mike could tell from what she said that her mind was still traveling through time.

The following week, he started taking her to familiar places in San Francisco, trying to reacquaint her with the neighborhood near her apartment. They had lunch at the Buena Vista Café and fed the ducks at the Palace of Fine Arts. She seemed to be enjoying herself and smiling more. *Maybe she's starting to feel safe enough to come out of her shell.*

On a bright, sunny day, Mike decided to risk having Cecelia revisit her apartment. She had already reconnected with the past— maybe it was time to let her live again in the present.

Telling her that he needed to gather a few more things, he began to drive her across the bridge. Next, he chose a route through San Francisco that would pass by things she might recognize. As they neared her building, he watched her closely: no reaction, no signs of recognition. At least she was sitting calmly, a serene look on her face.

Mike parked the car near the front entrance and they walked the short distance to the door and into the lobby. *She seems fine, maybe even peaceful.* Standing in front of the elevator, he reached forward and pressed the button. She watched as the numbers lit up in decreasing order, waiting patiently for the car to arrive.

When the elevator door opened, two large men stepped out, talking to each other. Mike had no idea Cecelia could scream so loud or run so fast. She was out the front door and running up the street before he even realized what had happened. It took three blocks for him to catch up with her, and another twenty minutes to calm her down. They made their way through a nearby park, Mike trying to answer each nearly hysteric statement with a calming, soothing tone and a reassurance that she was all right, that things were going to be fine.

Suddenly, he realized that they were talking about the present, about what had just happened. Cecelia was scared, all right, but she was in the present, instead of locked inside herself or wandering in the past.

"Cecelia! Do you realize you're talking to me about what you just saw?"

"Of course, you idiot, what else would I be talking about?"

Despite her words, he grinned. It was the first flash of the old Cecelia he'd seen since her rescue. He didn't know how long it would last, but it gave him hope that Cecelia was coming back into possession of herself.

Mike walked her slowly back to the car and helped her inside. Not wanting to subject her to another traumatic experience, he decided to get her away from the city.

When they were crossing back over the Bay Bridge, he asked, "How would you like to visit Tony? This is the time of year when they prune the vines, and the drive should be beautiful. I know he would love to see you, too. He was calling the hospital almost every day. In his own way, I think Tony cares about you almost as much as I do."

She just stared ahead.

That's okay. I saw the real Cecelia, for just a second, back there. I know she's still in there, somewhere.

———

Driving up the Silverado Trail, Tony was proudly sitting behind the wheel of his old Lincoln Continental convertible. Built before the war, the elegant car could be easily recognized by its unusual design and the external casing of the spare tire on the rear of the trunk. Mike sometimes thought Tony loved the Continental like a member of his family.

Tony was born to be a tour director. He was telling stories nonstop, chattering away to Cecelia and Jacques, who sat up front with him. The top of the car was down on this warm, sunny day. The four of them were all together, touring the Napa Valley and listening to Tony narrate his dreams, many of which Mike had heard before.

Tony was in his element, pointing out pieces of land he planned to purchase. He had given them a map marked with small, numbered dots used to index each parcel of interest.

Tony continued his running commentary. "Without their leaves, the trunks and limbs of the vineyards are clearly visible. They remind me of the cardiovascular system. Look at the dark brown soil, the green, rolling hills studded with California live oak trees, and the cloudless, blue sky. Don't you think this is the kind of scene the impressionist painters were trying to capture?"

Cecelia didn't say much, but she seemed interested in Tony's stories and enchanted by the scenery; she was even the first one to hop out, when the car stopped, to stretch her legs and take in the view.

Noticing how well Cecelia was reacting to his stories, Tony decided to describe Claudine's role in helping him when they had done the original research about each of the parcels. "She helped me collect so much information on our weekend field trips. You should have seen her. With that heavy survey instrument balanced on her shoulder, she hiked all over these hills like a mountain goat. It's entirely possible that she was the most attractive pack animal that this land will ever see."

Tony started to point out the different restaurants and bed and breakfasts that he and Claudine had frequented. Mike thought he heard a tinge of regret mixed with Tony's nostalgia.

Eventually, they left that area and came upon Rutherford Hills, for which Tony had a whole new set of tales. "Someday, wines made from grapes grown in this region will be among the most acclaimed of all the California wines. Mark my words," he said, "one day, in the not-so-distant future, cabernet sauvignon from this valley will sell for twenty-five dollars a bottle!"

"Come on, Tony, be realistic," Mike said. "Do you realize how few of even the finest wines have ever sold for that kind of price?"

"That's exactly my point. There will come a time when the very best wines produced here will be regarded as comparable to the world's best. And that's coming from someone who was born in Italy!"

Next, they drove on through Calistoga to St. Helena and Yountville—more dots and more stories.

When they entered Alexander Valley, Mike was amazed at how much larger it was than all the others. Tony began to explain how, unlike the Napa and Sonoma valleys, this valley ran from east to west. For grape-growing purposes, the experts had divided the valley into three separate zones, he told them: the valley floor, the foothills to the north, and the bench ground to the south. Tony explained how the unique air drainage patterns, microclimates, and soils distinguished one zone from another and how each section was specially suited for growing distinct varieties of grapes.

Suddenly, Jacques spoke up. "Wow, Tony, this place is really vast. This would be some hiding place. I mean, they could look for you for years and never find you, I'll bet."

"You don't know how right you are, Jacques. Even if someone came snooping around, they would be noticed." Traveling farther down the road, Tony continued, "Today this valley is mostly cattle country, but someday it will be as important as the developed wine regions, even in Europe. You'll note that there aren't any dots here on the map."

Turning south into the Sonoma Valley, they drove toward Healdsburg. "Lots of dots here," Mike noted, leaning forward to look at the map Tony had just handed to Cecelia.

"About thirty percent of our proposed acreage is located in the Sonoma Valley, fifty percent in the Napa Valley, and the remaining twenty percent in the Russian River Valley and Carneros region," Tony said. They turned west and gradually made their way toward the Dry Creek Reservoir and the small river resort town of Rio Nido. From there, Tony turned on to a highway marked "River Road." They followed the Russian River Valley eastward. "There's something I want to show Cecelia," Tony said. Almost immediately they were suddenly surrounded by giant redwoods. Cecelia's eyes gazed up at them in wonder.

"No matter how many times I've driven through here," Tony said, turning to look at her, "I'm always impressed by these ancient trees. I hope the federal government has the sense to protect them from any further logging. These redwoods certainly should be considered an endangered species."

It was one-thirty when they stopped at the Washoe House, an old bar and restaurant, long one of Tony's favorites. Upon entering, they were greeted by the intoxicating aromas coming from the kitchen. Mike, however, was more interested in what he saw on the ceiling.

"What on earth is all that?" he asked, staring up at the ceiling, which was covered with dollar bills.

"If you're going to eat here, you have to give me a dollar," said a voice from behind the bar.

Tony nodded his head, encouraging Mike to do as he was told. He walked over to the bartender, handed him a dollar bill, then watched as he took a fifty-cent coin from the cash register, placed the flat side of a tack against it, and carefully wrapped the bill around the coin with the sharp point of the tack sticking out. With a quick flick of his wrist, he threw the whole thing up toward the ceiling. The tack and the dollar bill stuck there, and the coin dropped down toward the bar. The bartender snatched it in midair and dropped it into the open cash register.

Mike and Jacques clapped their hands in appreciation and astonishment. Amazingly, so did Cecelia.

"Thank you, thank you." The man bowed as if he were quite the magician. He then gave them a friendly smile and said, "Each year, just before Christmas, we take the money down and give it to the local boys' home. Thank you for your contribution."

After a leisurely lunch, the foursome headed east, passing through the Carneros region, the last area marked on Tony's map.

"This region is particularly well suited for growing the kind of grapes that make good champagne. Someday, the champagnes produced here will compete with the ones produced in France, mark my words."

"Didn't you say the same thing about the cabernet?" Mike laughed.

By the time they reached Tony's ranch, the sun had begun to set. Cecelia was tired and went to the guest room to take a nap. Mike and Jacques followed Tony into his office. The walls were covered with topographical maps of each of the areas that they had just driven through. The maps were riddled with numbered pins, corresponding to the numbered dots on the diagrams they'd been using.

Moving over to an open walk-in safe, Tony pointed inside to the file cabinets neatly arranged along both walls.

"Each number refers to a file, and each file contains all the information about each parcel marked on the maps. I've been collecting and updating this information ever since I was at Davis," he said, managing to sound both proud and exhausted.

Mike let out a low whistle, obviously impressed. "Tony, this has to be the finest data bank on Northern California's vineyard land in existence. How do you find the time to upgrade the information and keep everything current?"

"That's what a bachelor does, way out here in the country."

"Well, Tony," Jacques said, putting a hand on his shoulder, "it's about time we discussed the details of your proposed plan.

"I must say, I've been impressed with the boldness of your ideas ever since Mike first presented your investment summary to me. Before we get into the details, I need to ask you a question. Developing five thousand acres of grapes is an enormous undertaking. Are you certain that it's what you really want to do? Your plan represents an enormous commitment. I'm curious why you are so certain that it's the right thing for you."

Tony smiled. "Ever since our Berkeley days, I couldn't help but notice how similar our thoughts were regarding the spread of fascism and how different each of our interests were. Just look at the different paths our lives have taken since graduation. Ian is doing his thing in London. Claudine has introduced a new global system of wealth transfer. Cecelia has been helping people threatened by the Japanese. You two have become recognized experts in gold transfer and currency exchange, and I would like to think that I have been making progress in developing a new premium wine business here in Northern California. I find it interesting that each of us has developed the means, when combined, to pursue our original objective.

"Developing vineyards into an income-producing and appreciating capital asset to support your efforts just happens to be my contribution.

"The addition of twenty-five million dollars' worth of Sentinel land to my family's holdings will put the American wine industry on the world map."

"Tony, let me ask you something," Mike said. "In your opinion, how many acres of vineyards can be put into production without upsetting the market or creating unwanted attention?"

"I'd have to do some calculations, but off the top of my head, I would guess not more than five hundred acres a year. If we buy this five-thousand-acre package," Tony pointed to a place on the map, "we will be acquiring about a ten-year supply of land. Each year, we should be able to establish approximately one hundred acres of vineyards in each of the five regions that I showed you.

"At that rate," Tony concluded, "we could maintain a good balance between varieties, not oversupply the market, and not overburden the management team I've been developing—all without drawing too much attention to ourselves. After all, we're not exactly newcomers to the business."

Making certain that he had Tony's complete attention, Mike asked, "But why so much? Couldn't you accomplish what you want to do and take a smaller bite?" He paused, looking his friend straight in the eye. "Your optimism aside, how do you know that there will be a market for so much premium-quality wine?"

"It depends on how fast the postwar market in America develops a taste for good wines, similar to the prewar markets in Europe," Tony said. "Prior to the war, the yearly consumption of these wines in England, Italy, France, and Germany was approximately twenty gallons per capita. Consumption of wine in the United States is less than one gallon per person. When the war is won, a lot of people believe life in America will become increasingly concentrated in the cities, similar to Europe. As the urbanization of America occurs, the experts believe that national wine consumption will increase. If American consumption increases to just one-fifth of prewar European levels, or five gallons per capita over the next ten years, the demand for premium wine could be enormous. According to my calculations it will take a minimum of five thousand acres of fully producing vineyards to supply only five percent of the needs of a national market. I don't think our biggest problem will be adequate demand; it will be creating an adequate supply."

"Tony, what's so important about supplying a national market? Wouldn't the penetration of a limited number of regional markets suffice—and be less risky?"

"I think the distribution of food and alcohol is going to evolve into a business dominated by stores with multiple locations across the country—like a chain, you might say. Since the promotion and consumption of premium wine requires reliable consistency of carefully developed taste, only wineries capable of supplying a national market will be able to compete."

"You're talking about a very capital-intensive business," Mike said, suddenly sounding like his father. "How did you arrive at an investment of approximately five thousand dollars per acre as a requirement to pay for all the costs, including the construction of a modern wine-making facility?"

"The time required to convert new production into properly aged wine ranges from three to seven years, depending upon the variety," Tony said. "According to my calculations, I believe it will take seven to ten years before the revenues from the sale of Sentinel wines are adequate to show a profit and cover the annual costs of continued development. My best guess is twenty-five million dollars.

"And, in an unproven market like the one for American premium wines, the problems of organizing such a large amount of capital should protect us from competition, at least for the first few years. And with that kind of lead time, we should be able to establish ourselves as the industry leader."

"You really have thought this through," Jacques said. "Now I understand how you could absorb twenty-five million dollars without it being noticeable. But I have another question. Can you organize the operation so that the identity of the owners remains anonymous?"

"Are you serious?" Tony grinned. "In California, the title of land ownership can rest with a company of undisclosed shareholders. To be really careful, specially structured trusts should be organized."

Tony grinned, clearly proud of the way he had answered their questions with such apparent ease. Jacques found himself wishing that Claudine were there to enjoy the moment with them.

There was a knock at Tony's front door.

"Funny, I wasn't expecting anyone," he said, exchanging concerned looks with Mike.

Tony walked to the front door and swung it open.

"Dr. Tom? What are you doing here?"

"Thank God you're all safe," Dr. Tom said. After a brief exchange of greetings and inquiries about Cecelia's condition, he revealed the reason for his unexpected visit.

"A few days ago, I received an important message for all of you. When Mike missed our appointment awhile ago, I got worried. I didn't know how to get in touch with the rest of you, so I decided to hand deliver it. I hope you don't mind my unexpected call."

"What could be so important to cause you to drive clear up here?" Tony asked.

"This," said Dr. Tom, pulling Karl's telegram from his pocket. The creases were already well worn, as if it had been read, folded, and reread numerous times.

Jacques read the note out loud, including its warning about Samson. "Tony," he said, "it appears that we have something new to discuss. Why don't you pour us some of your best wine? In fact, this could take some time—maybe you'd better bring a few bottles."

———

The three young men took their former mentor into their total confidence, telling Dr. Tom everything, from the inception of the duplicate bond idea to what they intended to do with the money.

"I thought we'd have more time," Mike said, shaking his head. "They're already looking for us."

Dr. Tom sat stunned for a few minutes, looking at the faces around him at the table. "What you did was brave, and believe me, I couldn't be any prouder of all of you. But I think you should take Karl's warning very seriously."

"Dr. Tom is right," said a voice from the doorway. They had been so immersed in their conversation that nobody had noticed Cecelia standing there, listening to them. They stared at her as if she had just risen from the dead.

"I think I'm the resident expert here on this Samson organization, and I say, if the Japanese were able to hire them, the Germans could, too."

"Cecelia!" Mike said, knocking over his chair in his haste to run to her and hug her. It was *his* Cecelia who spoke, the one he had loved for so long. It was so good to hear her speak naturally that he didn't even care about the danger her words implied.

"Do you have any way of getting in touch with Ian?" Dr. Tom asked. "I assume that if Karl knows what's happening, Claudine is aware of her danger."

"I'm headed to London the day after tomorrow," Jacques said. "If I can't reach him in the meantime, I'll be able to warn him in person."

Dr. Tom explained his use of the bank courier system. "It's been working pretty well, even during the war."

"You're using the same courier systems that we use at the bank?" Mike asked.

Dr. Tom nodded. "Your father, Pete Ferrari, Roger Malone, Pierre Roth, and Henri Demaureux worked out the details a long time ago. They have been kind enough to allow me to piggyback on their system. I would have thought you knew. Now, if you don't mind, I need to leave. It's getting late and I have a long drive. Just promise me one thing." He looked at each of them in turn.

"What's that?" Jacques asked.

"Be very careful."

He hugged them all good-bye and left. They watched his tail-lights disappear as he drove away down the empty road.

As they reentered the house, Tony said, "Mike, Cecelia, I think the two of you should stay here with me at the ranch. Jacques said it earlier: it's a good place to hide. Even if someone might find you, I have access to some very unusual and effective sources of protection. We should be quite safe. Besides, I could always use a couple of extra hands around here."

"Believe me, I don't need a second invitation," Cecelia said. "After that last episode, it will be some time before I feel safe staying at my apartment in San Francisco. Tony, if your invitation is sincere, I accept—on one condition." She looked at Tony and Mike with intensity. "I want to do my part in this plan."

Chapter 24

CLAUDINE'S ESCAPE

Thoroughly shaken by what Jacques had told her, Claudine took a few minutes to collect her thoughts. For some time, she had been thinking about what she would do if it became necessary for her to suddenly disappear. She had decided that she couldn't take anything too personal or anything from the office. She looked reluctantly at a framed photo of her father. *Make it look as if you are returning.*

She remembered what her father had told her—that if these people caught up to them, they wouldn't be left alive. Her heart ached. She knew she wouldn't have a chance to tell him good-bye.

She decided that her best chance was to drive directly to Chamonix and take whatever belongings she had left at the chalet. She walked out of her office and went to her car.

From the chalet, I can ski southward from the summit of Mont Blanc, 235 miles to Pugent-Theniers; that's only 55 miles from the Riviera. Once I get there, I should be able to disappear into the world of southern France. My friends there will take me in.

As she pulled into the street, her mind was only partially focused on her driving. She was mentally skiing down the same tract that she and the other members of the Swiss national team had undertaken each year as part of their endurance training.

The first day's run to Courmeyer will be the easiest . . . nothing very demanding. I can use the smooth, open terrain to become accustomed to my skis and the weight of my pack. But what if the Germans are already there, waiting for me? How will I be able to identify them?

She felt the panic setting in and forced it out of her mind. *I need to focus on familiar things, things I know. What will I need to take? It should be a four- or five-day journey, but I should be prepared to run into problems along the way.*

She knew she would be able to take just one pair of skis. After considering the varying terrain, she decided on a pair of medium-length, medium-soft skis for the short, quick turns she would make skiing close to the fall line, but which she could also use when she wanted to sit back and let the skis do the work.

She thought about where she might stay along the route. Ski resorts would be easy places to blend in, but they didn't connect with the route very well. It was either cross-country skiing or the local trains, but the train stations would be the first place the Germans would be looking for her. *I'll have to climb over some of the terrain, so I can't forget to take a set of climbing skins.*

As she pictured herself skiing—for her life, this time, instead of for bronze, silver, or gold—doubt began to creep in. *How long will it be before they find my car in the garage and figure out that I'm skiing southward? How much of a head start will I have? And the most important question of all—can I really do this?*

Claudine's mind was reeling from all that she had to consider when she stopped for gas and to call her friend, Denise Cumberledge. Denise had been a member of the English women's ski team, and she and Claudine had competed against each other on numerous occasions, all the time becoming close friends. Over the years, Claudine had been a frequent guest at La Garoupe, a hundred-acre estate with five stately homes, owned by Lady Cumberledge and operated by her daughter. A perfect hiding place, the estate lay on the French coast, halfway between Nice and Cannes, adjacent to Cap d'Antibes.

Famous as the summer home of the duke and duchess of Windsor, La Garoupe was the vacation choice for some of the world's wealthiest and most famous people. Claudine, however, hoped to use it for purposes other than escaping the paparazzi.

She dialed her friend's number and waited to hear her voice. "Denise, this is Claudine. I'm in real trouble and I need your help. Could you give me a call back at this number from a public telephone?"

She hung up after Denise promised to call right back, then started to pace around the phone box. *I'm sure that she'll go to the public phone just outside the gates of the estate, near the Plage du Garoupe*, Claudine thought. *That should take about ten minutes.*

Despite her correct calculation, Claudine jumped when the phone rang exactly ten minutes later.

"Denise? Thank goodness! I don't have much time to talk. I need a place to hide," she explained in a rush.

"What's happened?" Denise asked.

"Let's just say that I have some information that is greatly desired by some very powerful German industrialists, so they've hired special agents to find me. I can't tell you any more right now, but I'm planning to ski down the same route to Puget-Theniers that we used for training. I was hoping La Garoupe could use one more French maid."

"Claudine, you know that German officers stay here," Denise said in a whisper. "On the other hand, I suppose, disguised as a maid, you should be quite safe. I can't recall any of them ever questioning members of my staff, and I'm sure that one more attractive French maid will be most welcome."

"What about the staff?" Claudine asked. "Do you think some of them will recognize me?"

"Oh, I wouldn't worry about them," Denise answered. "None of those who might remember you would ever say anything. In fact, most of them are members of the French Underground. They are so involved with the resistance that protecting you would be an honor."

"Okay," Claudine said. "I'm going to start for Puget-Theniers today. I think it will take me about three days, perhaps four. Could you possibly pick me up there?"

"Yes, of course."

"I'll be in the back of that old church at the far end of town. I won't have any way of calling you, so please just check for me there on the third night."

"Of course," Denise said. "No worries about anything on this end. Just be safe on the slopes . . . and ski like you're trying to catch me."

"Oh, really? Which race was that?"

Claudine heard Denise's laugh and smiled as she hung up the phone. As she pulled out of the gas station, she began to refocus her mind on the rest of the things she would need—clothes, food, liquid, and shelter for four days. *Can't take too much, can't take too little. I need to be careful about the clothes. This time of year, the weather is changeable—cold blizzards, warm sun, and everything in between. Multiple thin layers, that's it, and a couple changes of underwear.*

She felt better focusing on the more mundane aspects of her journey. She decided she should carry at least one day's water supply. Two canteens in the rucksack, one for each of the two side pockets.

About the time she completed her mental list, she found herself pulling into the driveway of the chalet.

Once inside, she quickly assembled all that she needed and packed her rucksack. She placed it on the bathroom scale and saw that it weighed just a little less than ten kilos. *That'll be a bit of a strain on my back.*

Straightening up, she looked directly into the bathroom mirror. She placed a hand firmly on both sides of the sink and stared hard at her reflection. Quickly, she reached into the nearest drawer and pulled out a pair of scissors. With one last look in the mirror, she thought about Jacques stroking her hair as they lay on the sofa near the fireplace. She hesitated for a second, then pulled down on her locks and cut them into a short, blunt style. She rummaged through the rest of the drawers until she found some dye, left there by one of the servants. She grabbed it and rushed toward the shower. When she emerged and looked in the mirror once again, she had become a brunette.

She was ready to go.

Walking the short distance from the chalet to the base station of the overhead cable telepherique, she stood in line anonymously with the other skiers, purchased her ticket, and entered the tram that would carry her just below the fourteen-thousand-foot summit of Mont Blanc.

A bit later, Claudine stood on the summit, looking southward toward Italy and France, thinking about her journey. *If these guys want me, they are going to have to catch me!*

She hoisted her rucksack onto her shoulders, inserted her hands through the loops of her poles, took a deep breath, and pushed off.

Ski conservatively, make smooth, connected turns, compensate for the weight of your pack, and conserve your energy.

Skiing smoothly at about twenty miles per hour, she made her way down the top third of the mountain. As she developed a feel for her skis, she started to search around for an old fire trail that led through a heavily forested area to a long, twisting run and, eventually, across the Italian frontier to the village of Courmeyer.

Where are those two broken trees that mark the entrance to the fire trail?

Worried about missing the marker and having to climb back up the hill with her rucksack, Claudine slowed her pace and followed the right side of the run until she found the markers.

Leaving the broad expanse of the open run, she entered the narrow trail that wound through thick forest. Below the surface of the snow lay broken trees and limbs, silently waiting to capture the errant skier who dared to veer even slightly from the path.

Any mistake skiing down here could be disastrous . . . and they could certainly catch up to me if I had a broken leg.

At that thought, Claudine threw a quick glance behind her. She remembered a place just ahead that would give her a view of her back trail. She stopped there and waited, the clouds of her breath puffing before her, slowing as she collected her wind.

After waiting ten minutes and seeing no one appear, she continued, feeling somewhat foolish and paranoid. After all, I don't even know for certain that anyone's after me. She took the trail gingerly and, a few minutes later, emerged from the trees onto a long, gradual descent that would deliver her to her first night's destination miles away.

I remember this part of the run. All I have to do is sit back, keep my tips up, let my skis run, and lean from side to side when I need to turn. Piece of cake.

Mile after mile, she slowly descended the mountain, finally arriving at a small, deserted train station about thirty kilometers from Courmeyer.

She was the only person waiting for the train. *So far so good.*

———

Back in Chamonix, the Samson agents discovered her car in the middle of the afternoon, just hours after her departure.

After conducting a thorough search of the village, the two agents began showing her picture to shop owners and restaurant staff. It soon became apparent, however, that Claudine was no longer in Chamonix.

They returned to the chalet, picked the lock on the front door, and began searching the Demaureux house for clues. In the basement, one of the agents noticed a space between the other skis neatly arranged along a wall.

"One set is missing," he said. "She must have gone skiing."

"Let's just wait for her to get back."

When she failed to return by nightfall, they realized that she must have been using the skis to escape.

It was getting dark and the lifts had closed. Near the base lift, there was a large, well-lit sign that showed all the trails. Unfamiliar with the area, the agents had trouble at first deciphering the complicated network. After a while, they began to make out how someone could start in Chamonix and ski into southern France or, by a different route, Italy. They were amazed that the southbound route continued almost all the way to the Riviera.

"She surely wouldn't be trying to escape into Italy," one agent said. "So she must be trying to get to the Riviera."

"We have to catch her before she gets there."

Studying the map more closely, he said, "It looks as if she has to pass through four villages before she reaches the Riviera. If she gets that far, there'll be a thousand places she can hide. It's imperative to stop her before she gets to Puget-Theniers."

"Let's head back to the chalet and place a call," the other man said, turning back. "It's best to put a team in each of those villages, and employ extra agents to ski the trails she will be using. If we don't get her out in the open, we'll find her in one of the towns as she passes through."

———

Very early the next morning, Claudine awakened in her soft, down bed at the pension in Courmeyer. With the benefit of a good dinner, a hot shower, and a full night's sleep, she felt recharged and ready to go, despite the long and difficult day ahead.

Getting to the top of Gran Paradiso isn't going to be easy, and the run down to Lanslebourg is long and technical. But since when have I ever taken the easy way?

Claudine was one of the first skiers in line. She rode up three connecting chairlifts, then skied down a way and took two more lifts to a mountain chalet resting just below the peak of Gran Paradiso. Not pausing for the traditional hot lemonade, she put her skis over her shoulder and started hiking up the sunlit side of the steep peak, toward the summit.

On reaching the thirteen-thousand-foot peak, she thrust her skis securely into the snow, took off her backpack, and sat down in the bright sunlight to have a small lunch and take in the 360-degree view of France, Italy, and Switzerland. Up here, a person could forget about all her worries . . . almost.

She lingered for a full minute more, then roused herself. Claudine knew that the deep, sun-crusted powder and the steep pitch of the southern-oriented slopes required skiing down the fall line, making quick, short turns. *Even under normal circumstances, it would be a real test of my skiing ability and stamina. With the added weight of a heavy pack, it is going to be much more difficult.*

But, the minute she had completed the first few turns, the exhilaration of the powdery snow, the warm sunshine, and the steep mountain took over and more than compensated for the weight on her back. Down she went, one turn after another. Her legs were beginning to burn; her lungs were screaming for oxygen, yet she kept telling herself, *Keep going, girl. You're doing great.*

When she couldn't make another turn, she finally swung to a stop and realized that she had just skied down the entire upper portion of the mountain without so much as a pause. *Now, there's something you were never able to do, even when you weren't carrying a ten-kilo pack. Not bad for a thirty-five-year-old woman!*

She turned back to admire her achievement and saw two men just starting down the steep upper slope.

After watching them for a few moments, Claudine was certain that they were not accomplished skiers. In one sense, that was good: lacking her skill, they wouldn't be able to negotiate the quick-linked turns of deep powder, skiing along the fall line. In another way, it was bad: novices ordinarily wouldn't take this route.

Are they after me? If they are, they'll never come close. But they aren't the problem—it's the men who might be waiting for me in Lanslebourg that I need to worry about.

Claudine turned back around and forced herself to concentrate on what lay in front of her. She knew she would need to use long-radius turns to cover the sun-baked snow on the lower, gentler portion of the mountain. *If Jacques were here, he'd think I was copying his style.* The thought surprised her, coming out of nowhere as it did, and she realized that she was slightly smiling. *Okay, fine. If you ever want to see him again, go!*

Claudine skied in the direction of a small village to the south, which she was certain must be Lanslebourg. On the lower slopes, practically out of sight of her pursuers, she chose a combination of runs that would deposit her at the far end of town, opposite the end where skiers from Courmeyer would normally arrive.

Upon reaching the south end of the small village, she took off her skis, put them over her shoulder, and began walking slowly, along with other skiers, toward the center of town. She kept her eyes moving, watching for anything or anyone who seemed out of place. She noticed a pension that she and her father had stayed in last year, and the thought of a hot shower suddenly made her feel very tired.

She started for the lodging, then stopped, taking a step back. Two men were standing in front of the entrance.

She slowed her steps and glanced over in their direction. The snow was packed down around where they was standing, one of them smoking a cigarette.

Judging from the ring of cigarette butts on the snow, they must have been standing there for some time. *They are obviously waiting for someone. Could that person be me?*

Suddenly, her dreams of a hot shower disappeared and a knot of fear formed in her stomach. Walking into the alley diagonally across the street from the pension, she watched the two men and waited to see if any more showed up. Thirty minutes later, the two skiers from the slope appeared from the opposite end of town and walked toward the other men.

Claudine could feel desperation chilling her body. There are four agents who must have a pretty good idea of where I'm going. Where can I hide in this small town?

The sky was clouding up, a cold south wind was beginning to blow, and temperatures were dropping—a storm was on the way. That meant the lifts would be shutting down within the hour. Claudine considered her options.

It's too late to finish the next leg into Italy, and the tricky descent off Mont Cenis is the one place I don't want to be caught out in the open.

She closed her eyes and visualized the route: After descending the peak, the trail led across the crest of a long cornice. Following the exact line was absolutely critical—and good visibility was essential. Too far to the left and she could fall off the cornice. Too far to the right and she could end up below the crest, and it would take hours to climb out. And getting caught in a whiteout? It would be impossible.

When she opened her eyes again, the men were all standing exactly where they had been, waiting.

It's obvious those two on skis are not equipped to spend a night on the mountain. *Maybe I should go up to the summit and ski down the uppermost pitch before night and the storm sets in. I can camp there and wait until tomorrow before crossing the cornice.*

She looked up at the darkening sky and the summit in the distance. *That's probably the only place I'll be safe tonight.*

Resigned, Claudine walked down the alley, slipped out of town, and reached the top of Mont Cenis with the help of several lifts. The storm was setting in and deep shadows were beginning to appear. By the time she had skied down the pitch to the east, above the crest of the cornice, visibility was limited to less than twenty feet. She soon found herself in a real whiteout.

The one good thing is that the lifts will have closed already, and I should be safe here . . . if not from the weather, at least from the agents.

She skied a short way to the base of two large rocks and unloaded her pack. Then she used one ski to dig a hole large enough for her, her gear, and room to stretch out. Lining it with her tarp, she placed her skis across the hole and pulled the remaining portion of the tarp over them, creating a makeshift roof with a small opening to see through. She squinted through it but couldn't make out much of anything.

If I do see someone, they'll already be within ten feet of me, she thought with some despair, nestling down into the hole. *Then it will be too late.*

Totally protected from the wind, Claudine wrestled with the clothing from her rucksack, putting it all on, and placed her small sterno on top of the emptied bag. She lit it, made a cup of coffee, sat back, and surveyed her belongings.

Here I am, on top of a mountain, caught in a blizzard, but I have a gourmet dinner of salami, cheese, and French bread, followed by the great Swiss dessert—a chocolate bar. What could be greater?

Not long after, satiated, warm, and tired, Claudine waited for sleep to come. No matter how hard she tried to turn off her brain, though, she couldn't stop thinking about her immediate situation and the fates of her friends.

Clearly, we aren't spies. We aren't criminals, at least not in the classical sense. And we aren't soldiers of war. If we aren't any of those things, what are we and why are we being chased?

We are the enemies of fascism.

She thought about the vastness of that word, the lengths to which the agents would go to find her and the resources they had at their disposal.

There are already men in Lanslebourg looking for me. Most likely, there are men waiting for me in Sestriere, and by tomorrow, there will be men searching for me all along the way. *I could become trapped up here.*

That's when the true terror of the situation began to sink in. She was wide-awake, and she was scared. *What would Jacques do? He'd get a good night's sleep, then, the next day, search for a solution with a well-rested brain.* Finally, she drifted off to sleep.

The next morning, Claudine awakened to clear weather and a six-inch layer of snow covering the roof of her hastily built shelter. The storm had erased any signs of her presence.

She stretched out and was about to make some coffee when she heard voices. Her heart racing, she peered through the small opening and saw the same two men who had skied after her. They were standing within a couple hundred feet of her makeshift igloo, studying a map and discussing their options.

She strained to hear their words.

"From the look of the snow, she hasn't passed here, at least not this morning. She has to still be in Lanslebourg or tried to ski on to Sestriere yesterday, which means she arrived there by now or is holed up somewhere en route."

Seemingly satisfied, the men adjusted their goggles and bent to tighten their boots and adjust their bindings before starting their trek across the dangerous cornice.

Still carefully hidden, Claudine took a deep breath in an effort to calm down.

There's nothing I can do until they are well out of sight, and even then, they may find a hiding place ahead and wait for me to ski into them. So, if I can't go forward and I can't stay here, what am I going to do? Jacques would find a third choice, but what other choices do I have?

Settling back into her small shelter, she extracted her father's old map from her pack and began to study it for some other way off the mountain. Her finger traced a possible path. *What is this, the Mont Cenis tunnel?* It looked to be eight miles long, connecting Bardonecchia, Italy, to Modane, France.

She felt a glimmer of hope and her mind began racing.

To reach Bardonecchia, I would have to climb back up that steep pitch and ski eastward into Italy. From there, I could pass through the tunnel back into France.

But what good would that do me? I'd have to start this journey all over again. Wait a minute . . . They're looking for a single woman skiing toward the Riviera, not a young female hitchhiking through Provence.

She would call Denise and explain the change in plans tomorrow. For now, she was sure that the last thing in the world the German agents would expect was for her to ski away from the Riviera route.

This is exactly what Jacques would have done.

Realizing that the climb up the pitch was going to be difficult enough, she decided to lighten the load. Dumping most of her food, one water bottle, her extra clothing, and the tarp into the hole, she carefully covered it up. Next, she shouldered her lightened rucksack, placed her skis on one shoulder, holding her poles in the other hand, and began her climb back up to the summit of Mont Cenis.

The terrain was steep and the snow was deep. It was tough climbing. To make it easier for herself, she forced her mind to concentrate on one step at a time.

Sweat-soaked and exhausted, Claudine finally allowed herself the luxury of stopping when she reached the summit. Kneeling down in the snow, she ate her last chocolate bar, drank some water, and put on her skis, careful not to take too long and let her legs cramp up.

The storm had left everything covered with inches of fresh, dry powder. Under normal circumstances, these were exactly the conditions Claudine would have gone to any length to experience. Now, though, she simply looked downward, hoping to hit the bottom shortly.

Her graceful descent left her about five miles short of Bardonecchia. To avoid exposure, she steered clear of the direct route, deciding, instead, to ski cross-country up and down the sloping terrain that led to the small Italian village. As she approached the first hill, she stopped to attach the fur-lined skins to her skis before starting the laborious trek up the first of what would be three gradual slopes.

It was late afternoon when Claudine arrived on the outskirts of the village. She was too exhausted to think about being discovered or to take any satisfaction in having escaped their trap for the time being.

Tonight, I'm going to treat myself to a warm shower, a good dinner, and a soft bed. Tomorrow, I'll worry about the rest of the trip. I'm certain the new day will bring an entirely new set of problems to face.

Chapter 25

TROUBLE IN LONDON

Jacques stared out the windows of the Pan Am Clipper at the clouds over the North Atlantic. Worried thoughts tumbled through his mind, one after the other. Was Claudine somewhere safe by now? How much did the Germans know? Did he do the right thing, leaving Tony, Mike, and Cecelia? What about Ian? Jacques was, in some ways, more concerned for Ian than for Claudine. Claudine had an inner strength and a quick intelligence that would serve her well in dicey situations. But Ian was the least pragmatic and the most methodical and habitual of the six of them. Jacques just hoped he could warn him in time. *Is this the way it's going to be? Are we going to live the rest of our lives with some faceless posse constantly pursuing us?* As soon as Jacques disembarked, he found a pay phone and called Ian, who answered after the first ring.

"Jacques, I'm so glad it's you! Something's going on . . . That man whom I hired to do the duplications, Duncan Melvin, seems to have gone missing. I don't know who may have been after him but . . . what if they're coming for me?" Ian gushed in a voice on the edge of hysteria.

"First of all, you're going to have to calm down," Jacques said. "The Germans already know about us, or at least suspect enough to make them come after us. That's why I've come—to get you out of here. You are no longer safe in London. You must leave your apartment immediately. Take nothing with you. I want you to go to a movie. Appear as casual as you can, like you're just going on a whim. Then go to the French Club." Jacques gave him Maggie's private phone number, then looked at his watch. "I'll meet you there in three hours. I've got to straighten something out with Sir Desmond first, but I'll be at the club to meet you. You got all that?"

"Right. A movie, then the French Club in three hours."

To Jacques, Ian's voice still sounded shaky. "Ian, are you sure you can remember what I've told you?"

"I wrote it down. I'll keep the note in my pocket."

"Okay, buddy. Let's see some of that famous British stiff upper lip, okay?"

———

As his cab pulled away from the curb, Ian turned to look back at his flat. His heart began hammering at his ribs: two big men in overcoats were charging up the steps. Unable to take his eyes from the rear window, he instructed the cabbie to turn every few blocks. Only when he was finally convinced that no one was following them did he give the driver the name of the movie theater he'd selected.

———

The two men had no trouble picking the lock and entering Ian's flat. A quick search of the apartment turned up nothing. The bed was made, the dishes were all washed and stacked neatly in the cabinets, and a book had been left open near a large sofa chair. Ian's toothbrush was in its holder, his hairbrush was next to the sink, and his razor was in the medicine cabinet. Nothing seemed missing or out of order. Everything indicated that the owner would be returning.

Just as they were ready to leave, one of the men noticed the note pad next to the telephone. "Hang on."

He picked up the pad and peered carefully at it. The paper was blank, but there were a series of depressions across the page. He picked up the pencil lying next to the pad and ran the side of its sharpened end against the indentation. "Looks like a phone number."

He picked up Ian's phone, called the number, and, on the third ring, heard someone answer, "French Club."

———

Jacques wasted no time getting to Sir Desmond's office. Upon arrival, he was immediately shown into the chairman's office.

"Jacques, I can't tell you how distressed we were to receive your cable warning us about unauthorized auditors," Sir Desmond said, shaking Jacques' hand but otherwise forgoing his usual pleasantries. "We checked our records, and sure enough, they revealed that someone had been here around the time those gold bearer bonds from Mr. Meyer's, ah, client were cashed."

He suspects something.

"I'm sorry, Sir Desmond. That's exactly what happened to us at Stone City. Someone is searching for evidence of large deposits to try to find out the identity of the bonds' owners. Mr. Stone, Mr. Lee, Mr. Meyer, and myself are all quite upset at this, but no further disturbances have been made."

"Yes, well," Sir Desmond said, turning around to pace the well-worn carpet on his office floor. "We decided to do some investigation on our own, which revealed that the IFIC had been hired by the Schmidt family solicitors right here in London." He stopped and faced Jacques. "You may not know this, but the English branch of the Schmidts is related to some of Germany's top industrial families."

Before Jacques could speak, Sir Desmond approached him, putting a hand on his shoulder. "This situation with the bonds could turn very ugly indeed for all of us involved."

———

Jacques left Sir Desmond's office as soon as he possibly could, more and more concerned about the implications. He arrived at the French Club and hurried inside. In his haste, he failed to notice two large men standing across the street.

Maggie came toward him, smiling, but saw the look on his face. "What's the matter, love?"

"Maggie, I need an enormous favor. For reasons I can't explain, some very unsavory characters are after Ian and maybe me. We need the use of a safe house for a couple of weeks until things cool off. Do you know anyone who could help us?"

Maggie spun on her heel and went into her private office to make a call. Jacques could see her but couldn't hear what she was saying. At one point, she set the phone down, reentered the bar, walked toward the front, and looked out the window. Then, returning to her office, she finished the call.

Minutes later, she exited the room and walked over to Jacques. Before she could tell him anything, her private phone rang and she went back into her office, this time leaving the door open. She picked up the receiver and quickly motioned Jacques inside. "It's Ian," she mouthed at Jacques, silently. "Come ahead, love," she said into the phone. "Jacques is already here waiting. I'll have someone meet you."

———

Ian had just turned the corner and started up Maiden Lane toward the club when a man approached him.

Holding up his hands to stop Ian, he said, "There are two men waiting across the street from the club's front entrance. Maggie believes they may be waiting for you. She asked me to escort you up the alley to the rear door."

Ian nodded and followed the man.

Maggie and Jacques were waiting just inside the opened back door of the club, watching as Ian and his escort made their way down the alley.

Suddenly, two men emerged from behind a large garbage container. The first man shot Ian's escort and the second one pushed Ian through the back door of a grocery lorry that was parked nearby. The lorry squealed out of the alley even before the rear panel had been properly closed. It turned right, covered the short block that led to the Strand, and disappeared into heavy traffic.

Jacques wasn't sure if Maggie had screamed. He was too shocked by what he had just seen to realize much. All he knew was that she had pulled him back into the club and locked the door. In a matter of seconds, his close friend had vanished.

Chapter 26

A WAR WITHIN A WAR

Maggie had wide contacts with the London cells of the French resistance, and it wasn't difficult to persuade a few of them to look after Jacques. They moved him to a safe house, and at least one of them was practically at his elbow twenty-four hours a day.

On the afternoon of Jacques' second day in hiding, the leader of the cell approached him. "We've seen some fellows roaming the neighborhood lately, asking questions. We need to make you disappear."

"I thought I already did," Jacques said.

"No, *mon ami*, I mean permanently disappear. Just sit tight, and we'll let you know the next move."

The next morning, the headline in the *London Times* read:

BOMB DESTROYS SOHO NIGHT CLUB—PROMINENT FRENCH BANK HEIR FEARED DEAD

Jacques put down the paper and looked at his new French friend.

"Alain, isn't this a rather grim way to protect me?"

"It's not as grim as you think." Alain smiled. "The term 'feared dead' has a different meaning to our governments and friends than it does to your enemies—at least, we hope so. Those who need to know realize that you are still very much alive and under our protection."

"That's all well and good, but what about my family and friends?"

"I admit that this news is a bit harsh, but think about it. You wouldn't be able to communicate with them anyway, for your own safety and theirs. This is the best way to make sure that no one tries to contact you."

Jacques considered this for a moment. "And without Samson after me, I suppose I'll be able to rest in peace."

"That's the idea."

A few days later, Jacques was given the go-ahead to arrange his escape to the United States. When his French protectors were able to provide a secure overseas phone line, he knew what call he would have to make.

The five of us aren't going to be able to do this alone. We're going to need some assistance from higher up.

A voice on the other end answered, "Chairman Malone's office. How can I help you?"

———

Two days later, Jacques was traveling as an unlisted passenger on an outbound U.S. Army cargo plane. Roger Malone had arranged everything, even getting in touch with Mike to tell him the truth about his friend's whereabouts.

There was a lot of time to think on the flight to Washington, especially since sleep was out of the question. Jacques thought about Ian and how he'd hold up under questioning. *Certainly not as well as Cecelia. Samson may know everything by now—which means the Germans do, too.*

Unable to figure out any solution to the situation they had gotten themselves into, Jacques was growing frustrated. He was not accustomed to being unable to think his way through any issue. In fact, although he'd never admit it to others, he had always believed that by focusing all his mental energy on a problem, he could generally bore through the barriers and find a solution.

What's wrong with me? Why can't I see a way through this minefield? Perhaps I'm too close to it this time.

Picturing Ian being pushed into the back of Samson's truck, Jacques thought, *This is the kind of exchange we're caught up in—human bodies for bars of gold. We have allies and enemies, victims and victors. There is certainly no doubt that what we've ignited is a war within a war.*

———

Hours later, Jacques emerged from the cargo bay door and spotted what he believed to be an unmarked government car. *Roger must have called in the first team.*

Seated in the passenger seat, Jacques watched the familiar sights of Washington, D.C., glide past. A short time later, the driver turned into a side street that led to the lower level of the United States Treasury building.

Roger Malone was waiting near the elevator shaft and walked forward to greet Jacques as he stepped from the car.

"Jacques, what a pleasure it is to see you alive and well and here in Washington."

"Thank you, sir. I can't tell you how good it is to be here."

"You had us worried," Roger continued. "And it sounds as if we have a lot to talk about. Henry Ainsworth, the Secretary of the Treasury, is waiting for us upstairs. I hope you don't mind, but I took the liberty of filling him in on the industrialists' plan. He wants to hear every detail."

Before Jacques could entirely fathom what was happening, they were seated in the secretary's innermost private office.

"As you know," Roger started, by way of introduction, "Secretary Ainsworth has complete control over the United States Secret Service and the FBI."

"Mr. Roth, you have no idea how repugnant this administration considers the idea of the reestablishment of another Reich," the secretary began. "In fact, our instructions are coming directly from the president himself. If memory serves, I believe his exact words were, 'I want you to make sure we neutralize the Germans' capital, put Samson out of business, and send a clear message to the industrial elite that this government is not going to tolerate any future abuses of power.'"

Jacques nodded, impressed.

"You and your friends have done a good job so far, but Mr. Malone tells me you could use our help."

"Knowing this young man, he has a plan," Roger said. "Jacques, do you mind sharing it with us?"

"I haven't had a lot of time to think through what I'm about to say, sir, but here goes. By now, my guess is the Germans and Samson know who we are, how we duplicated the bonds, and where they are hidden, but so do we. Why can't you use that information to lure the Samson agents into the open and capture as many of them as you can? We'll have the bonds sent to us in the books, cash a few of them, and leave a trail. As much as I hate to say it, it may be necessary for you to use the remaining five of us as bait."

Turning toward Secretary Ainsworth, Roger said, "Henry, that's a lot of bait. Do we have the manpower to protect it all?"

"We have the manpower, but the real question is, do we have enough men whom we can trust? I'm not sure how leakproof the FBI is. It's been reported that the director has some very . . . *interesting* relationships with certain American industrialists who were involved with their German counterparts before the war. I need to give this matter some more thought, but to be on the safe side, the best course of action may be for me to obtain an executive order from the president and use the Secret Service."

"Secretary Ainsworth, maybe we can make your job easier, at least at first," Jacques said. "My friends and I are pretty resourceful. Cecelia and her network of contacts can move our cash and bonds around. That shouldn't be too much of a challenge for her. Right now, she's holed up at a friend's ranch in Napa. It has a massive switchboard and it's built like a fort, so protecting the two of them shouldn't require too many men. The rest of us will find a way to take care of ourselves. I'll get in touch with my friend, Mike, and work out a safe place to stay."

The secretary was clearly impressed. But before everything could be agreed upon, Jacques added, "There's just one more thing, Mr. Ainsworth. My friend, Ian, who's being held in London, is the one I'm most worried about. If there's anything you can do to help the French Underground find him—"

"We'll do everything possible."

———

After arriving at Grand Central Terminal in New York a few days after the meeting in Washington, Jacques phoned his doorman for messages. He finally read the one Jacques had been waiting to hear: "All's well in Napa. Received your message. Know you need help. See you in Boston next Thursday. Meet me at Jimmy's Harborside at one o'clock, and come hungry. Mike."

Chapter 27

QUEENIE AND GEORGE

Having skied cross-country over the five miles of hilly terrain that separated the base of Mont Cenis from the small alpine village of Bardonecchia, Claudine arrived in the mid-afternoon, tired, hungry, and unsure of what to expect.

Are they here waiting for me? Every so often, she would stop, pretending to look at the contents displayed in the front windows of the shops, and study the reflections of the people around her. Slowly, she moved from store window to store window like any other tourist, occasionally entering one of the shops to inquire about some object on display. That gave her an opportunity to look out the window and obtain a better view of the street.

Unable to detect the presence of any suspicious people, she walked across the street and entered a small tea shop that had a window facing the street and the local train station. As she sat down at a table near the front, Claudine realized just how hungry she was and ordered a selection of finger sandwiches and a pot of tea. This was the closest she had come to normalcy in three days.

As she ate, no one entered or left the train station. There weren't any men loitering on the street. Everyone she saw seemed intent on going someplace.

Convinced that she wasn't being watched, she finished her tea, ate the last of her sandwiches, and stood up to pay the bill. She left the shop and crossed the street on the way to the seemingly deserted train station. Looking up, she studied the steep, serpentine path of the rail bed that wound its way up four thousand feet before disappearing into Mont Vallon, approximately three thousand feet below its summit. That would be her way out, but it wasn't exactly a comforting thought.

The ticket agent sat dozing behind his counter. She tapped quietly on the booth window.

"Yes, my dear," the agent said, suddenly coming to life. "The next train is leaving for Modane at ten tomorrow morning. You can clear Italian customs right here in the station with me. May I see your passport?"

Claudine hadn't given much thought to border-crossing problems. As a skier, it hadn't been an issue. But here she was, faced with a strange man asking questions.

Don't panic. It's not the German, Italian, or French governments that are after you.

"Ah, Swiss," the man said happily, looking at her passport photo. "We don't see many Swiss down here this time of year. Are you traveling on business or pleasure?"

"I've been skiing, but now I'm afraid my vacation is over. I have to call on some clients, so I guess you would say that I am traveling on business." She smiled, handing him one of her business cards. "Even in wartime, banking must go on."

The agent handed her the ticket and her stamped passport, then walked out of the booth and pointed up at the tunnel. He had a captive audience.

"This tunnel and the railroad were conceived in the 1840s to provide a more-efficient overland route from London to India and a better connection between Italy and France. Prior to its construction, goods were transported over water from Marseille to Alexandria—a twenty-seven-hundred-kilometer journey that required seven to eight days. These rails reduced that to two or three days and allowed cargo sizes to be increased."

Claudine smiled warmly at the man standing at her side. It was the first conversation she'd had in days, and it made her feel human.

Encouraged, he continued. "This route represents some unbelievable engineering accomplishments. Before it could even be selected, the owners had to agree on what form of energy and equipment could bore an eight-kilometer hole through a mountain. There were only two known sources of energy: steam and compressed air. The final solution involved the hydraulic use of water taken from natural streams to compress air, then the use of pipe lines to transport the air to the point of excavation. The final route was determined by the existence of these naturally occurring streams. That's why it's so winding," he concluded.

Oddly, being in possession of that information made Claudine feel better about the vertiginous trip. "How are trains able to go up and come down such steep slopes?" she asked.

Walking over to a picture of the train on the wall, the ticket master said, "That's the best part. The engineers designed two horizontal wheels with beveled teeth to mesh with a third rail built between the two regular rails. You can see from this picture how the whole thing works. On the way up, power is applied to these wheels to help the train ascend eight- to twelve-degree inclines—and on the way down, extra brake power is used to control the rate of descent."

Satisfied with the explanation, and less wary about her approaching morning commute, Claudine thanked the man, left the station, and began her search for a pension, complete with clean sheets and a hot shower.

As she walked away, the ticket agent picked up a phone and dialed a number. It had been written on a piece of paper, next to a photograph of her that had been left with him earlier that day.

═══

The next morning, Claudine contacted Denise to relay her change of plans. Then she returned to her usual window seat in the tea shop to continue her surveillance of the train depot. About thirty minutes later, encouraged by the empty streets, Claudine got up and crossed to the depot.

At precisely ten o'clock, the train left the station. The two engines, the coal-carrying cars, the freight cars, and the one passenger car all looked like something out of an Old West movie. The rail bed itself had been constructed over a system of switchbacks carved out of the steep eastern face of the Alps.

When the train rounded an outside corner, Claudine looked down. *My God, it looks like a thousand-foot drop.* On the inside turns, she felt as if she could put her arm out the window and touch the granite face of the mountain.

Relax, girl. If this were so dangerous, they wouldn't still be running the train.

Slowly, it plodded its way up the approach to the Mont Cenis tunnel. After a time, Claudine decided to stop worrying about the risk and start concentrating on the view. From her vantage point ten thousand feet up in the air, she could see well into Italy. On a clear day, she had heard that you could see all the way to Turin.

Apparently, today is not going to be one of those days.

Content to watch the scenery, Claudine was surprised by the sudden darkness of the tunnel as they began the eight-mile run under Mont Vallon.

Her eyes readjusted as the train emerged from the tunnel, beginning its slow descent down the western slope of the Italian Alps, toward the little French village of Madone—and French customs.

If there is going to be a problem, it will occur at the customs station at the point of entry into France. For some reason she couldn't explain to herself, she suddenly felt panicked about having changed her plans.

Finally, the train started slowing for its stop in Madone. Peering out the window, Claudine couldn't see anything strange or out of place.

There doesn't seem to be anyone who looks like an enemy agent or a member of the Gestapo . . . whatever they're supposed to look like.

Stepping from the train, Claudine began to make her way to the small customs shack, located on the far end of the station platform. Heart beating fast, she presented her passport to the lone official standing behind the counter.

Typical bureaucrat, taking his sweet time.

The agent twisted around in his booth, searching for the stamp.

It was at that moment that she felt something press into her right rib cage. "Excuse me, Miss Demaureux, would you mind coming with us?" said a quiet voice next to her ear.

The passport official was still searching for his stamp, and he didn't even look up as the Samson agents moved her well out of sight of the customs shack. She heard a "cough, cough" sound and the two men dropped to the ground, blood quickly spreading from holes in the front of their coats. Staring wildly about, Claudine saw a man and a woman, pistols in hand, approaching at a quick walk. She clenched her fists, expecting it all to be over soon.

Instead, they rushed past her, toward the bodies. "This one's dead," said the short, stout woman with yellow, peroxided hair.

"So is this one," said the large, swarthy man with her. "Nice shooting, old girl."

Claudine was bewildered, trying to comprehend what had just happened. She was standing motionless when the woman seemed to first notice her and extended her hand. "Miss Demaureux, we're friends of Denise. I'm Queenie and this is George, my husband. We're part of the Resistance, sent to fetch you and deal with any . . . uh . . . problems that might occur."

Queenie looked down. "George, I hate to say it, but I think we need to take the bodies with us so they aren't associated with Miss Demaureux. Let's roll them up in that old tarp you keep in the boot. Between here and Cap d'Antibes, we should find a suitable place to dump 'em." She smiled at Claudine. It was as if she had been discussing a way to get rid of broken kitchen appliances.

It was late, well after dark, when the old French Citroën, minus two bodies, drove through the gate marking the entrance to La Garoupe. Denise was waiting as they pulled to a stop at the servants' entrance, at the rear of the chateau. She gave Claudine a hug, then listened quietly as Queenie and George delivered their report.

She seemed to take everything they were saying in stride, thanked them, then turned her full attention to Claudine, grabbing her by the hand and leading her into the house, almost as if Claudine were the final guest to arrive for a slumber party.

Too excited to wait until the next morning, Denise woke up all the servants. "Everyone, I'd like to introduce you to Claudine, the new French maid."

Chapter 28

ATTACK AT NAPA

Mike, Cecelia, and Tony were waiting on the porch of the ranch house in Napa when the unmarked motorcade of the Secret Service agents entered through the front gates.

A portion of the ranch bunkhouse had been cleared to provide accommodations. Farm and winery working apparel had been laid out on the bunks. The government cars were hidden in the barn.

An hour or two later, a careful inspection of the ranch workforce would reveal that there were several new faces. Their lack of a tan identified them as people who were used to making a living indoors. A look at their soft, pink hands was further evidence that these men weren't used to earning their living on a ranch. But Samson agents wouldn't have a chance for such careful inspection, since twenty-four-hour protection was now in place.

Taking no chances that the government's manpower was adequate, Tony had called his family back east, asking for more help, and a few of his "cousins" had arrived. Under different circumstances, the two groups sent to Napa to protect Tony and his friends would have been natural enemies. But here, they shared common goals.

However, pragmatic planning called for the two teams to be kept intact and away from each other. Each group was assigned different duties, shifts, and locations throughout the vineyards—the bottling plant, the ranch house, the winery, and the dining facility in the limestone cave.

With every inch of the ranch covered, Tony, Mike, and Cecelia decided not to allow the threat of trouble to interfere with their daily routines. Today was the day Tony had chosen to demonstrate how he'd be selling Sentinel wines. Lunch had been prepared and would be served on the heavy oak tables normally used for entertaining wine buyers, owners of fine restaurants, and managers of leading hotels. Today, there would just be two special guests: Mike and Cecelia.

The area for entertaining was located in the limestone caves, midway between the big oak barrels used for the aging of wine and the mouth of the cave. The atmosphere was a cool sixty-two degrees, the perfect temperature for aging wine. In this incredible environment, Mike and Cecelia were enjoying the opportunity to play the role of visiting buyers.

Tony greeted them the same way he would have welcomed any of his other guests, making them temporarily forget that they were virtually being held prisoners for their own protection.

"Welcome to the Garibaldi Vineyards." Handing them a small folder, he continued, "Here is a list of all of our wines. A reservation sheet has been included in your folder." He smiled charmingly, causing Cecelia to cover her mouth to hide her own grin. She was acting the part of a wine buyer, and this was supposed to be all business.

"After our tour of the facilities, we will be serving a three-course lunch specially prepared for you today," Tony announced. "For that, I have selected three of our newer wines that we are eager for you to taste. At Sentinel Vineyards, we believe that the food should be chosen to best suit the wine."

"For a guy who can be so quiet," Mike said to Cecelia when Tony walked away toward the vats, "he can be a hell of a talker when he chooses to be." They followed him, staying in character throughout the rest of the tour, but the three of them cut loose over lunch, laughing and sharing bottles of wine at the communal oak tables.

"This," Cecelia said, standing for a toast, "is the right way to spend an afternoon."

The Samson agents timed their attack on the caves to coincide with their raid on the ranch house. They approached the compound through the vineyards, and then split into two groups. One went toward the cookhouse and the other toward the caves.

Quietly, the first group took up their positions around the cookhouse, waiting for the workers to take their places at the long, picnic-style tables. On cue, with their automatic weapons loaded and cocked, they entered the narrow building from both ends.

Sitting alongside the other workers, the surprised federal agents were stuck. Firing would have been too risky in such crowded quarters. They had no choice but to submit to the Samson gunmen.

Intent on guarding the people inside the cookhouse, the Samson agents failed to see a separate contingent of Secret Service men coming out of the barn and taking up positions directly behind them. Quietly and without gunfire, they disarmed the intruders, handcuffed them, and marched them into the barn, out of sight of the second group of intruders, who were concentrating on the cave.

Four heavily armed men discreetly entered the wine storage facility where Tony and his friends were having lunch. Flattening themselves against the walls, they made their way into the dining area.

Tony was the first to see the Samson agents enter the room. At first, he wasn't alarmed, since he was used to seeing the agents on duty carrying guns while performing their drills. But something was wrong about this scene. Squinting carefully at their faces, he couldn't recognize any of these men as they advanced.

Without warning, two of the waiters serving lunch tipped over the heavy oak table where Mike was seated and Cecelia was making her toast. Cecelia's eyes grew wide when she saw pistols, automatic weapons, and shotguns fastened to the underside of the table. It was at that moment that they all realized that this was no drill.

More men, dressed in farm-laborer clothing, entered the cave behind the Samson agents. They dropped to a kneeling position and pointed their weapons toward the gunmen. Mike was partially shielded by the overturned table, but Tony and Cecelia found themselves standing between the intruders and their protectors, directly in the line of fire.

Tony launched himself toward Cecelia, hitting his petite friend with the full force of his weight, knocking her to the floor, and covering her with his own body. It all seemed to go in slow motion, until the first shots were fired.

The first rounds were quickly followed by the sound of automatic weapons being unloaded. Tony could hear what was happening, but he couldn't move, shielding Cecelia until the gunfire stopped. One bullet hit his shoulder, another hit his arm, and a third lodged in his thigh.

The intruders were caught in the cross fire between Tony's cousins, who had been working as waiters inside the cave, and the federal agents who had been positioned in the bottling plant. Two of Samson's agents were killed instantly; another one was wounded and lying on the floor, not more than ten feet from Cecelia and Tony. The fourth threw down his gun and raised his arms.

For a moment, the silence seemed surreal. Then, Tony rolled off Cecelia and inspected her for any signs of wounds, unconcerned about his own condition. When Cecelia saw the blood, she screamed.

Looking down at his thigh, Tony became conscious of the bullet holes in his body. His vision started to blur, but he could make out someone running toward him from the bottling plant. In seconds, ambulances, squad cars, and unmarked government vehicles squealed to a halt just outside the entrance to the limestone cave.

Mike and Cecelia rode in the ambulance that was taking Tony to the emergency room. Sitting in the confined space, Mike was just beginning to comprehend what had happened and understand the ruthless nature of the war in which they were now engaged. Cecelia, crying softly, didn't require any additional reality lessons.

———

Two days later, under the care of Mike and Cecelia, Tony was released from the hospital and taken back to the ranch. They cared for him, cooked for him, and handled the day-to-day operations activities of the winery. Before long, without realizing what was happening, both of them were learning a great deal about Garibaldi Vineyards.

There was something very idyllic about this sort of life, especially after all the spy games they had been involved in. But, all too soon for Mike, there was an appointment he had to keep in Boston.

Chapter 29

BURNING BOTH ENDS

Kevin sat on the edge of Cricket's desk. It had been a long, frustrating day. All his efforts to locate any of the remaining Six Sentinels had produced no results; he was hearing rumors that the Germans were ready to buy back their bonds, costing him his finders' fees; and his sure bet at the racetrack had failed to finish in the money.

"If the Germans make a deal to buy back the remaining duplicates, they don't pass through our hands," he said.

"We're the ones who discovered the forgers' identities and found the location of the bonds. Samson's failure to recover them doesn't excuse the Germans from paying us our fee," Cricket said.

"Absolutely not," Kevin responded. "But just in case they don't feel the same way, do you have any backup plans?"

"Well," Cricket said, studying the pencil she was twirling in her hand, "how much do you suppose the rest of the six would be willing to pay to know where the Meyer lad is being held?"

Kevin nodded his head, thinking about the last names of the six kids he had seen in that photo. "Their families have got some swag, right enough. You might be on to something, love."

Erhart Schmidt gripped the phone receiver, listening carefully to the argument the president of IFIC had been making. He waited for the man to finish before exploding: "What do you mean you expected to be paid your fee up front? Six hundred thousand dollars is a lot of money for us to just give away, particularly before we have the bonds in our hands. Your people didn't do much of anything! If we fail to recover them ourselves, *we're* the ones who'll be forced to negotiate with those forgers . . . and have you considered what will happen if they decide not to sell?"

It was something that Herr Schmidt himself did not like to consider, but he answered his own rhetorical question nonetheless. "No one will see any money then!" He slammed the phone back into its cradle.

This astonishingly bad phone call was followed by a meeting with a European Samson agent. "According to our people on the West Coast, two more of our agents have been killed, one was seriously wounded, and six have been captured . . . bringing the death toll up to six, if you count the two missing agents sent to capture Claudine Demaureux. These are very significant losses."

"Yes, well, you have the Meyer boy, don't you? Have you been able to learn anything from him?"

"Nothing that we haven't already put in our reports to you."

"Yes. I now know that my bonds are sewn into some old books. But have you done anything about locating the books themselves?"

"So far, that task has proven more complicated . . ."

"I can see that, you fool! Why don't you put some pressure on Meyer—make him tell you where the books are."

"We have, Herr Schmidt. Once the books left the Meyer & Co. warehouse, they were dispersed among a host of locations, in

private libraries throughout England and America . . . and probably other countries, from what we can tell. Very widely dispersed,
mein Herr. We've used our most . . . reliable methods of questioning, and I am convinced he is telling us all he knows. And we can't
very well make direct inquiries, can we, *mein Herr*? I mean, going
up to the house, knocking on the door, and asking to look at the
book collection? Oh, no. Very complicated, indeed. Rather clever,
actually."

Schmidt's face was reddening as he rubbed it with his hands,
but the Samson agent bravely ventured on to the main purpose of
his appointment. "When we accepted this assignment, we didn't
count on the French Resistance and the American Secret Service
being involved. I am not sure how much longer our people will be
willing to continue our contract with you."

"I am not asking for much longer," Schmidt said, pounding a
fist upon his desk. "In fact, I am asking that you find them fast!"

———

Since Claudine's arrival at La Garoupe months earlier, time had
seemed to crawl.

In the beginning, the staff, many of whom were members of
the French Resistance, knew not to ask questions. They took her
in and treated her like one of their family. Before long, however,
Claudine was deeply involved with what appeared to be her new
family's principal activity: espionage.

In addition to her regular tasks of going to the market, serving cocktails and meals, and cleaning up in the kitchen, Claudine
soon had a new assignment—gathering information from the
German officer-guests.

For the most part, the colonels and generals were battle-hard-
ened veterans who had seen action in Russia, North Africa, and

Italy. On duty, they were the feared masters of the German army that had invaded and occupied most of Western Europe. On their rest and recovery assignments at La Garoupe, however, dressed in nonmilitary clothes and with no one to intimidate, these same men acted in a civil and polite manner befitting their privileged backgrounds in Germany before Hitler came to power.

Some were just lonely; they had been away from home for a long time. Others were tired and depressed from the war and the change in its direction. They were all worried about their next assignments. And they all enjoyed Claudine's seemingly sunny disposition. They looked forward to her company and treated her with dignity and respect.

When she first began her new job, the officers were very guarded about speaking with one another whenever she entered the room. In less time than she imagined, they began to relax and let down their guards, especially after Claudine served them a few drinks. From experience, Claudine knew that men of this class often regarded the staff as nonpersons. Often, they would continue their conversations about wives, girlfriends, and children as if they were alone. That was a benefit to Claudine, since they sometimes also talked about the war.

Each night, in the privacy of her small room, Claudine made notes about anything she had heard and believed to be important. When the last of the lights went out, she went outside and hid her notes in the tubes of her bicycle handlebars, concealed behind the rubber handle grips.

The next day, when she went to market in Antibes, she'd pedal her bicycle the extra distance to the markets in Nice. If she were asked by one of the officers why she didn't do all her shopping in Cap d'Antibes, she would simply say, "The markets are better in Nice."

After some quick shopping, she would stop at Queenie's gelato shop near the beach and order a cool, smooth dessert. Queenie was always there to greet her and accept the messages she had for George. Once the notes were delivered, Claudine never knew what happened to them. She just assumed they were passed along to the appropriate people, and hoped that they'd help shorten the war.

Claudine became comforted by her daily routine. It was the nights that she dreaded. In her small room, she felt vulnerable and utterly alone. That was when she'd think about the German officers sleeping such a short distance away. During the day, they seemed to be lonely men, tired of war and wanting to go home. At night, however, in her mind, they transformed into the evil villains that had captured, killed, and exterminated so many of their enemies.

Sleeping only meters away, she couldn't help but realize how exposed she really was. If any one of those officers began to suspect why she was there, there was absolutely nothing she could do to protect herself. She had no papers, no work permit, not even a French passport. She was literally sleeping with the enemy. Terrified of what might happen if she were discovered, she would try to shift her mind to more pleasant subjects.

Every night for months, she had been forcing herself to think about her home life with her father and fantasize about her future with Jacques. It was the thoughts of their life together after the war that gave her the hope and strength to continue her French maid charade there, in enemy territory.

Ian huddled in the corner of the damp cellar room. They kept him blindfolded, but he had learned to tell the time of day from the traffic sounds that filtered in from the street above. He had lost track of how many days he'd been at this particular location. It was better than some of the others. Not too many rats, at least.

Maybe they'd finally believed him that he'd told them all he knew. At least, the interrogation sessions had become less frequent. For the thousandth time, he thanked his lucky stars that he'd hit on the book idea for the disposition of the bonds. The moment he was shoved into the lorry in the alley behind the French Club, he'd known that he didn't have the emotional strength or the physical courage to withhold information from someone who didn't care if he lived or died. Ian knew his limitations, and the idea of betraying his friends through his own weakness was unthinkable. Fortunately, he really didn't know enough to betray them—not quite.

He prayed that his captors hadn't completely given up hope that he still knew something useful. From what he could tell, that uncertainty was the only thing keeping him alive.

Chapter 30

REPORTING FOR DUTY

Mike came walking into Jimmy's Harborside Restaurant in downtown Boston as if he owned the place. It was obvious he had been there many times.

Jacques was sitting at a corner booth that commanded a view of the entire dining area. Mike crossed to him, tossed down the hanging garment bag and sports duffle he carried, and gripped his friend in a long hug. He slid into the booth.

"Jacques, my old friend, the cat with nine lives. How is it that you are still kicking?"

Over lunch, Jacques brought Mike up to date. "They've got Ian. I think I'm almost more worried about him than I am about Claudine."

Mike nodded. "You know, between what I witnessed in Napa and what you're telling me now, there is one thing I'm sure of—we need a very safe place to hide. And that's why I brought these," Mike said, patting the bags he'd brought.

"Should I ask what's in them?"

"Only if you're prepared to say how brilliant I am. They're genuine U.S. Navy uniforms! Where we're going, they'll be our passports to obscurity . . . and maybe a lot of fun."

Jacques ordered a bottle of wine. "Okay, buddy, I'll bite. How do the sailor suits figure into our safety—or our fun?"

"You remember that place my family has, on the bluffs overlooking Newport harbor? Before the war, I used to spend the summer there with some friends of mine from Yale and Harvard whose families also own homes in Newport. But since the start of the war, not many people go there to vacation anymore. The bluffs will be practically deserted—and we should be safe, at least for a little while."

"You mean I'm going to finally see the great Stone mansion that I've heard so much about?"

"Well . . . not quite. If we went to my parents' house, we'd make it too easy for Samson to find us; that's probably one of the first places they'd look. I have something else in mind that may make their job a little more difficult."

They finished eating and polished off the wine. As they stood up to leave, Mike grabbed the check.

"There's nothing better than fresh New England seafood, especially when someone else pays the tab," Jacques said.

"Well, if you like fresh seafood, you're going to love this next part." They left the restaurant and headed down to the docks, where sleek powerboats were moored and waiting.

Mike spotted the dock manager and walked over to him. "Hey, Metro, it's nice to see you again. I believe Pete Ashby sent you a note asking that my friend and I be allowed to use his boat?"

"Yes, sir, Mr. Stone. The boat's been fueled and wiped down. She's all set to go. I tied her up at the guest dock, just over there."

"Metro, some people may come looking for me and my friend. It's very important to me, and very profitable for you, that they not be able to find us."

"I completely understand, Mr. Mike, sir. You can count on me."

The boat was different from anything Jacques had ever seen. It appeared to have been converted from an old plank-bottom, forty-two-foot luxury oceangoing cruiser into a commercial fishing boat. At the stern, there was a large deck, significantly larger than anything normally required to support two sportfishing fighting chairs. It ran from the stern to the aft portion of the captain's bridge. Upon closer inspection, Jacques could see the extra reinforcing on the sides. Two cranes were anchored near the outer edges of the deck, the kind of cranes that would be used to handle fishing nets or lift heavy cargo. Wide hatches in the middle of the deck appeared to lead to below-deck storage. A large dinghy lay on top of the bridge. The outside was lined with plate steel; windows were constructed of double-thick, bulletproof glass; and there were what looked like turrets where weapons could have been attached.

"This doesn't look like any fishing vessel I've ever seen," Jacques said, "unless the fish are packing bazookas. This thing is like a floating tank."

Mike smiled and nodded.

A few minutes later, Mike was maneuvering the vessel between the other boats in the harbor. Between checking the nautical chart and looking around to find landmarks, he ignored Jacques' nonstop questions.

"Who's Pete Ashby and how are we able to use this boat?"

"What's with this boat, anyway? This sure isn't a fishing boat."

"If we're not going to your family's place, where are we headed?"

With his course set to put Allerton Point to starboard in about ten miles, Mike began to focus on Jacques' questions.

"At Yale, Pete Ashby was a Deke fraternity brother of mine. We actually roomed together for two years. He's one of the friends

I spent summers with in Newport. His family's mansion is near ours."

"And that's where we're going to stay, at the Ashby mansion?"

"No, that would still make it too easy for them to find us. That's the second place they'd come looking for me, if they keep doing their homework like they have so far."

"Then where are we going?"

"Another place, the Maddox mansion. It's just around the point from the Ashby place. Maddox was an old rumrunner during Prohibition. His son, Parker, and I went to Harvard Business School together. The parties we had in his house when his parents were out of town were legendary, even by our standards. There's rack after rack of some of the world's best wine and liquor in his cellars, all left over from the days of Prohibition. When we get there, it may be our responsibility to make sure that none of that stuff has spoiled."

"And this boat?"

"It's a relic of that same era," Mike said. "You might be surprised at some of the folks who were involved in rum-running during Prohibition."

"Then again, maybe I wouldn't."

Jacques smiled and tilted his face to the wind, enjoying the sea air. When they cleared the harbor, Mike pushed both throttles forward and the two Rolls Royce engines roared louder. Surprised by the power and acceleration, Jacques said, "What the hell is going on?"

"Find a seat and enjoy the view! We've got a long way to go and there's no sense in taking all day."

The fishing craft had risen up out of the water and was skimming over the light, afternoon chop at nearly fifty knots.

"Is this some kind of boat or what?" Mike yelled above the engines. "The Ashbys bought it from the Maddox family after the repeal of Prohibition. This is what he used to make his offshore pickups. Even fully loaded, it could outrun any police boat from here to Maine."

"What's with all the fishing equipment?"

"Nowadays, all these waters around the Cape—Nantucket Sound and Buzzards Bay and the entrance to Newport harbor— are patrolled by the Coast Guard on the lookout for German U-boats. Only registered fishing boats are allowed to pass."

Jacques nodded. "What happens when it gets dark? Are you going to get us lost?"

Mike grinned and shook his head. "Not likely. It's easier than you think. See this chart? That light over there to starboard is at Allerton Point. Once we pass it, we turn south-southeast for the next forty miles, until we see the lighthouse at Provincetown. From there, we turn south along the eastern coast of Cape Cod for another forty miles or so until we approach Chatham harbor. We'll work through some islands and shallows and enter Nantucket Sound. Another fifty miles along, we'll come to Woods Hole Point and the opening to Buzzard Bay. Across the bay maybe thirty miles toward the light at Skonnet Point, we'll be within ten miles or so of Brenton Point, close to our destination.

"Look, it's a beautiful moonlit night. Why don't you grab us a couple of beers, then shut up with all the questions and just enjoy the ride?"

When the bluffs overlooking Newport harbor finally came into view, Mike began pointing out the magnificent mansions illuminated by the full moon, naming each of their owners. To Jacques, the list sounded like a Who's Who of the East Coast establishment. To Mike, they were simply old friends and neighbors.

Mike slowed the boat as they neared the bluff. "Watch this," he said with a grin. Slowing the boat to a snail's pace, he maneuvered it around a large outcropping of rocks and into a cave completely hidden from the sea. On the right side, cleverly hidden just inside the entrance, was a light switch. He reached out and turned it on, and the cave and rocks marking the path under the cliff were suddenly illuminated. The light seemed to come from below the water.

"This is astonishing!" Jacques said. "What a perfect way to hide a dock!"

After turning off the engine, Mike handed Jacques a large, wooden pole. It was low tide, and the rocks on the bottom of the entrance were exposed. Standing on opposite sides of the boat, they used the poles to maneuver the boat between the rocks. It was slow, difficult work.

"I can tell you one thing," Jacques said, wiping off his brow. "Getting through this cave would be impossible for anyone not familiar with the rocks. But at high tide, I'll bet you could drive a boat through at full speed."

"You're right," Mike said. "We generally time our trips to take advantage of that fact."

They poled the boat for another hundred yards until they reached a well-illuminated, deep lagoon. Jacques stared, his mouth open. On both sides of the cavern were concrete docks, equipped with large, heavy-duty overhead cranes. Behind each crane was a large, empty warehouse that had obviously been excavated out of the stone cliffs. Freight elevators, leading to the upper stories, were located on either side of each warehouse, and groups of hand trucks lay idle in each storage area. Jacques could visualize the cases of liquor that must have been stored there during a bygone time.

After securing the boat, Mike led the way toward the nearest elevator. "These were used to transport liquor to the smaller quarters located in the rear of the house. From there, it was transported to major eastern cities in the many service vehicles that came and went each day. It was a beautiful operation . . . and apparently, it worked well for a very long time. To my knowledge, it was never discovered."

"That bodes well for us, then," Jacques said.

"My thoughts exactly. We're going up to the servants' quarters," Mike said, pressing a button. "They know we're coming. I had Parker call ahead, and everything has been arranged."

"Why the servants' quarters?"

"It's still off season, and most of the houses are closed except for skeleton staff. It would look strange if lights or residents were seen in the main part of the house, especially on the upper floors. In a small community like this, that's cause for the local police to investigate. Tomorrow, we'll check the blackout curtains in the main bedrooms, and if everything seems okay, we'll move upstairs."

As the elevator began its ascent, Mike went on. "The staff here aren't the normal servants you'd expect in a Newport mansion. Paul is their leader—still very strong for an older guy. He was Mr. Maddox's personal bodyguard. On their runs to supply ships, Paul manned the machine gun attached to the top of the cockpit. Rhoda, his wife, drove the boat. The other two servants handled the cargo, loaded the service trucks, and did odd jobs around the estate. Wait until you hear some of their stories! Incidentally, they're all very accustomed to *not* asking questions, so they don't know the real reason we're here."

When the elevator reached Level S, Mike rotated the wheel to a stop. Paul, Rhoda, and two other servants were waiting to greet them.

After the introductions were completed, Jacques asked, "How did you know when we'd be arriving?"

"Oh, we didn't. You set off a silent alarm the minute you entered the cave," Paul said. "We have them everywhere. Look up there on the wall. See the flashing light and the plaque below it? When the light over the 'Cave Entrance' sign began to flash, we knew you had arrived. Those alarms haven't been used in years, but we still test them every week—out of habit, I suppose."

Rhoda showed them where they'd be bunking for the night and told them that cocktails would be served at six. "You'll be eating very well here. We appreciate the opportunity to dust off some of our old skills. But tonight, it will have to be dinner in the kitchen with the rest of us."

The next morning, Mike and Jacques made their way upstairs. With the blackout curtains carefully inspected and securely closed, the two visitors began to inspect their new quarters.

Each had his own master suite—complete with balconies opening onto the sea. At night, with the lights out, they could open the balcony doors and enjoy the sound of the waves crashing on the bluffs below, the soft sea breezes, and the lights of Newport in the distance.

Noticing the sad look on Jacques' face, Mike asked, "Are you thinking about Ian and Claudine? Here we are, seemingly safe in this fortress of luxury and comfort, not knowing what's happened to them."

"Mike, you read my mind. I've been thinking that as soon as it's safe, I need to return to Europe and see what I can do."

Gradually, over the next few weeks, they grew accustomed to their surroundings—and the staff became accustomed to their peculiar habit of leaving score sheets from cribbage and other card games scattered everywhere. Paul and the others looked on, convinced that the two friends were playing for great sums of money. But on the fifth night, over dinner, when Mike was totaling up the score, they were astounded to hear, "Well, Jacques, it looks like you're the big winner. According to my scoring, which is not open for audit, you have won a grand total of five dollars and seventeen cents."

Accepting the money, Jacques said, "I'm quite grateful for all of this. But," he added, lowering his voice, "rolling around in this grand old mansion is becoming a bit boring. Haven't we waited long enough to try out those uniforms?"

Smiling, Mike responded, "Jacques, my old pal, you are about to understand why those U.S. Navy uniforms are about to become our passports to the world of anti-boredom. Less than a quarter mile away, down some unmarked path, there is a very nasty town that has everything a sailor could wish for: booze, wild women, hot jazz, and at least one good fight every night."

"Reporting for duty, sir," Jacques said, snapping off a salute.

From that day forward, they fell into a daily routine. After sleeping late, they would awaken to breakfast cooked by the staff, read the local newspapers, then conduct daily gin rummy, dominoes, cribbage, and backgammon tournaments. The loser was expected to pay that night's bar bill at the winner's honky-tonk of choice.

In the afternoon, they would work out in the fully equipped gym, followed by a growing number of laps in the indoor pool, a steam bath, and a massage administered by Rhoda and her surprisingly strong hands.

Following a nap, they would shower, shave, and put on their freshly laundered uniforms. Already half-smashed from the richness of dinner and the grand assortment of vintage wines, Jacques and Mike would make their way down the path to Newport and the world of the swabbies from whatever ship happened to be in port.

Though the atmosphere of each of the bars was similarly tawdry, for reasons Mike and Jacques could never quite fathom, the crew of one ship would favor a different bar from the crew of another ship. Fights were generally limited to those places frequented by sailors from separate ships, or else they occurred over any one of the ladies of the night, who were always in attendance.

Gradually, Mike and Jacques learned which bars to avoid and which ones to frequent. Their choices normally centered on what musicians were in town and where they were playing. Lately, a real hot horn man had been hanging out in Shanty Malone's, which was fast becoming one of their favorite hangouts. As word spread, other musicians began to appear and sit in for jam sessions. Dixieland jazz, swing, the blues . . . whatever the impromptu band played fit like a hand in a glove.

One night, a tall, slight, bespectacled man with long, graceful hands sat in at the piano. The horn man usually waited a few bars before coming in. As the pianist started to play, everyone in the club knew something was different. They were hearing the same tunes they'd heard many times, but the pianist had improvised the music and played it in an entirely new way. Even the horn man forgot to start playing, he was so fascinated by what the pianist was doing. The room became amazingly quiet.

Waving to the horn man and the other musician, the jazz pianist indicated his desire to have them join in. At first they would play an old standard swing song straight. The second time through, they would begin to improvise. By the fourth time, you had to listen carefully to hear the notes of the original melody.

Word about this special talent spread quickly. From that night forward, Jacques and Mike learned that if you didn't get to the bar early, you couldn't get a seat.

———

One night, while Jacques and Mike soaked up jazz and whiskey in equal quantities, one of the Maddox staff members noticed a strange vehicle parked outside the nearby Stone mansion. Two men sat inside the car, watching the house intently.

Paul said to his wife, while looking out the window, "Look at those men in that parked car. They are obviously looking for somebody. I don't know what kind of trouble those two young men are in, but I'm ready to do whatever's required to protect them. Quite frankly, our current domestic duties have become a little boring. I'd appreciate some action!"

Paul assigned one of the staff to watch the men in the car for a couple of hours. Before the first shift ended, the men had left their vehicle and were going from mansion to mansion, knocking on doors and, with the aid of their heavy flashlights, looking around the grounds. Seeing the men headed in his direction, the staff member barely had time to warn Paul before there was a knock on the front door.

Paul greeted the pair. "How can I help you gentlemen?"

"Well, we're looking for a close friend of ours—Mike Stone," said one of the men. "We were supposed to meet him in town, and he hasn't arrived yet."

"I'm sorry, sir, this is the Maddox residence. The Stone mansion is over there, on the opposite side of the bluff. Maybe you can find him there."

"We've already been there and it seems that no one's home. Do you mind if we come in and use your telephone?"

Paul's instincts, honed by years of operating as a Prohibition rumrunner, kicked in immediately. "I'm afraid my employer has left specific instructions not to let anyone in—at least without a search warrant."

———

While the two Samson agents went door to door, another pair was looking around the yacht club where Mike and Jacques had taken the boat from. Unfortunately, this was the one day in the month that Metro had off.

Approaching the attendant, a Samson agent reached into his pocket and withdrew what appeared to be an FBI badge and identification. "Excuse me, do you have the Stone yacht moored here?"

Trained to please, the substitute attendant answered, "Yes, sir, you can see it berthed over there. It's the big white one with the teak decks, moored in 3B."

"Do you know if it has been used within the last few weeks?"

"No, sir, it's been here the entire time. Just look at the dust on it."

Glancing over at the boat, the agent scanned the other berths, noticing only one empty space. "Whose boat belongs there?"

"That's the Ashby boat. I believe it's being borrowed by a family friend," the young man answered.

"Thank you," the agent said, shoving a few dollars into the attendant's hand. With no way to talk to the agents that were already in Newport, the two men began the two-hour drive to the Ashby mansion, stopping en route in Boston to pick up two other agents.

As the Samson operatives searched the Ashby house and its deserted boat dock, one of them noticed that the Maddox mansion next door didn't have a docking facility.

"Strange," he said, studying the adjacent property more carefully. "Why would only one of the mansions not have a boat dock?" It was then that they saw the large exhaust vents that emerged out of the stony cliff connecting the mansion to the water below.

The smallest of the four agents agreed to climb down the cliff to inspect the closest vent. Pulling off the cover, he carefully climbed down the iron ladder welded to the inside of the large vent. Almost immediately upon reaching the hidden dock area below, the agent spotted the docking lines hanging in the water, which suggested that a boat must have left in such haste, the captain or crew failed to coil and place them in their accustomed spot. The agent suspected that those on board were the two men the FBI were hunting, namely, Mike Stone and Jacques Roth. He hurriedly retraced his steps and headed back to report what he had discovered.

———

A yellow, blinking light inside the mansion told Paul that someone had crawled through the air duct to the boat dock. He had just enough time to stash away all of Mike and Jacques' belongings and alert Rhoda to head out down the back path before the four Samson agents made a second call on the Maddox residence.

As Paul opened the door, a pistol was pointed directly into his face. The same agent who had been there before said, "Will this warrant suffice?"

"Come in, fellows. You were looking for someone, weren't you? Well, feel free to look."

The Samson agents began searching the house. They couldn't find any trace of visitors in the immaculate master bedrooms upstairs. In fact, they were beginning to think they had made a mistake until one agent held up a sheet of paper—a scorecard with Jacques' and Mike's names written on it.

The agent's eyes widened when he saw Jacques' name and knew for certain that he was still alive. "Where are they?" he asked, shoving his gun into the side of Paul's face.

"Don't . . . don't shoot me, okay, buddy? When they saw you pull up outside the Ashby home, they took the speedboat and headed out. You can probably catch up with them at the yacht club."

The agents raced out the front door. A moment later, Paul went to the door and closed it quietly. Rhoda came up behind him. "Think they bought it?"

"I hope so. We've got to get Mike and Jacques out of here."

———

It had been a great night at Shanty's. Sitting at the bar, Mike and Jacques had been served immediately and frequently. Musicians from various ships moored in port had joined in on the horn man and pianist's session, knowing it would be their last night there. They were determined to make it a great gig. The music was loud, and the excited crowd was even louder.

It was past midnight before the first fight broke out, signaling that it was time for Mike and Jacques to leave and begin their unsteady trek up the path back home. They were still laughing and discussing the events of the evening when they noticed Rhoda standing quietly in the shadows, waiting for them.

"You two need to come with me," she said.

After quickly explaining what had happened, she led them up a different path to a fourth mansion, whose staff had already been informed and was waiting for them. Without comment and without belongings, Mike and Jacques were led into an old service van. They lay down in the rear cargo area, where Rhoda pulled some old blankets over them and gave each a silent pat good-bye.

Two hours later, the van came to a halt outside Boston's old produce warehouse near a dock, a short walking distance from Sculley Square. The driver handed them the name of a "no questions asked" hotel, neatly written on a scrap of paper.

Stepping out of the van, Jacques smoothed out his crinkled sailor's uniform, then looked down at the address. "Mike, I think we've just gone down in rank."

Chapter 31

TIME TO MAKE A DEAL

As Henri Demaureux read the papers, Karl Schagel looked out the window of Henri's office in Geneva. He had laid out all of his documents on the small conference table in front of a window overlooking the lake. Outside, the April sun made everything look especially crisp and bright. But here, inside Henri's office, the mood was somber and serious.

Henri carefully studied each document in front of him. Taking off his glasses to clean them, he stared directly into Karl's eyes.

"Although this agreement is an accurate reflection of what we discussed on your last visit, things have changed . . . and these terms are no longer satisfactory." Henri leaned back in his chair. "Ian Meyer is still missing, and there was that attack in Napa. Two Samson agents who were captured have divulged that they were in the employ of a German client. Karl, what additional information do you need to understand that the people you're working for are not to be trusted?"

"Henri, you have to believe me—I was not informed of any of these plans. It has become apparent that since Herr Schmidt learned about Claudine and the others, they no longer welcome me in their inner circle. I have simply become an errand boy . . .

and they have instructed me that this is our last chance to come to an agreement. Henri," he said, leaning forward over the small table, "this may be the only way to make it all stop."

"Karl, can't you see that the game has changed? Forgive me, but obviously you are no longer authorized to speak for your clients, so why should I even discuss this deal with you?"

"I know money alone won't convince you that we—they—can be trusted," Karl said. "But they have sent me here to offer an additional hundred and ten million dollars in escrow to buy back the duplicate bonds. They are also willing to wait ten years before collecting their own savings. Doesn't that indicate my clients' good faith?"

"No, Karl. This is not an issue of money. It never was. Your clients have already demonstrated that they are willing to abuse their power to get their way. That is exactly what my daughter and her friends are trying, in their way, to prevent."

"Henri," Karl said, an alarmed look on his face, "sign this agreement and Claudine can come out of hiding. She can be safe again, here with you. Isn't that what you want?"

"More than anything. But it's not my decision to make. Let me be clear: Events are not in your clients' favor. Since the beginning of 1944, the Allies have opened a front at Anzio, Berlin and Hamburg have been bombed, and the Soviet army is moving in the Crimea. The Allied invasion of France is days, perhaps hours, away. You and I both know that your clients have precious little time left in their country before they are either discovered and prosecuted—and likely executed very quickly—or forced to flee the Allied forces. My six charges may just be willing to wait out the clock."

Karl's mouth opened and closed. Henri felt a deep pang of pity for his old friend, who was in an impossible situation. But he had little room for compassion for the man. This was, after all, about his only daughter, Claudine.

"But, Henri, is that smart?" Karl said, finally. "The men I'm dealing with . . . This is their last chance. If you reject their offer, I'm afraid they'll lash out in any way they can."

Henri knew that Karl was not only concerned about the fate of Claudine and her friends; he was scared for his own life as well.

Henri stared at his friend for a full minute, studying his face. "Very well," Henri said at last. "They do have a bargaining chip with Ian Meyer in captivity. I'll try to convince my daughter's friends to agree to these terms. Place the funds in escrow, and I will advise them to start collecting all the duplicate bonds as soon as possible. But tell your clients that if there is any more trouble, I can guarantee the deal won't go through."

"Thank you," Karl said, visibly relieved. "You are making the correct choice for everyone concerned."

Henri stood to shake his friend's hand. "Be very careful, Karl. It is clear to me that your clients make decisions based more on desperation and revenge than on reason."

———

Karl stood in Erhart Schmidt's inner office. Schmidt was treating him like a truant schoolboy in front of the headmaster; he had not even suggested his guest sit down. He stared at Karl, silently waiting for his report on the meeting with Henri.

"The documents have been completed, the funds are on deposit, and the time has come for them to start assembling the duplicate bonds," he told Schmidt. "That process will require a few more weeks to complete—providing there are no more threats or attacks directed at any of the people involved. It is also imperative that Ian Meyer be released unhurt."

Schmidt folded his hands and spoke in a calm voice. "Karl, so far, all of our attempts to locate them have failed. The U.S. Secret

Service is heavily guarding some of their members and others have disappeared under the protection of the French Resistance. I am no longer employing any outside services. Therefore, there is nothing I can do."

He threw up his hands theatrically and gave Karl a tight smile. "At this point, we are totally dependent upon the completion of this deal if we are to ever recover our bonds and access our savings. Believe me, we will do nothing to jeopardize that."

Karl left the office. He wished he could believe Schmidt was telling the truth.

Through Dr. Tom's special courier system, Henri was able to send word stateside that the bonds should be retrieved immediately from their hiding places around the world and shipped to the Demaureux Bank in Geneva. Dr. Tom personally delivered this message to Cecelia at the ranch.

"Getting the bonds back is the easy part," Cecelia said to Dr. Tom and Tony as they sat around the kitchen table, drinking coffee. "The more difficult problem is finding some safe way to communicate with my old network for assistance. As tempting as it is to use your switchboard system, I'm afraid we have to assume Samson has it tapped."

"Remember, I've been able to correspond with Henri and Karl von Schagel during wartime by using commercial bank courier systems," Dr. Tom said. "Friends of mine have allowed me to use regular bank envelopes to include the letters of a bunch of old, harmless academics with interbank deliveries. Once they arrive at the designated bank, they're placed in the regular mail for their final destination. The system is all quite simple and seems to work very well."

"That's a great idea. I can ask Mr. Ferrari to let me use the outgoing envelopes from the Napa branch of the American West National Bank," Cecelia said. "Since I send out payroll for the ranch each Friday, that would be an opportune time to deliver and receive any special letters without raising suspicions."

"If you think your communication system is tapped, how are you getting in touch with Mike and Jacques?" Dr. Tom asked.

"We're not." Cecelia's face was downcast.

"But we've made it this far, and this is the final phase," Tony said, putting a hand on her shoulder. "We just have to believe that all of us will be all right."

"You have to do more than believe it," Dr. Tom said. "The six of you have to *ensure* it. Everything is in your hands now."

Chapter 32

AN OLD FRIEND

One look at their new accommodations was all it took to convince Mike and Jacques that within the space of a few hours, they had managed to slide down from the top rung of the social ladder, alongside the rich and famous, to the bottom rung, alongside the disenfranchised.

Pressed in between a strip joint and a tattoo shop, the hotel where they were staying was frequented by an endless stream of hookers and their wartime supply of lonely, drunk sailors. Rooms were let by the hour on a cash-up-front basis, with no questions asked and no written registrations required. The seedy front lobby—with its stained carpet, broken furniture, and encaged front desk—was outdone only by their second-story room, which overlooked the street below.

Entering the room, Mike and Jacques first noticed the eerie patterns that the blue-and-pink, blinking neon lights made through the cracked window on the unadorned, peeling wall. They preferred not to think about the soiled, dirty linen on the beds and how it got that way. The room was lit by one naked lightbulb hanging through a hole in the ceiling. The furniture had seen better days; chipped paint, drawers that didn't fit their cases, broken handles, and missing legs represented the latest in Sculley Square decor.

Too exhausted to care, Mike and Jacques lay down, fully clothed, on top of the dirty beds. Using their pea jackets for pillows, they found sleep almost immediately.

The next morning, they awoke to the reality of their new environment. Standing in front of the broken window, Jacques studied the activity on the street below. After twenty minutes of seeing nothing suspicious, he suggested, "Why don't we take a chance and leave this hotel for some fresh air? Somewhere around here there must be a place to get a cup of coffee."

Just around the corner, they were able to find a twenty-four-hour shop that sold bad coffee, stale doughnuts, and newspapers. Retreating with their precious bounty to the safety of their room, the two old friends gagged over the cooling coffee and the hardened doughnuts.

"Try dipping them," Mike said, mouth full. "They're not as bad that way."

As in the Maddox mansion, they began to adjust to their new environment. Mornings would start with the same bad coffee, day-old doughnuts, and copies of the *Boston Globe* and *New York Times*. Having arrived with only the clothes on their backs, days were spent in search of naval surplus stores, Laundromats, and better places to eat.

Late in the afternoon, they would carry paper bags filled with cleaning supplies and tools back to their den of iniquity. As unaccustomed as they were to repairing things, they began to enjoy the process.

"I don't know how it was with you growing up in France," Mike said, "but fixing up this room reminds me of some of the tree forts I used to build in my backyard."

Hammering away, with extra nails clamped between his lips, Jacques smiled as best he could at Mike's nostalgia.

Nights were still their favorite time. After some initial hesitation about entering certain establishments, they were able to find the bars and nightclubs most often frequented by wartime musicians. But this time, they were more careful to mix up their pattern, never visiting the same bar on a regular basis.

For weeks, their days in solitude drifted along in the same way, until one morning, while Mike was reading the *Globe*, Jacques heard him say, "Well, I'll be damned. Guess who's coming to town?"

Jacques walked over to Mike's cot and peered over his shoulder. "I can't believe it! Natalie and her new show are coming to Boston for an out-of-town rehearsal."

"Maybe your luck is beginning to change," Mike said.

"What do you think?" Jacques asked excitedly. "Should we take the risk of attending at such a high-profile place?"

"Jacques, you and I both know that there is absolutely no way we are not attending that show . . . and going backstage afterward!"

———

No one noticed two more sailors sitting in the audience for the road performance of Natalie's Rodgers and Hammerstein musical. As the curtain rose, all eyes were riveted on the stage, anticipating the appearance of the new face from England.

Dressed in a white sailor suit perfectly tailored to fit her shapely figure, Natalie emerged from the wings to a thunderous ovation. To Jacques, she seemed more beautiful than ever. Even her voice had changed; it was deeper and stronger, perfectly suited to Rodgers' music. Somehow, she had managed to make herself into what Jacques knew she could become, an international star of the musical stage.

The final curtain came down all too soon. Jacques wished he could go on watching her forever. From the audience's reaction, he was certain that the show would be a huge hit on Broadway.

Mike and Jacques worked their way backstage and waited for Natalie. Flushed with excitement, she failed to notice the two sailors quietly standing in the wings. She was absorbed in conversation with the play's producer and director when she suddenly felt his eyes upon her. She turned and saw Jacques.

He could almost read her thoughts on her face: *How could it be! I thought he'd been killed in London! But there's no mistaking that stupid-looking grin.*

Even if Natalie hadn't let out a Maggie-style "whoop!" everyone backstage would have taken notice when she flew across the room to Jacques, threw her arms around him, and began kissing him and crying at the same time.

Standing behind some scenery, giving notes to one of the actors, Emily hadn't noticed what had happened. She turned to see what all the excitement was about and couldn't believe her eyes. She ran up and started hugging Jacques and Natalie together, then turned and grabbed Mike.

The old mahogany-walled bar at the Milner Hotel was their tavern of choice after the theater. It also happened to be where Natalie was staying. The four friends ordered too many bottles of Dom Perignon, and all started talking at once. But the celebration quickly began to wind down when Emily, no longer able to hide being distraught over the lack of news as to Ian's whereabouts, tearfully excused herself and went to bed.

Mike's attention had long since drifted away from the conversation. The more he drank, the more he thought about Cecilia— and the more convinced he became of his need to hear her voice.

He suddenly excused himself from the table, found a pay phone, and placed a call to Tony's ranch.

A yellow light started to shine in the basement of a small house in Napa. The on-duty Samson agent put on his earphones and heard Cecelia say, "Hello?"

"Cecelia, I have to talk to you."

"Mike! Are you okay?"

"Yes. No. Listen, I know I'm breaking the rules by calling, but Jacques and I just saw Natalie's new play, and when I saw how hard this has all been on her and Emily, I just knew I needed to call."

"I miss you, too, Mike. But this should all be over soon. We got word to start collecting the bonds."

Their conversation lasted just a little while longer as Cecelia explained the message from Henri that Dr. Tom had brought.

By the time they hung up, another phone call had been placed.

"Stone and Roth have just seen some new play that has a girl named Natalie in it. They are having drinks at the Milner Hotel. Find out where it is and get some agents on it right away."

———

Midnight came all too soon. Mike started his lonely trek back to the hotel. Jacques and Natalie, taking a bottle of champagne with them, found the elevator and disappeared upstairs, in search of her room. They had a lot of catching up to do.

The door had barely closed before they were in each other's arms. Natalie still couldn't believe that her prince had returned.

"Jacques Roth, I hope you haven't forgotten about the healthy girl with healthy appetites! Welcome back."

Once Natalie closed and locked the door to her hotel room they just stood there, holding each other while he kissed her lips, her neck, her eyes, and her forehead. Suddenly, she pulled back from him and, eyes twinkling, asked, "Have you ever noticed how unnecessary clothes are?"

On cue, articles of clothing were flung everywhere. Not waiting to turn off the lights or pull back the covers, they found themselves fully engulfed in each other on top of the bed. Natalie was as glamorous naked as she was in full costume.

Stretching out full length, she said, "Well, sailor boy, see anything you like?"

———

Lying spent on the bed, Jacques watched as Natalie sat up, crossing her legs. Unaware of the effect the sight of her nakedness was having on him, this unbelievably sexy woman wanted more than anything else to tell him all about her new life in the theater.

"Jacques, you wouldn't believe the things that have happened. When Mr. Rodgers came to London, he had me sing some of the early songs he'd written for the play. It seemed like we were on another planet! He played the piano and I sat beside him, reading the music and singing. His new score perfectly fit my voice, or was it the other way around? I've never been able to decide." She laughed. "Anyway, afterward, he called his producers in New York and convinced them that the play should open there, not London. So here we are. Tomorrow, we return to New York, and we open next Friday. Is there any chance you could be there?"

"Nothing would please me more, Natalie," Jacques said, "but things are happening in my life that make it necessary for me to return to Europe."

She looked shocked for a moment, then recovered, giving him a slow, seductive smile.

Jacques was surprised when she suddenly pushed him over backward with both hands. "The appetizer was fine," she said, "but what are we going to do about the main course?"

The full moon had come up and was shining through the window when they finally rolled away from each other, covered with sweat and gasping for air.

"My dear, don't you think some nourishment is in order?" Jacques asked.

"Nothing too filling. Remember, we wouldn't want to destroy our appetite for dessert," she answered, smiling that devilish grin he had learned to understand so well.

———

As Mike was walking slowly back to the room in Sculley Square, thoughts of Cecilia occupied his mind. So, he was caught totally off guard when a woman of the night approached him, pulling him into the entrance of a nearby alley. Before he could react, she peeled back a section of her coat lapel, revealing a gold badge.

"Mike Stone, listen very closely to what I am going to tell you," she said, her mouth close to his ear. "Your call to Cecelia Chang was intercepted. The Samson agents have discovered that you and Jacques Roth were in the vicinity of the Milner Hotel. Their agents are on their way. It's important you do exactly as I say."

She pressed her body closer to Mike's. "We need to make it appear as if you are taking me back to your room. It's the only way we can get me there without alerting Samson's suspicions. Our agents are already there, taking up their assigned positions."

It took Mike a moment to collect his thoughts. "What about Jacques?"

"He's fine where he is. We have agents stationed outside his location. My guess is that men from Samson will wait to follow him back to your hotel, wanting to catch the two of you together. If you don't mind my being blunt, we were hoping they'd make one last move like this."

"Are you saying you used us as bait?"

"Keep your voice down!" she hissed. "Just do as I say. You can talk to your friend about it when you see him. It was Jacques' idea."

━━━

It was eleven o'clock the next morning when Jacques and Natalie finished breakfast. They had spent an incredible time together, but Jacques knew—and something told him Natalie did, too— that things between them were about to change. Her career was taking off and he would have to remain in hiding until the war was over.

For a short while, they sat on the edge of the bed together, looking into each other's eyes.

"Natalie, I wish the best for you," Jacques said, pushing a stray strand of hair away from her eyes. "It may be a long time before we see each other again. Why do I believe that while I'm gone, you're going to be busy conquering the world?"

She smiled. "And I think you're about to save it."

Jacques stood up, lifted her hand, and reluctantly walked her to the door. With a final kiss, she said, "You know where I'll be, if you ever want to find me. And I want you to know I'd give it all up . . . for the right guy."

Jacques looked into her brown eyes, which were beginning to tear up. "Natalie, I probably won't be able to see your beautiful face for a long while, except on billboards," he said, taking her face in his hands and kissing her gently. "Be happy, and know that I wouldn't trade our time together for anything."

With that, she shut the door behind him, before the tears started streaming down her face.

━━━

Jacques was walking back to his shabby room in Sculley Square, his mind still on Natalie and the evening they had spent together. *How does she manage to be so smart and witty, yet stay so uncomplicated? Life with her could be very interesting. Maybe someday, I could meet her back in New York, where we would both be free to pursue our occupations. She would be the center of attention in public, and we would have our private life together. Isn't that what I always wanted?*

Wrapped up in his thoughts, Jacques failed to notice the men following him. He entered the hotel, took out his room key to open the door, and stepped fully inside before noticing the cheap-looking woman seated at his and Mike's three-legged table.

Confused, he turned toward Mike.

"Things are not as they appear," Mike whispered, putting his finger to his lips.

Mike motioned for Jacques to follow him into the small bathroom. Turning on the water in the sink, he began to whisper into Jacques' ear.

"That hooker is actually an undercover Secret Service agent sent here to protect us. Last night, I foolishly made a call to Cecelia, alerting Samson of our presence here."

"How did the Secret Service know where we were?"

"According to the agent, we've been under their surveillance since we left Newport. She said that Mr. Ainsworth decided to follow your advice."

Jacques nodded his understanding, patting his friend on the back for assurance. He returned to the main room, where the agent had been raising and lowering the torn curtain partially covering the cracked window. She was watching intently but remained silent, as if waiting for something to happen.

In less than a minute, a military patrol wagon pulled in front of the old hotel. Watching through the window, Jacques couldn't help but notice how none of the people on the street paid particular attention. Must be a common occurrence around here.

Four big U.S. Navy patrolmen exited from the rear of the van and made their way into the hotel, up the stairs, and to Mike and Jacques' room. Hearing three short raps on the door, followed by another two, the agent turned toward Mike and Jacques.

"The cavalry has just arrived," she said.

"You mean we're going to be rescued?" Mike asked.

"Sort of. You're going to be arrested."

Chapter 33

TROUBLE AT LA GAROUPE

As was her usual custom on her day off, Claudine had accepted an invitation to join a group of the officer-guests for dinner at a small bistro near La Garoupe, in the village of Juan les Pins. The general seated to her right, who was the senior officer present, had been drinking heavily. When he leaned over to pick up his napkin, she felt his hand brush her thigh. At first, she thought it was just a careless error. When he reached over and began to stroke her thigh, she knew it had not been a mistake.

Claudine could understand why he had decided to get drunk. For Germany and the Axis, the news was almost unfailingly bad since the Allied landing at Normandy earlier in the month. The German army had abandoned Paris and the Italian front had broken down; the Allied forces now occupied Rome. British and American troops were moving steadily toward the western border of Germany, and the Soviet army was in Romania, bringing pressure to bear upon the east. Though Hitler and the other top-ranking officials in the Reich continued to preach and crow about the inevitability of the Reich's victory, clearly the general seated beside her didn't share their optimism.

Not wanting to embarrass the general in front of the junior officers, she removed his hand. Not dissuaded, the general continued his groping. Finally, she reached down, picked up his hand, raised it above the table, and announced in a very loud voice, "There will be no more of that. Keep your *fishy hands off the mutton*!"

She rose from the table and exited the restaurant. Using a bicycle borrowed from one of her waiter friends, she began to pedal back to La Garoupe.

Lying in her bed in her small room at the end of the hall, not far from the rooms where the German officers were billeted, Claudine was thinking of Jacques when she heard the door handle slowly start to turn. When the door failed to open, a massive force slammed against it. The extra latch was no match for the powerful blow. With a loud crash, the door flew open, and in charged the enraged general.

Claudine's scream and the sound of the crashing door woke up the rest of the officers. They rushed into her room. Sizing up the situation, the officers pulled the half-naked general off Claudine. Forcefully, they escorted the embarrassed officer back to his room. After placing a guard in front of her door, they retired for the night.

———

The next morning, Claudine, her meager belongings, and her bicycle were nowhere to be found at La Garoupe. The ensuing attempts by Denise, her mother, Queenie and George, as well as the Germans, all failed to locate her. She had vanished, leaving no clues as to where she might have gone.

Chapter 34

CHANGING THE STAKES

The pressure caused by the deteriorating military situation and the urgency of the situation required Erhart Schmidt to meet with his coinvestors once more. Negative reports were frustrating the investors and driving him crazy.

The Reich was dying, and anyone who wasn't deluded—like Hitler and his inner circle—could see it. The Romanian oil fields at Ploesti had been bombed again in the spring, and this time, the Soviet army was closing in to finish the job. In the west, Cherbourg had fallen and the Allied forces had landed in southern France.

The only good news Herr Schmidt had received was that the German government appeared to be so distracted by its war problems, little if any progress had been made in their missing-accounts investigation.

When he arrived, the atmosphere in the bank boardroom was one of numbing fear and deep depression. Herr Schmidt and his six colleagues knew they were in trouble. Unlike almost everything else in their lives, which they had been able to control, the problem with the duplicate bonds was beyond their sphere of influence and power. Not knowing who to trust or how to solve their problem was adding fuel to a very dangerous fire.

The thought of losing their fortunes, their influence, and their industries had created an entirely new feeling of uncertainty and insecurity. Tempers were short. The pitch in their voices and the frequency of foul language in their speech revealed their growing tension. Unwilling to listen now, they only waited to talk.

The German automaker was the first on his feet when Schmidt entered the room. "Schmidt, what do you mean you failed to capture the Demaureux woman? Having her would have forced her father into negotiations—on *our* terms. How can this girl slip through the fingers of your supposedly well-trained Samson agents?"

The normally reserved, bespectacled shipbuilder interrupted before Herr Schmidt could answer Bimmler. "I've also heard that Jacques Roth has been discovered alive and eluded you once again. Is it true that after this last effort, Samson has resigned?" concluded Herr Klein.

"You've managed to take one hostage, that Meyer character, but he seems completely out of the loop," Herr Fleischer said. "None of the information he's told us is accurate or probably even current anymore. That's how quickly *they* operate!"

Herr von Steuben spoke out. "Herr Schmidt's attempts at espionage speak for themselves, but I think we should be focusing on agreeing to a better deal that will ensure that we get our bonds back. We can worry about *les six cochons* at a later date."

Gritting his teeth against the words he wanted to say, Schmidt motioned for a chance to speak. "Gentlemen, believe it or not, there is some good news. Mr. Demaureux has informed me that the duplicate bonds are arriving in Geneva. If they aren't planning to make a deal, why would they have gone to all the trouble of collecting their bonds and delivering them to Geneva? Meyer, worthless as he has proven to be, will be our best tool in securing a rearrangement of certain terms and conditions . . . if they want his release. For now, there is no sense in becoming more frustrated than we already are. We have no alternative but to wait for the shipment of the bonds. Only this time, I will go with Karl when he meets his connection, to make sure nothing goes wrong."

———

As the female Secret Service agent had explained, placing Mike and Jacques under arrest got them out of the hotel without Samson making a move.

Unfortunately, the federal agents also felt that placing them under protective custody in a holding cell at the sheriff's office was a necessary precaution. Sitting there in the double cell, the two old friends had plenty of time to think and talk.

"You know, Mike, when we checked into that old hotel, I was sure that our elevator in life had just hit bottom. I wouldn't have believed it, but sitting here now, I think it has actually gotten worse."

Despite his exhaustion and partial hangover, Mike laughed for a solid minute, wiping his eyes at the end. He looked at his friend. "Jacques, how would you feel about losing me to the West Coast? You're safe, and our problem appears to be solved. It seems that Tony could still use my help at the ranch, and as you know, I've gotten handier lately. I could also be with Cecelia. Now that she's doing better, I want to spend as much time with her as I can."

"Mike, I think your timing works. I need to get over to Europe and help Henri with the agreement to end this whole thing. I'll book a passage on the clipper to South Hampton, then see if the Demaureux plane can pick me up. That is, if they ever let us out of this joint."

———

Two days later, seated on the Demaureux plane on the last leg of his trip to Geneva, Jacques read a newspaper headline announcing that an attempt to assassinate Hitler at his Rustenburg headquarters had failed.

The backlash in Berlin was going to be fierce. No doubt, there would be massive arrests, quick trials, and busy firing squads. The German industrialists would need to get out of there as soon as possible, making it even more important to recover their bonds.

That may give us even more of an advantage . . .

Jacques' thoughts were interrupted by the appearance of the copilot. "Excuse me, Mr. Roth, but we have been asked to land at an Allied military base just outside of Paris. Apparently, there is something of importance that the bank wants picked up."

"Is it a good idea to land out of the safe-fly zone?"

"The Allies have advanced and are using the airfield as a resupply depot. If you look out the window, you'll see two British Spitfires starting to firm up off each wing. It looks like we have an escort. Whatever it is that we're picking up must be pretty important."

Secure with the escort, Jacques continued to study the newspaper until the pilot announced the final approach. He looked out the window, beyond the lowered end of the wing, as the plane made its turn.

My God, there are bomb craters everywhere. The Germans must have been using this very same airfield. Jacques noticed big, smoking piles of scrap metal pushed together on the edge of the runway.

That's undoubtedly what's left of the local attachment of the Luftwaffe. *What could be so important that a private bank plane would be landing here?*

Jacques forced himself to concentrate on the newspaper articles so he'd be current with the political climate for his meeting with Henri in a couple of hours.

I could be making some of the most important decisions of my life—and my friends' lives. I can't screw up.

Focused on his reading, Jacques didn't look up as the plane's cargo door was opened. "Hey, buddy, does this plane go to Geneva?" asked somebody climbing up the metal ladder.

I know that voice!

Jacques stared in amazement at the person now standing before him in the door of the plane. He had to look twice to be certain it really was Ian.

Chapter 35

SHOWDOWN

Erhart Schmidt spoke without pause as he and Karl Schagel approached Geneva from the east in Schmidt's private plane.

"I can't believe that bomb didn't kill Hitler! According to my reports, it blew up inside the bunker while they were all inside. This is going to trigger an unbelievable reaction in Berlin. There's no way to overestimate Hitler's rage and paranoia. None of us is safe."

He turned to Karl. "It is essential that this deal go through *exactly* as I'm planning. Do you understand, Karl?"

———

The next day, Henri, Karl, and Erhart were seated around the conference table in Henri's office at the Demaureux Bank. Placed in front of them were copies of each of the contracts and details about how the industrialists had deposited the sixty million dollars in cash in the designated escrow account, along with the additional hundred million dollars in gold bearer bonds required to fund the contingency account.

Henri had reviewed the contracts and deemed them to be complete. They were simply awaiting execution.

Schmidt leaned forward as if about to speak, but Henri held up a hand.

"Excuse me, gentlemen. Before we sign anything, there is someone I'd like to introduce you to."

Von Schagel and Schmidt stared in disbelief as Jacques entered the room. Although they were aware that he was alive, they weren't expecting to see him at their meeting.

Despite his surprise, Herr Schmidt reluctantly rose out of his chair and extended his hand. "Young man, it's not often that I shake the hand of someone who has caused me so much trouble. If we may begin this meeting, I believe I have a way to put it all behind us."

Jacques ignored Schmidt's outstretched hand.

"Strange as it may seem, I am not willing to shake the hand of a man responsible for so much death and destruction. Frankly, it disturbs me to be in the same room with you. But I have come here with something to say, so I strongly suggest you return to your chair and listen carefully."

Never in his entire life had Schmidt been treated so rudely— not even when Hitler was acting his worst. His face reddening, he dropped into his chair, speechless. Karl and Henri had never seen anything like it, either. All eyes were on Jacques, standing calm and confident on one side of the long conference table, staring directly into the eyes of Herr Schmidt, a powerful, rich, and influential man who was now frustrated and utterly confused.

"Well, what is it that's so important?"

"Herr Schmidt, Herr von Schagel, Monsieur Demaureux . . . I have come to tell you that we are no longer prepared to complete the deal."

Schmidt's jaw dropped.

"Originally, my colleagues and I were prepared to go ahead with the proposed transaction, going so far as to deliver the bonds as promised. But on my way here, I started to think about how, despite Henri's warning, you have continued to authorize attacks against us. In fact, the United States Secret Service has all the evidence they need to prove the connection between you and the Samson organization. Samson's files have been confiscated and arrests are being made as we speak."

Schmidt opened his mouth to say something but seemed to choke on the words.

"In addition to everything else," Jacques continued, "that means you are going to have some very disturbed friends in America as well."

Jacques picked up one of the documents before him. "No one would ever disagree that a hundred million dollars is a lot of money to turn down. But you have to understand that this situation was never about money. It's an issue of what kind of world we want to live in. When this war is over, everyone around the globe will undoubtedly accuse Hitler and his National Socialist German Workers Party of responsibility for all that has happened. But there are some of us who will know the truth."

Leaning across the table, Jacques looked Schmidt straight in the eye. "We believe, now more than ever, that it is absolutely critical that you and your other elitist friends be prohibited from using your wealth and influence to corrupt the political process. We are going to use your own funds to make sure that never happens."

He walked over to Schmidt's side of the table. "Let me make myself clear. Unless you accept our terms, we will continue to use our duplicate bonds to freeze your entire two billion dollars in savings long after you have been arrested for your crimes of war."

The silence in the room was startling. Schmidt, swallowing his anger, finally asked, "What is it you have in mind?"

"There will be no further effort to harm Henri, myself, or any of my colleagues. If, at the end of each year, we are satisfied with your compliance with that rule, we will allow you to cash your ten-percent annual allotment. If we are not satisfied, we are in a position to create so much confusion with the gold center banks that you will never touch a cent of your entire fortune."

Schmidt hit the table with his fist. "Just who do you think you are, dictating to me? We know who is responsible for all of this, and we are prepared to track you down, kill you, and recover our bonds, no matter how long it takes. In fact, I think we will start with Ian Meyer."

There was an ominous silence all around the room. Then, Jacques spoke again, his voice firm and steady. "Herr Schmidt, Once the war is over—if Hitler hasn't killed you—it will be you and your colleagues who will be hunted down, arrested, and tried as common war criminals. You will be so consumed with protecting yourselves that my friends and I will be the least of your problems."

A slight grin appeared on Jacques' face. "Years from now, if you survive, we will know where you are the moment you cash a bond and deposit the money into any part of the world's banking system. *You* will be leaving footprints for *us* to track. You will never be free of us."

Jacques took out of his briefcase the contract he had prepared that morning and placed it in front of the red-faced Schmidt, along with a pen. "Don't you understand that you are alone? The world's appetite for the misdirected ambitions of the elite has changed. Your kind of wealth and influence is no longer welcome."

Schmidt was apoplectic. He finally recovered himself enough to say, "You say *I'm* a monster, yet you are willing to trade your friend's life for some useless theories you learned in school."

"For such a powerful man, it seems there's a lot you don't know, Herr Schmidt," Jacques said. "For one thing, those 'useless theories' were able to predict your actions and put us onto you in the first place."

Schmidt scoffed, then watched silently as Jacques abruptly turned and walked toward the door leading to the hallway. "Where do you think you're going?" he shouted.

"There's something else you obviously don't know," Jacques said, opening the door. "Herr Schmidt, I'd like you to meet my old friend, Ian Meyer."

Chapter 36

PERSONIFICATION OF EVIL

Following the meeting in Henri's office, the plane ride back to Berlin was the worst experience that Karl had ever lived through. Being with Erhart Schmidt was like sitting next to a time bomb that he knew was going to explode. It was only a question of when.

Schmidt had been wrapped in a cloak of silence, waiting to mull over the meeting and the agreement he was forced to sign until they were safely on his private plane, fortified with more than a few drinks.

The alcohol and the news that Schmidt received once on board only amplified his depression and fears. Reports of the failed attempt to assassinate Hitler were still coming in. It was said that he was in sufficient health to attend a planned meeting with his old friend and ally, Benito Mussolini.

Warrants had already been issued for all suspected conspirators, including some members of Hitler's High Command. Colonel von Stauffenberg, the leader of the attempt, was shot the same day. Those once considered the closest to Hitler were now the ones most closely watched. This was the climate to which Schmidt was returning.

This may be my last chance to persuade Schmidt to see reason, Karl thought.

"Herr Schmidt," he began, "perhaps it is time for you to look at things from a more-positive point of view. All you have to do is live up to your side of the deal, and you will have the use of ninety-five percent of your two billion dollars. Although your losses approach a hundred million dollars, that is only five percent of the total funds they helped us transfer out of Germany. When you think about it, a five-percent fee is not such a great deal to pay for their services."

Schmidt gave Karl a piercing look, but he said nothing.

"Once the war is over," Karl went on, "you and the others will be able to return to Germany, and gradually, over the next ten years, regain complete control of your money. There is always the possibility that by then, in peacetime, you and your friends will be able to accomplish economically what you failed to do in wartime."

Karl allowed his rhetoric to reach new heights. It was the best way he could think of to protect Claudine and her friends from Schmidt's seething rage. "Think about it . . . the reconstruction of Germany is going to require your individual and collective knowledge, influence, and capital. You won't even need to try to gain more control of Germany's government—the new leaders will be coming to *you*. In that way, you will enjoy the support of not only the German people but also the entire Allied community."

No response was forthcoming.

After hours of strained silence, the two men returned to a city in total chaos. Hitler's revenge on the conspirators and suspected conspirators was unyielding. More than 7,000 people were arrested. Courts were hastily organized to provide short trials and maximum sentences: 4,980 of the convicted were hanged.

The exodus had begun. Many of Herr Schmidt's friends had already left. Flights out of Germany on private planes, passages on private yachts, and crossings over the frontier into Switzerland were becoming commonplace. No one trusted anyone. Today's friend could become tomorrow's informant.

The next day, sitting on the deck of his chalet, Henri Demaureux read in the *Berliner*: "DEPUTY MINISTER OF FINANCE, KARL von SCHAGEL, FOUND SHOT TO DEATH." He closed his eyes and rested his forehead on his fingertips. *Karl, my old friend . . .*

He wondered how many of Germany's best citizens had been or would soon be killed by their own countrymen during the chaos of the Reich's death throes. He suspected that there had never been any doubt in Karl's mind that he'd pay with his life for his perceived disloyalty. *His death was a waste of one of Germany's true patriots.*

Raising his wine glass, Henri said out loud, "Bon voyage, old friend. May you find the peace for yourself that has eluded your homeland."

Minutes later, the sound of tires crunching on gravel jarred Henri from his thoughts. Setting down his glass, he made his way to the front door and opened it at the same time that Jacques and Ian were just about to knock.

As a greeting, Henri gave both of the young men a strong and silent hug, then ushered them out to the veranda, where he poured two more glasses of the Garibaldi reserve.

Sitting back in their chairs, savoring the fine wine and the magnificent view, no one seemed to want to talk. They were all reflecting on the same thing—the events of the last twenty-four hours.

Finally, Jacques spoke up. "Henri, we were sorry to read about Karl. He was the one who sent word to us about how dangerous our situation was getting. Do you think . . . "

"That Schmidt was responsible?" Henri said, finishing Jacques' thought. "Directly or indirectly, I have no doubt. He either pulled the trigger himself, to compensate for his feelings of frustration and powerlessness, or else he murdered Karl with a few well-placed words in the right ears."

"If he informed on Karl, wouldn't he be exposing himself in the process?" Jacques asked.

"On the contrary, I think he may have been trying to protect himself. I admit that I wouldn't put it past him to kill Karl right after signing your agreement, but it would be a very foolish move, even for someone with Schmidt's temper," Henri said. "But the Gestapo has tactics for getting even the strongest men to talk."

"You think they tortured him for information?" Jacques asked.

Henri nodded. "Most likely, they at last found out that Schmidt's money was among the missing, and they used him to get the others involved. After he told them what they wanted to know, I am sure they had no further use for him."

For a moment, the men silently considered Schmidt's fate. Then Ian exhaled loudly. "I thought Schmidt's Samson agents were going to use some of those same tactics on me. Henri, how were you able to get me out of there like that?"

"Oh, that was easier than it seemed. On Karl's last visit here, he told me that some IFIC agents were the ones who had discovered your part in the plan. I figured that they might also know something about your whereabouts. It turns out that in this day and age, almost anything can be bought . . . especially information."

Reaching into his pocket, Henri extracted a small piece of paper. "This receipt requires reimbursement of three hundred thousand dollars from the funds of your new organization. That's what I paid the two IFIC agents—a rather unsavory woman and an Irishman, I believe—in exchange for word of Ian's location. I trust you will be good for the payment?"

"A bargain at that," Jacques said, taking the receipt and grinning at Ian, who now looked a bit embarrassed. "But what I still don't understand is how you were able to get to him."

"Well, we have our friend, Chairman Roger Malone, to thank for that. I contacted him with the information, hoping there was something he could do to help. He said he had told you he'd do everything possible."

Henri poured another round before continuing. "The timing had to be just right. If he sent men in too soon, it could have ruined our dealings with the depositors. Too late and Ian might have been killed."

Noticing that Ian had turned completely pale, Henri added, "Mr. Malone felt that you'd be perfectly safe as long as Schmidt believed you could be used as a chip in his game."

"Unfortunately for Herr Schmidt, he didn't serve any such purpose himself," Jacques said. "I warned him that there was no longer a place in this world for people like him."

"Jacques, what I would like to know is what was going through your mind when you confronted Schmidt like that. That was one of the bravest and most impressive displays I've ever witnessed," Henri said.

"Honestly, Henri, all I could see in front of me when I looked at Schmidt was the *personification of evil* itself. He represents everything I've learned to despise. By using his influence over an already unstable political environment, he made matters much worse, and it's entirely possible that he, along with the other industrialists, have had to pay the ultimate price for what they have done. The same will go for Hitler, someday soon. But how does that compare to the terrible price their victims have had to pay? Think about the cost that now falls upon us to undo the damage they caused with their abuse of power."

Jacques looked down for a brief moment before collecting himself to answer Henri's question. "You ask me if it was difficult to stand up to Herr Schmidt. I can tell you, Henri, it was the easiest thing I've ever done."

Henri nodded. "Yes, I believe you. My only wish is that Claudine could be here to enjoy this moment with us."

Chapter 37

FINDING CLAUDINE

Henri asked his two tired guests to spend the night, and they agreed. As Jacques walked inside, he spotted the fireplace and the sofa where he and Claudine had spent the evening together so many months past. The memory still lingered warmly inside him.

He waited for Ian to retire upstairs before pulling Henri gently aside. "Henri, it seems so strange for Claudine not to be here. I assume she's been in hiding, but it should be okay for her to come back now. Where is she?"

"Jacques, all I can tell you is that she disappeared a few hours after receiving your call. She left before I arrived home, without even a note telling me that she was leaving. She must have thought she'd be compromising me with that information."

"So you don't even know if she's safe?"

"A few weeks after she left, I found this in the *Paris Herald Tribune*," Henri said, withdrawing a small classified advertisement from his wallet.

Geneva, June 23, 1944
Please notify owner of silver Mercedes that problems
with car have been fixed. It is now in storage.

Jacques stared at the scrap of newspaper for several moments before handing it back to Henri. "I don't get it."

"It's a code she and I worked out at the onset of the war, in case we were separated in our travels and communication became impossible."

"How do you know for certain it's her?"

"Have you ever noticed how her hair shines like silver in the sunlight?" Jacques' look was all the confirmation Henri needed. "If I had to guess," Henri continued, "I'd say it means she ran into some problems and was forced into hiding. Some of her ski equipment is missing, so she could have made it down to a number of small villages along the Riviera, where she has plenty of friends."

"Ian and I will go there to find her. Now that the Allies occupy the western and southern regions of France, it shouldn't be too hard for us to find our way to Nice and look around. After all, there can't be too many places where a woman like Claudine can hide without being noticed."

Henri saw the look of concern—and something more—on Jacques' face. "It could take months," he said, knowing that would not dissuade Jacques. "How about if I take out an ad of my own, telling her to drive the car to Geneva? Maybe she'll see it and come home."

"Okay, but I'm still going. I wouldn't be able to return to the States without knowing she's safe."

"I understand," Henri said. In fact, he understood more than Jacques was saying.

———

It was August. Mike, wrapping up his work in preparation for leaving New York, hadn't heard anything from Jacques for a few weeks. He didn't know how things were progressing in Geneva, but he couldn't sit still any longer to find out.

When deciding on his itinerary, Mike decided to break up his train ride to California into several separate legs, turning a three-day trip into a six-day journey. During this time, he had lots of time to think about what was happening in another part of the world and what kind of life he wanted with Cecelia.

The news he read from Europe was encouraging enough. Hitler's armies appeared to be in full retreat on all fronts. Yet he couldn't help but wonder if the news would make the depositors even more desperate.

Mike felt tired. He was exhausted from all of the running, the coded messages, and the fear that was his almost constant companion since the six of them had begun this whole thing. While he had every intention of continuing his work with the Sentinels, he'd need a more-relaxing occupation with which to balance it out—and banking wasn't it.

He began really considering talking to Tony about partnering with him at the ranch. There was no doubt that when fully developed, Sentinel Vineyards was going to be a very large business with national markets to develop, service, and protect. It would be a challenge from production, marketing, and financial management points of view, but it would be a good kind of challenge, one that could grow with the help of his own two hands. He stared out the train window, trying to keep his hopes down.

Having a business partner might have seemed to be a good idea to Tony while he was still recovering, but how will he feel about it now that he's almost back to full strength? After all, it's been his dream, his baby.

━━━

Cecelia and Tony were standing in front of the main house, watching the taxi drive up the long driveway. Without waiting for Mike to get all the way out of the car, Cecelia rushed toward him, threw her arms around him, and gave him the kind of kiss he needed.

"Come on, Cecelia, let's take a walk," he said when she finally let go.

Lost among rows of grapevines, Mike stopped suddenly and reached out to take Cecelia's hand.

"I've had six days on a train with nothing to do except think about us. It's time for you and me to resolve things once and for all. For five years, we have been living on opposite coasts, separated by more than just geography. But when you were missing, I promised myself that if you were returned safely to me, I would never let you go."

Cecelia stared at him, her eyes moistening.

"Cecelia, I've given my father my resignation, which he accepted gracefully. I'd like to see if Tony meant it when he said he could use some help here at the ranch."

Unable to hold her tears any longer, Cecelia sobbed. "Oh, Mike, you finally made the decision I've been hoping to hear. But are you sure that someday you won't resent giving up your life in New York to be with me on the West Coast?"

"I've never regretted a moment I've spent with you, so how could this be any different? Besides, my father, of all people, seemed to support my decision. He said there's always been a side of him that wanted to leave the world of big banking and be a part of some independent company that he could help build up."

"I'm sure Tony will say yes. He and I did a lot of talking about it after you left. He knows what a great financial manager you'd make for his operation," Cecelia said. She took a deep breath, steadied herself, and said, "Then it's settled. I can count on you being here and on our being Sentinels, side by side?"

"Of course," Mike said, leaning in to kiss her.

"Wait, there's one more thing," Cecelia said, backing away. "I've been thinking, too. After the war is over, the economic reconstruction of Asia will require an enormous amount of assistance, and I'm in a good position to help."

"You want to continue your government work?"

"I want us to include it on the Sentinels' agenda. After all, it's just another piece of the same problem."

"Well, you'll have to ask the others, but as always, Cecelia, you've got my support."

"And you've got mine," she said, gently pushing him toward the house. "Now, go in and ask Tony what you came all this way to ask."

———

Jacques' and Ian's inquiries along the docks of the Côte d'Azur, at the train stations, in the bus depots, and on the frontiers into Italy and Spain failed to yield any useful information about Claudine's whereabouts. They went up into the small hillside villages behind Cannes and Nice and began asking around there, with similar results.

During one such outing, Ian turned toward Jacques, walking beside him, and asked, "When you find her, are you finally going to stop looking?"

"What do you mean?"

"I mean, when you find Claudine, are you finally going to admit you love her and stop looking around at other girls?"

"Ian, I don't know what you're talking about. Why are you asking me that, anyway?"

"Because that's what I'm going to do . . . with Emily," Ian said. "After the war, I think I'll return to London, get a job with one of the art auction houses, and be with her. That is, if she'll still have me."

"I'm sure she will, Ian. From what I know of her—and of you—she must be a very patient lady."

"There's just one problem," Ian said, stopping short. "Emily will never understand our 'side work' or live with all the secrecy involved. I must make a decision: either give up active participation with the Sentinels or give up Emily. Don't get me wrong, Jacques . . . I'm very proud of all that we've accomplished. It's just that I think it's time for me to settle down and enjoy a simpler kind of life."

"I understand completely. That's the kind of decision that sooner or later, all of us are going to have to make."

"I'm fortunate in that I found the right girl to help me make it. So what about Claudine?"

Jacques started walking up the hill toward the next town. "Let's just *find* her first. Then I'll worry about finding out if she's the right girl."

———

By the end of October, their search had extended well up into the Alps, as far north as Grenoble. They had by then already completed their search of the French and Italian rivieras, Genoa, and the Lake Como area. They had explored all the small villages westward as far as Marseille before turning their attention northward to Avignon and on to Lyon. Finally, they headed southwest, crossing the Spanish frontier into Barcelona. Weeks of searching and waiting had failed to turn up even the smallest hint of where Claudine was hiding.

One afternoon, returning to their hotel, tired, disappointed, and depressed, Ian said, "Well, I guess if she didn't want the Germans to locate her, what made us think we'd be able to?"

Jacques didn't have an answer for his friend. He only knew that if he didn't find Claudine, nothing else would matter.

Chapter 38

RETURN TO CHAMONIX

It was a chilly day in the late fall when Ian and Jacques finally returned, frustrated and in despair, to the Demaureux chalet in Chamonix. They sat on the veranda with Henri, trying to figure out a way to explain their lack of success in finding Claudine, when they heard the sound of gravel scrunching beneath the wheels of a car. The sound drew them to the front of the chalet.

"My God," Ian said, watching a woman get out of the taxi. "It's Claudine."

She looked so different. It was more than her hair being darker and cut very short; she looked tired, dirty, and much thinner. She had deep circles under her eyes. Gone was her eternal sense of well-being. She seemed sad and scared.

Jacques was the first to move. He strode toward her, looking into her eyes for a long time before pulling her to him so closely that he could feel her heart beating.

"Hey, you two, can't an old man give his daughter a kiss?" Henri said, holding out his arms as he came toward her.

After Claudine gave them all a proper greeting, Jacques took her arm and slowly escorted her through the chalet, out to the warm, sun-filled veranda. Facing her chair toward her beloved

Mont Blanc, he slowly lowered her into it and held her hand as she focused on the beauty and comfort of being home, surrounded by her father and friends.

All three men were sitting quietly near her, watching her closely and refraining from any conversation that would interrupt whatever monologue was going on in her mind. After about ten minutes of silence, she said, "What's the matter with all of you? Is this any way to welcome a girl home?"

Henri went inside the chalet with the stated purpose of returning with a good deal of champagne. After assuring her that the six of them were all safe now, Jacques and Ian slowly started to ask her questions.

After about half an hour, she said, "Enough of my stories. I would think you would grow tired of hearing about German generals. With one exception, they all seemed human, just like everyone else." She rose to go to her room when her father stopped her with a gentle touch of his hand.

"Just one more thing," Henri said. "Where the hell have you been hiding since you left La Garoupe, young lady? These two young men have spent the last few months combing the countryside of the Riviera looking for you. We've been so worried—then, without warning, you step out of a cab."

Claudine smiled. "Put yourselves in my place. What's a girl without papers supposed to do when a German general breaks into her room? What if they all started asking questions? Who could I trust to help me? Denise and her mother would have been the first people they would have interrogated. So, with very few choices, where could I go without leaving a trail, jeopardizing my friends, or having to answer too many questions?"

Leaning forward, she helped herself to another glass of champagne and watched, with some amusement, as the three of them searched for a reply.

"Come on," she said, "I don't understand how three such intelligent men can't solve the dilemma that I was forced to solve for myself."

Their looks of confusion were entertaining her. "Take your time," she said, pouring another drink. "I think there's still enough for one more glass."

Having finished the last of the champagne and no longer able to stand the suspense, she said, "Okay, I'll give you a clue. Say hello to Sister Claudine."

When the men's jaws dropped, she continued. "I've been in a convent, you dummies! And, by the way, I think we need to open another bottle of champagne. This one seems to be empty."

———

It was a different Claudine, clean and well scrubbed, with some of the dark dye washed out of her hair, who came skipping down the stairs a few hours later.

"Okay, that's enough talk for one day," she announced. "I have done nothing for the last few months but serve dinners, clean dishes, and make beds for German officers and Catholic nuns. I don't suppose I could interest you in a night out on the town with three of my favorite men? Father, is that little restaurant that serves *pommes soufflé* still there? You may not believe this, but convent food leaves something to be desired."

"I'll call and make the reservations," Henri said, going toward the phone.

She turned to Jacques. "If you don't mind, let's take two cars so I can spend the ride convincing my father that I'm all right." When Henri returned, she said, "Father, can we take the Mercedes?"

———

A bit later, as Henri pulled out of the driveway, Claudine put her hand on his arm.

"Father, you would have been proud of me. At one time or another, I thought about everything you taught me, including how to build a snow cave. How did you know that would ever become useful? There I was, near the top of Mont Cenis, hidden in a snow fort. I was all alone, very tired, and scared to death."

Henri glanced over at her. "Well, you're here now. You are safe, and all that is behind you."

"No, it isn't. For months, I have been going to sleep at night and waking up in the morning with the same two fears. One was being caught and the other was the fear of never seeing Jacques again. Here I am, a mature woman with a schoolgirl crush on an old friend, a professional colleague . . . and a world-class womanizer! Oh, Father, I tried not to fall in love with him. You don't know how hard I tried, but I'm afraid I've failed miserably. All those lonely nights at La Garoupe, I couldn't get him out of my mind. I don't know what I should do about it."

Henri smiled at her. "I am certain he is very fond of you, too. Why else would he drag Ian all over the south of Europe searching for you? Have you ever considered the possibility that both of you have been so afraid of losing each other as friends that you haven't been willing to express your true feelings to each other? Claudine, my love, you need to realize that you are in charge of the situation. Women are always in control—they just don't always know it."

Over dinner, more of the old Claudine began to reappear. Four bawdy jokes that she had learned from the nuns, three orders of *pommes soufflé,* and two bottles of wine later, Henri and Ian, feigning fatigue, asked to be excused. "You two stay," Henri said as they got up from the table. "Take your time. We'll even leave you the Mercedes."

How could I have ever lived without being able to look into these eyes? Jacques thought as they slowly polished off the last bottle of wine. A bit later, Claudine suggested, "Let's pay the bill and go outside for some air."

They donned their coats and left the restaurant. Claudine headed away from where the Mercedes was parked. "How would you like to take an old friend for a moonlight walk?"

"Sure thing, Sister Claudine."

"You can cut out all that sister stuff," she said. "In case you were worried, I wasn't there long enough to make it official."

She smiled and led him down a well-marked path, easy to see in the brightness of the full moon. It wasn't until they crossed the lower meadows of Mont Blanc and were heading up through the steeper, forested terrain that Jacques thought to ask, "Where are we going?"

"I have something special I want to show you."

By this time, he was having some difficulty keeping up with her. They emerged from the trees into a meadow; the moonlight was so bright that the winter-browned meadow grass was bathed in intense shades of silver, swaying in the breeze like ocean waves. Claudine didn't stop long enough for Jacques to enjoy the view— or to catch his breath. Passing through the meadow, she began to work her way through a steep rock field. Halfway up, he watched her disappear over the crest.

Damn, she's in good shape! I, on the other hand, am about to have a heart attack.

Even in daylight, ascending the upper portion of that part of the mountain would have been difficult for him. At night, it was even harder. He had to slow down and carefully pick his way through the rocks. Tired, slightly chilled, and panting, he finally reached the crest.

Pausing to regain his breath, bent over with his hands on his knees, he was sucking in deep, full gulps of the high mountain air. As his heart rate slowed down, he stood up and surveyed the scene. In front of him lay a small, snow-fed lake. On the far side, he could see a cabin for hikers and mountain climbers. To his right, Claudine was taking a trail that wound along the lake's edge, toward the cabin. She was looking back at him, urging him to follow.

Walking along the edge of the lake, with her heavy wool coat and scarf wrapped tight about her, she appeared to him like some trick of the moonlight and the mountain air—like an apparition, a vision. With nothing but the sound of his breathing to accompany his thoughts, he realized that he could not allow her to walk away from him anymore, even if just toward an isolated cabin on a lake.

Claudine, it's you. It's always been you.

He started jogging down the sloping meadow to catch up with her. The cold air punished his throat and chest, but he didn't care. She was almost halfway around the small lake when he caught up with her. She looked over her shoulder as he approached, and then turned to receive him. He held her to him, his chest heaving in and out.

"Claudine, I—"

She put a hand on his mouth. "Shut up, you. You don't have any breath to waste on something as useless as talking."

She took his face in her hands and kissed him. To Jacques, it was like the first drink of cool water after walking through five miles of desert.

As he caught his breath, they continued around the lake to the cabin. They went inside and Jacques laid a fire.

"Whose place are we invading?" he asked her.

"Actually, this is my father's cabin. He hasn't used it much these last few years, but he used to come here on weekends, with my mother." When the fire was blazing, Claudine brought some heavy blankets from the beds.

"I think we should get out of these clothes, don't you?"

Jacques nodded, his heart beginning to pound—but not because of exertion.

The next morning, he awoke to the warmth of a roaring fire and the smell of fresh, hot coffee brewing atop the wood-burning stove. He could hear Claudine moving around in the makeshift kitchen. Fully wrapped in the heavy blanket, Jacques raised himself up on one elbow.

He watched her preparing something with the emergency supplies that were always left in the cabin. "What are you making?" he asked, walking up behind her and kissing her neck.

Still wrapped in the blanket, he stood and watched while Claudine mixed flour, water, yeast, salt, and pepper into a sticky mass. She then used the mixture to line the inside of an old, cast-iron Dutch oven. After placing the heavy cover on the pot, she used the large, metal handle to pick it up and place it on the hook that extended into the fireplace, over the glowing coals. Next, she placed hot coals on top of the lid, stepped back, and said, "Give it a few minutes. You're in for a real treat."

She smiled at him. "Your clothes are over there on the chair. Why don't you put them on and pour yourself a cup of coffee? Breakfast will be ready in a few minutes."

While he got dressed, he watched Claudine set the table, then sniff the steam coming out of the cast-iron pot. Using an old set of gloves that had been left on top of the mantle, she lifted the heavy pot off the hook and carried it to the table. After lifting off the cover, she picked up a narrow knife and ran it around the inside edge of the pot, to separate the bread from its surface.

"Sheepherders' bread *au Claudine* is about to be served."

The bread smelled delicious and the coffee was doing its magic. But Jacques was still uncertain about what to say.

This is Claudine. The lines you've used on a hundred other girls will bounce off her like popcorn.

It was too important and, Jacques realized, he had too little experience at actually making himself vulnerable to a woman— especially one he couldn't afford to lose.

As he was playing with the bread she'd put on his plate, he felt her hand touch his arm.

"Maybe you should let me do the talking, Jacques."

Is she reading my mind?

"You have no idea how hard I've tried to ignore my feelings for you," she said. "During all those nights on the ski trail and at La Garoupe, all I could think about was you. Even when I felt trapped on Mont Cenis, I would find myself asking, 'What would Jacques do if he were here?' Jacques, I know that I love you and I want to spend the rest of my life with you. The question is, now that I have seduced you in my father's mountain shack, how do you feel about me? Are you willing to let me share in your life?"

He stared at her, hardly able to breathe. Of all the words she might have said, he would never have expected her to speak aloud the very idea he dreamed about, night and day.

Jacques, old boy, you need to think very carefully about what you are going to say next.

"Claudine, I . . ." Silence.

Come on, man! Don't seize up now!

"I guess I'm not too good at this," he said with a weak grin.

"Good at what?"

He reached across and took her hand. "Good at telling a woman I love her, without sounding like I'm just trying to get her in bed. Good at hanging on to someone, whatever it takes. Even before Ian and I started to try to find you, I knew that I had fallen in love with you—I just didn't know how bad it was."

"Bad?" She gave him a look of mock horror.

"You know what I mean. Every day Ian and I came home with no word of you, I became more certain of how I really felt. You have no idea how many times I promised myself that if I was fortunate enough to get you back, I would never let you go."

"Jacques, that's beautiful, but you still haven't answered my second question."

He stared at her blankly. "What's your second question?"

"Let me explain. Do you remember how hard I worked to help Tony with his vineyard research when we were at Berkeley? His dreams became my dreams. Did you ever realize how happy I was to share his work and support his dreams? If he had asked me to marry him, stay in California, and share his life, I probably would have done so."

Jacques stared at the tabletop. "Yeah. When we were in Napa last year, he couldn't stop talking about the way you looked, trekking up and down the hills with the equipment. I loved hearing it, and hated it at the same time. I loved thinking about you happy, but I hated thinking about how close I'd been to losing you—without even knowing how much I needed you."

She looked at him for a time. He wished he could read which way her thoughts were running.

"It was only when I realized that there wasn't enough room in his life for me *and* his dreams that I packed my bags and returned home," she said, finally. "Now do you understand my question?"

"Are you saying . . . asking if there's room in my life . . . my career, for you?" And then, the question was burning in his brain: "Are you . . . willing to come back to New York . . . with me?"

"Monsieur Jacques Roth, you have enough career for *both* of us," she said. "We make pretty good partners, no? Together we set up the gold bearer bond program. Together we solved the German transfer problem. Why can't I be a partner in your life?"

He left his seat then, going around and kneeling beside her chair. He put his arms around her. "I can't imagine any other partnership that would compare. Claudine, please . . . marry me."

She put a hand on his head; her eyes were glistening. "Jacques, you will never know how much that means to me. But not so fast, *mon cher.* The war is not over, and the Six Sentinels won't be completely in the clear until it is—if then.

"I want you to go back to New York. If, at the end of the war, you are absolutely certain that you still feel the same way, ask me, and I will join you there, or wherever you are, and marry you. I just need to know, when you have time to think everything through, that you feel the same way you do now."

"But, Claudine . . . I know how I feel, for the first time in my life."

The look on her face warned him.

Remember whom you're dealing with. This is Claudine, and these terms aren't negotiable.

Jacques and Claudine returned to the chalet early in the afternoon of the next day. They decided not to talk with the others about their new understanding. Jacques thought she might share it with her father, once he and Ian were gone, but that was her decision, not his. He had already decided that this was too important to be influenced by anything but his own certainty, free of persuasion even by his good friend. Ian was in love with Emily and, like all lovers, longed for the whole world to be in love, too.

That was fine as far as it went, but Claudine was too important a decision to make on any basis other than his own heart's dead-level surety.

At dinner that evening, Jacques asked, "Henri, how much confidence do you have in the Germans? Do you think they will live up to their end of the deal and leave us alone?"

"I've wondered the same thing. You would think, under the circumstances, that they wouldn't want to do anything that would adversely affect the liquidity of their bonds. On the other hand, that possibility certainly hasn't seemed to stop them in the past. If I had to guess, I think I would assume the worst. I strongly suggest that each of you return to your sanctuaries until the war is over. By then, you will have to make a decision regarding cashing the next allotment of your bonds. Maybe, by that time, you will know more."

"I can always go back to the convent," Claudine said. "Father and I can keep in touch by our classified ad code. If I fail to place an ad at the right time, he can send in the cavalry."

Jacques turned to Ian. "You can't return to London. And Mike and I can't return to Sculley Square. In fact, Mike has already moved out to California. I need a roommate and we need to find a new place to live. The question is, where can we go where we won't be noticed or can't be found?"

"Jacques, you never ask a question like that unless you already have an answer in mind. Do you mind sharing it with us?" Ian said.

"Well, I was just thinking . . . we've done almost everything there is to do in life. How would you like to get a divorce?"

"Get divorced? But darling," Ian said in falsetto, "we aren't even married. What the hell are you talking about?"

"I understand there are some dude ranches near Reno, Nevada, where people stay while completing their residency requirements so that they can obtain quick divorces. They come and go. There is a steady turnover. Why would anyone question two more male guests? We could register under assumed names and wait for the war to end."

"What can I say?" Ian said, finally. "My parents think I'm dead. And you're right about the risk of returning to London. It's too dangerous for me to see Emily. By now, they could be watching *her*, hoping I'll show up." He stared into the middle distance for a moment, sadness on his face. Then he gave them his best smile. "Maybe, when we are in Nevada, I can learn to ride a horse. Who knows? I might become a cowboy."

Chapter 39

THE SIX SENTINELS

Not wanting to take any chances with flying with a major airline back to New York, Jacques called Chairman Malone's office. Malone quickly arranged for a U.S. Army cargo plane to pick them up in Geneva. With the war effort at its zenith, Jacques and Ian's travel schedule had to be organized around the more pressing problems of military demands. Flying five different legs, they went to France, England, Ireland, Newfoundland, and finally to an Army/Air Force base on Long Island, New York.

The planes were slow; they were not pressurized; and they were cold, drafty, and very noisy. After six days, Ian and Jacques, exhausted and grimy, arrived safely. They were placed in one of the vacant officers' houses, where they could shower, change clothes, make phone calls, and, best of all, catch up on their sleep. The quarters were small, clean, and spartan, and the officers' club was only a short walk away. By noon of their third day, new identity papers had been placed on the kitchen table.

———

Monday was Natalie's one day off. She could sleep late, do her weekly shopping, and read one of the books or manuscripts that always seemed to be lying around her apartment. She routinely unplugged her phone, made no dates, and refused to attend meetings, script readings, or rehearsals. Dressed in sweat clothes, sneakers, and large, dark glasses, her hair tucked under a ball cap, she could do her shopping and come and go as she pleased without being recognized.

While she was standing in front of the meat counter at her favorite neighborhood grocery store, she noticed an attractive man wearing dark glasses and military fatigues. It was obvious that he was not an experienced shopper. Amused, she watched him searching for items, asking questions of the other patrons, and having a difficult time determining which of the multiple brands to select. She was so intrigued by him that she moved away from the meat counter to watch him proceed up the next aisle. *There's something familiar about him.* Moving quickly down a parallel aisle, she rounded the corner and stared as he approached her. *Well, I'll be damned. It's Jacques!*

Slowly, she started pushing her cart toward him. When he showed no sign of recognition, she shifted her attention to the canned goods, waiting for him to pass. "Statue of Liberty, two o'clock this afternoon," she heard him whisper as he passed by.

At two on the dot she was standing at the top of the Lady, looking at the skyline of Manhattan, when she heard Jacques say, "Natalie, don't turn around. It's important that we talk and avoid showing any signs of personal recognition. I could have been followed. I apologize for all the mystery. I am afraid there's not much I can do to explain. All I am allowed to say is that my friends and I are involved in some serious work that might bring the war in Europe to an early and successful conclusion. There have been some very nasty people trying to stop what we are doing. That night I left your hotel, I was followed by some dangerous people who were trying to kidnap me. Thanks to some alert work by members of the United States Secret Service, they were arrested and I was able to complete an important trip that I had to make to Geneva. I've just returned.

"It's not just me that I'm worried about. If these people learn of our relationship, you could be in danger as well. If it weren't for the fact that something has happened that we need to discuss, I wouldn't have taken the risk of tracking you down."

Natalie had been on Jacques' mind ever since he and Ian had left Geneva. No matter how hard he had tried, he couldn't figure out a way to tell her about Claudine without being hurtful. It had only been two months since they had spent the night together in Boston, and now he was supposed to tell her he had asked another woman to marry him?

Explaining things to Natalie was difficult enough, but not being able to face her, hold her hand, and look into her eyes made things a lot worse. It didn't take Natalie long before she began to understand what Jacques was trying to tell her. The realization of what he was saying was the worst pain she had ever experienced. She could sense his discomfort in his voice and in the quick glances she made from the corner of her eye. *What did I do wrong? How many times did I ask myself if I was making a mistake by falling in love with such a high-profile, worldly man? I can't even turn around or show any emotion. Whatever I do, I will not cry.*

Never one to express himself when it came to personal feelings, Jacques struggled along. Not knowing how Natalie was going to react, he was afraid to stop talking. His continuing babble gave her time to collect her composure and organize her thoughts.

"Jacques, I'm sure that what you and I had was real. I'll always remember those special occasions when it seemed we were on our own special planet and the world had stopped. I don't want to let what's happening ruin those memories."

Anyway, she thought, *how do I know it's really over? It could be that he's feeling guilty about having affairs with both of us at the same time. Things can change.*

"As hurtful as it has been to hear what you've been telling me, I will always love you. I know if you didn't care, you wouldn't have made the effort to personally explain what has happened. For that, I thank you. But I wish it could have been me. You are the only man I have ever loved. If it would have made you happy, I'd have gladly given up the theater. It wouldn't have been as much of a sacrifice as you might think."

She took a few steps away from him and whispered, "*Bon voyage*, my prince. Maybe we will meet in our next life."

———

From Reno, Jacques and Ian watched; from the convent, Claudine watched; from the well-guarded Sentinels' Vineyards, Cecelia, Mike, and Tony watched, along with the rest of the world, as Hitler's war efforts ground to a halt. In April 1945, Allied forces entered Berlin. Shortly afterward, Hitler killed himself, and what was left of his officer corps negotiated for peace.

The war in the Pacific was progressing. Allied forces, on their island-hopping campaign, were approaching Japan. Soon, the invasion of the Japanese mainland would become the last great battlefield of the Second World War. With the capture of islands well within the range of America's new, long-range B-29 bomber, the Allies were able to launch massive bombing raids on Japan's principal cities and military installations. But even the destruction of the once-proud Japanese navy, the costly loss of men and matériel during the island battles, and the firebombing of Tokyo itself failed to alter Japan's will to defend its homeland down to the last man.

American invasion plans were being developed. They fore-casted the loss of hundreds of thousands of men on both sides.

As part of a separate strategy, the Manhattan Project, America's most carefully guarded secret development of the atom bomb, had been completed. Hoping to avoid the loss of so many American lives, President Harry S. Truman authorized the bombing of Hiroshima on August 6, 1945. Two days later, they dropped a second bomb on Nagasaki. Shortly thereafter, the Japanese sur-rendered. After seven years, the war in Europe and the Pacific was finally at an end.

Walter Matthews, a leading war correspondent, reported, "An exhausted victor and the conquered enemy have both been forced to pay a terrible price to restore sovereign equilibrium to the world."

───

Jacques had scheduled the first formal meeting of the Six Sentinels for December 15, 1945, in New York City. The meeting would convene at nine o'clock sharp in a small conference room reserved in the Plaza Hotel. The war had been over for four months; the Sentinels needed to meet.

Everyone had been contacted, but as he sat in his old office at Stone City Bank the week before the meeting, Jacques knew there was one very special invitation he needed to extend personally. Although he had talked to Claudine on a regular basis, it had been fifteen months since he had last seen her, in Chamonix. For some part of every day, he had thought of her, imagined her being with him in whatever he was doing, imagined what she would say and how her voice would sound while saying it. And he was more certain than ever that life without her wouldn't be worth living. Talking to her was one thing, inviting her to New York was his invitation to marriage.

He stared at the phone on his desk. *Just do it, damn it! Pick up the phone and make the call. But what if she's changed her mind? This is Claudine, for God's sake! She could have any duke or baronet she wanted just by crooking her finger. Call her, you fool! This is the chance of your lifetime, and if you don't make the attempt, you have no right to call yourself a man.*

Finally, he dragged the phone from its cradle. After calculating the time difference for the thousandth time, he dialed the international operator and gave her the number for the chalet in Chamonix. The phone buzzed in his ear.

Come on! Answer, Claudine, Henri, anybody.

Two rings.

Damn! I don't know if I can do this again later . . .

Three . . .

Oh, dear God . . .

"Hello?"

The sound of her voice nearly made him fall over backward.

"Claudine . . . It's me, Jacques."

"Well, hello there, handsome."

He melted. "Claudine, this is the call that I have been waiting to make for fifteen months. Will you come to New York and marry me?"

"All right."

"What? What did you say?"

"I said, 'all right,' you silly man. I love you. Why wouldn't I marry you?"

He laughed aloud, right into the phone. "You do? I mean . . . You do! And I do!" Her laughter on the line was like a Mozart sonata.

Six days later—six agonizingly long days—Jacques arrived at the airport nearly two hours before Claudine's scheduled arrival. After watching her plane taxi up to the gate, his attention was riveted on the open door of the aircraft.

Come on, people! My God, these people are so slow . . .

Finally, Claudine appeared in the doorway.

There's something different about her. She's still wearing her hair short, and maybe she's regained a little weight, which she definitely needed after her ordeal, but . . .

Then, he saw it. The sad look in her eyes was gone. It had been replaced with the knowing look of a quiet, confident woman who was in love.

As she passed through the gate, he extended his arms. Almost immediately, he experienced the familiar feel of her sliding up against his body. He held her tightly, afraid to let go. The deplaning passengers and those waiting for them watched as Claudine and Jacques quietly held each other.

Once they collected her bags and cleared customs, they took a taxi to the Plaza. After checking in and sending her bags to her room, they strolled into the Oak Bar. Mike, Cecelia, Tony, and Ian were seated at a corner table. Beside the table was a line of champagne bottles turned upside down in the buckets.

As they walked to the table, Jacques realized that this was the first time the six of them had all been together in one place since their graduation.

What would any of us have thought if we'd known then what we know now? Would we have done things differently?

Jacques looked around at the smiling faces, each beaming like it was the first day of school. "Well, I see you declared war on the champagne supply while you were waiting for us," he said. "So glad you weren't worried."

"What the deuce are you talking about?" Ian said. "We've been shot at, kidnapped, on the run, arrested by the military police, and generally put through merry hell during the last two years. Why should we have lost any drinking time fretting about whether you and Claudine could find your way back from the airport?"

Everyone laughed. "Don't mind Ian," Tony said, grinning at his friend. "He's been giddy ever since he found out Emily is on her way here to meet him."

Jacques gave Ian a broad smile. "Congratulations, my friend! Though, frankly, I don't know how she had the patience to wait on you."

Ian shrugged, a foolish grin on his face. "I am a lucky man. And I shall dearly miss having fun with the rest of you, going forward with all this."

"You can always reconsider," Cecelia said.

"And risk losing Emily? No." Ian shook his head, a little sadly. "I'll leave saving the world to the rest of you. My forgery career is over." Everyone smiled and nodded.

Jacques looked around at them all.

Yes, that is the difference, isn't it? Ten years ago, our ideas were just a bunch of theories. Now, bloodied and battered, we are here to make a life commitment to those same ideas.

He found a bottle that still had some champagne, poured the balance into two glasses, one for Claudine and one for himself. Next he raised his drink. "To the Six Sentinels—five in number from now on, but always six in spirit."

"Now on a more personal note, let us toast Mike and Cecelia. Ian and Emily, may you share a long and loving journey. Tony, may all your dreams come true, and finally, to my future wife and my partner in everything I do, may our path be lined with love, adventure, and our great friends."